A NOVEL

Sleight of Hand

Book Three: The Weir Chronicles

Sue Duff

CROSSWINDS PUBLISHING / DENVER

*For Leah —
Now you can't
escape !
Happy reading !
Sue Duff*

CrossWinds Publishing
P.O. Box 630223
Littleton, Colorado 80163
www.sueduff.com

Book Layout © 2014 BookDesignTemplates.com

Sleight of Hand/ Sue Duff. -- 1st ed.
ISBN 978-0-9970156-1-4

For my son, Jonathan
Each sunrise is your promise of a new day—at every
sunset, I kiss you goodnight

Deception

In order to endure, one must be willing to either sacrifice, or choose to become something—someone—else. Then, and only then, will your quarry come within your grasp, unaware of their blunder until the fatal thrust.

The Pur Heir, Book of the Weir, Vol. II

Part One

Desperation transforms us into something unrecognizable—
willing to do the unthinkable

{1}

The forecast had promised a cloudless, bluebird sky for the ceremony. The threatening thunder and gray frosting overhead was anything but. Hordes of parents, carrying the weight of college loans on their backs, arrived in waves eager to see their offspring walk across a stage and receive the coveted piece of paper, its value equal to a decent-sized home. Their grumbles and curses floated down from the stands, blaming local weathermen for their failure to bring an umbrella.

Rayne knew better. The clueless humans couldn't predict the weather any more than the Pur Syndrion would know when their arch enemy, the Duach, would strike again, or where planet Earth's next calamity would appear.

Many of the seated crowd fixed their gazes on the heavens. Rayne kept her attention riveted on the surrounding college stadium, scanning for a hint of green from the recesses of a dark corner, any place Ian could shyft to the stadium and still remain hidden from the crowd. He promised he'd be there, but as the battle to protect the planet raged on, Ian's promises came and went as often as the tides.

Her cell phone chirped and Rayne glanced at the screen. *Any sign of him?*

Not yet, she texted back to Patrick.

Milo made jambalaya and cornbread.

Rayne scanned the sea of bodies searching for Patrick and Tara. The promise of her favorite meal and a celebration back at Ian's mansion barely made a dent in the emptiness she'd carried around for the past few weeks. The only graduation present she wanted was for Ian to share in her special moment.

It was at times like this she longed for her mother and imagined her seated among the other proud parents. Knowledge of the bigger battle to protect Earth from the Duach, the darker sect of the Weir, had Rayne second-guessing the worth of finishing her degree. But it was a goal she swore she'd see to the end. She ran her fingers across her sash. Pursuit of the summa cum laude ranking contributed to many a sleepless night during finals. She didn't mind; anything to fill the perpetual void.

Where are you sitting? she texted.

North side, mid-section, three rows up from the field.

Rayne twisted in her seat and swiped the swinging tassel out of her line of vision. She found them in the crowd thanks to Tara's snowy hair and early-twenties figure that stood out amongst the parents and grandparents. From this distance, Patrick's short-cropped, chocolate hair and not-so-lean torso blended with the bodies in the crowd. Rayne waved and her gown's sleeve swept back and forth like a flag caught in the wind. Tara nudged Patrick and pointed at Rayne. Tara stood and clapped. Patrick cupped his hands around his mouth and gave a resounding hoot, loud enough for Rayne to hear above the buzz of a couple thousand voices.

The ground beneath her chair shook. Rayne grabbed the seat back. A few standing graduates stumbled and fell into nearby seated classmates. The quake came to a halt as suddenly as it reared its head. Rayne looked to her friends in the stands. Tara had her cell phone out, no doubt checking her app to get an accurate reading. Ian's core fluctuations told him how serious each tremor was without the need to refer to a spiking graph. He often predicted the tremor's arrival a heartbeat before everyone else felt it.

Rayne's cell chimed. *Hold on!* Patrick's text message screamed on Rayne's screen. *Something BIG is coming.*

The ground beneath Rayne's feet gave a violent shake. A deafening roar came from beyond the plywood stage. High above the stands, the stadium's press booth shook from side to side as if suspended by rubber bands. *CRACK!* A corner of the booth crumbled and concrete crumbs rained toward the seats below. Rayne strained to see through the rising dust cloud.

Shrieks and screams filled the stadium as the undulating stands jolted people to their feet. The narrow rows swelled with families scrambling to escape. A large man fell into Patrick and he in turn stumbled into Tara as the row of people made to flee. Rayne shook her head in disbelief as Patrick's arms bobbed up and down in a futile attempt to calm the pressing crowd. Tara grasped Patrick's arm and jerked him to sit as the throng of people fought their way into the already packed staircase leading up and out of the stadium.

A tremor snaked up a lamppost and with a *POP,* the massive spotlight dislodged and swung downward from its thick cable like a wrecking ball. Sparks burst into the air and sizzled in a cascading waterfall as it slammed into the empty uppermost row of seats.

A collective shout came from the front of the stadium. An earthen wave raced toward them and uprooted the makeshift stage, splitting it in two. Squawking professors, their colorful gowns flapping like birds, took flight and landed in piles on the grassy field.

The wave reached the graduates and upended one row of chairs after another on a beeline course toward Rayne. Graduates piled up around her like a wall. Trapped!

A blinding emerald burst came from one row ahead. Ian appeared shielding his face with his arms. The closest graduates clamored over each other in retreat as chairs toppled amidst shrieks. Ian fell to one knee and raised a fist high above his head, then drove it against the ground. His power met Earth's wave head-on and with a thunderclap, they cancelled each other out.

Ian slowly rose to his feet but wobbled for a second from the tremendous energy drain. He looked haggard and gaunt. Thick stubble covered his face and the dark circles surrounding his eyes were enhanced by his ebony, disheveled hair. "Sorry I'm late," he said

Rayne strained to hear him over the shouts. "You made it," she said and gave him a smile that would have been wider if not for the near-brush with calamity.

"I can't stay," he said in a voice dripping with regret. The tremors had stopped but no one stood still long enough to notice. "There was a quake about fifty miles off the coast. I need to check on tidal wave threats along the—"

"Go," Rayne said, but her heart said stay.

"Don't let Patrick eat it all." Ian crouched low, between the piles of upturned chairs. A green burst, and he was gone.

Rayne stood still staring at the spot, committing his image to memory.

{2}

Ian didn't bother with the lights when he arrived at the mansion in the middle of the night. A floating mass blocked his way and he swiped a handful of balloons to the side as he stepped into the kitchen. A note on the oven door announced leftovers could be found in the refrigerator. He was too exhausted to see what he'd missed.

Movement on the back patio. Ian let himself out through the sliding glass door and discovered Patrick sitting on the concrete railing, smoking a cigar.

Ian descended the stairs but didn't pause until he reached the edge of the lake. Dust, with a hint of mildew had been kicked up by the quake. Ian would survey how much of the ocean cliffs had toppled into the surf in the morning. He watched the moonlight's glow across the still surface of the lake and made a feeble attempt to erase the devastation he'd witnessed over the past several hours.

Born without his full complement of powers, there was so little he could do to counter Mother Nature's pains. He'd been at a loss about how to stop what he and the Pur Syndrion could no longer control. The Primary's claims, that Earth's natural disasters were the result of the Weir Sars dying out, didn't stop Ian's hope that they—he—could somehow prevent the planet's gradual self-destruction.

At a shuffle from behind, he braced himself for Patrick's inevitable lecture.

Ian's friend stepped quietly next to him. "You look like shit," Patrick said under his breath, as if voicing it softly would ease the impact of his words.

"It goes with the mood." Ian picked up a stone and skipped it across the lake. It bounced several times, parting the small lake in tiny ripples. Gentle lapping soon reached the outer edges. "Any significant damage?"

"Not to the mansion. Milo checked the water purification system. Said it was intact," Patrick reported. "Otherwise, there's plenty of firewood for the upcoming winter."

Guilt at the mansion, untouched by the disaster when countless others lost so much, clawed at Ian's chest. The Syndrion's engineers had built the compound's structures to withstand all but the most devastating of quakes.

"I would have been here if I could," Ian said.

"We all understood, Ian, especially Rayne. Shake the guilt off and get some rest." He grabbed a stone and whipped it across the surface of the water. It landed with a plop.

"I feel like I've been swept up in a tidal wave." Ian picked up another rock and gripped it tight in his palm.

"Feeling helpless doesn't bode well with any of us. Rayne and I may not have a magical connection to planet Earth, but if there's any way we can help, you know to just ask," Patrick said. "You'll find a way to stop this, Ian. We haven't lost our faith in you."

A sigh escaped, carried by the breeze. "Rayne moved out," Ian said. There was an odd sensation, emptiness to the mansion when he had arrived home.

Patrick kicked at a muddy clump. "A couple of days ago. I helped. She wants to be on her own. No ties."

Not after losing her best friend to a Duach psychopath, Ian thought. Rayne's independence ran deep and fierce. Her ability to drain their power, Ian's included, coupled with his constant absences, didn't make bridging their chasm any easier. "Leave me her address," Ian said.

"She told me not to give it to you," Patrick mumbled. When Ian turned on him, Patrick threw his hands up. "She doesn't want you distracted. She said it's better this way."

"She could still be in danger," Ian said. "Ning may have told someone about her."

"He's been dead two months. If the Duach or the Pur Sars know about her, or cared, they'd have struck by now." Patrick shook his head. "Let her have her space. You both need to focus on other things right now. Eat some dinner, then get some rest. Tomorrow's another day," Patrick said.

"You're sounding more and more like Milo."

"If I become anything like that grumpy old caretaker, you have permission to put me out of my misery," Patrick said. "As painlessly as possible, of course."

"If I'm ever to take you out, it'll be when you least expect it," Ian added with a half smile.

"I take comfort in that." Patrick took a deep draw on his cigar, then headed up the steps.

Ian lingered at the edge of the lake. He craved the calm more than a warm meal, and he raised his face with closed eyes, mellowing to the tunes of the katydids. Thoughts drifted to Rayne. He yearned to stand in her doorway and watch her sleep, as he had countless times before, assured that she was safe. Even more, he ached for what they were forever denied: to gather her in his arms and feel her warmth against his skin.

Ian awoke with a jolt. A pressure built, deep in his chest. The Seal over his left breast grew increasingly warm, the triangle surrounding his sun glowed bright orange the second it turned searing. He threw aside the sheet and shyfted to the foyer at the base of the mansion stairs.

A message scroll spun on its end above the old, worn silver platter on the foyer table. Ian snatched it and unfurled the scroll. The branding iron heat at his chest ceased. As he read the Primary's message, the parchment crackled under his fist. He let it spring back, then held it up. The scroll burst into flame, turned to ash, and disappeared.

"Good god, they can't let you have even one day off?" Milo's grizzly-bear voice came from the hall leading to the kitchen. Ian's stomach did a cartwheel at the smell of bacon and freshly brewed coffee. "Where?"

"Africa," Ian said.

"You're not taking off until I've stuffed a decent meal in you."

"Throw in some of your sweet rolls, and you've got a deal." Ian brushed past Milo, headed for the kitchen. He needed some of that coffee.

"Unless it's a tribal council meeting, consider wearing clothes." Milo stepped up next to Ian at the counter and extended his half-drained mug.

It wasn't until Milo's remark that Ian realized he was naked. He finished topping off the old caretaker's cup, poured himself one, and took a few sips without turning around. The pungent brew fired more than a few brain cells.

"Did you use your boost last night?" Milo gave Ian a discerning eye.

"It barely makes a dent anymore."

"The boost was designed to heal in case you're ill or injured. You're exhausted, Ian, pure and simple. Try re-energizing your core in the northern vortex structure before you leave."

Arms wrapped around Ian from behind. Tara's welcoming embrace was filled with loving warmth. Welcome home, stranger, she channeled, pulling away and rustling his hair.

"I'd turn around and return the hug, but . . ." he said.

"Such a target and no dish towel in sight," she quipped.

Scrapes across the tile floor. Saxon greeted Ian with a sniffing, cold nose to his butt. Ian sidestepped, then half turned and gave the massive, snow-colored wolf a scruff around the ears.

"You're up early," Milo said as Tara took a seat at the kitchen island.

"You're off to somewhere and wherever it is, Saxon and I are coming with you, Ian. The edge in Tara's voice was razor sharp. "You need me." Saxon snorted at Ian's leg. "You need us both," she amended.

"I don't have it in me to argue with you anymore," Ian said.

"Bring back some fresh fruit and spices," Milo said. "My pantry is getting low."

"We'll rendezvous in the foyer within the hour." Ian shyfted to his bedroom and fought the urge to collapse on his bed. He stepped into his bathroom, set his coffee mug down and studied the dark circles under his eyes. He did look like shit, a far cry from his meticulous performance days. How he missed his illusions and the control he had in his life during those years.

His thoughts fell to this latest assignment. He was to connect with a Doctor Willoughsby in the heart of the African Congo. The Weir geophysicist claimed he could stop the increasing earthquakes across Earth. But he would only share this knowledge with the Pur Heir.

{3}

Jaered pulled the Jeep onto the interstate and soon reached the stretch along the ocean cliff. The smell of exhaust and garbage morphed into the salty sea and he inhaled deep, filling his lungs. The morning haze had given way to the intense glare of the natural sun. Jaered turned his face toward the heavens and absorbed the energy's warmth, a constant reminder of his mission on Earth.

A remote overlook offered the privacy Jaered sought. He crossed the vacant lot and came to a stop at the concrete barrier separating the overlook from the sheer drop on the other side. He shut off the engine and studied his surroundings to verify that he hadn't been followed.

Jaered withdrew the cell from his pocket and stared at Eve's text. *It's time.* He thought of the hundreds of rebels scattered across the globe. Each one had received the identical message. How many stared at their screens, wallowing in the significance of those two simple words? Were they prepared to see this to the end, understanding they were about to change Earth forever?

A gust of wind whipped through the open cab. Jaered grasped the steering wheel to steady himself. At the horizon, a steel blanket rose from the ocean. It billowed and swirled. The dark mass soon obliterated the sun and transformed the blues of the sky to a palate of overlapping grays.

Jaered tapped out his response. *Rec'd.* His finger hovered over the send button. A heartbeat later, he touched the screen.

He left the Jeep, approached the edge of the overlook and threw the burner phone over the side.

There was no reason to stay in contact with Eve in the days ahead. Jaered was well versed in his next assignment.

He needed to close out his affairs and erase any lingering sign he'd ever been in San Francisco. It would be disastrous if Aeros, Jaered's father, discovered his association with the rebel forces or his hand in the events to follow.

The sun's rays poked through the overcast sky and ignited Jaered's core. He relished the afterburn while his thoughts fell to his assignment. Kill the Pur Heir.

{4}

Ian shyfted Tara and Saxon to the coordinates. They appeared in the middle of a small outcropping of boulders on a high plateau. Moist, sweltering air doused them in an instant. Tara wiped her brow with the sleeve of her shirt. Saxon snorted and shook his thick coat. Ian feared the wolf might topple over from heatstroke.

A tall man leaned against the rocks. His skin and clothes were so dark Ian took him for a shadow. "Welcome to the Democratic Republic of the Congo, Pur Heir," he said in a French accent. They shook hands.

The scientist was much younger than Ian had expected. "Dr. Willoughsby."

He laughed, full and hearty. "I'm sorry, you have me mistaken. I am Dr. Bhutto Masani, Dr. Willoughsby's associate. The others are setting up an experiment below. I am to take you to them."

"Is your entire research team Weir?" Tara asked.

"Yes, everyone here," Bhutto said. "There are many Weir in Africa."

"This is Tara, my Channel," Ian said. "And Saxon."

Bhutto offered Tara a toothy grin and hearty handshake. His outstretched hand toward Saxon was rewarded with a paw. Bhutto led them out of the clearing. "We are honored by your arrival, Sire." He gestured toward a mud-clotted Rover and, with a slight bow, Bhutto held a door for Ian. They got in and headed down a narrow winding dirt road that promised more ruts than smooth surfaces.

"How long has Dr. Willoughsby been doing this research?" Ian asked.

"Which one?" Bhutto said. "The father or the daughter?"

"I didn't know there were two." Ian grabbed the roll bar when the vehicle veered close to the edge of a two-hundred-foot drop-off.

"Both are acclaimed scientists," Bhutto said jerking the steering wheel back and forth. "They study the same thing from two different directions."

"What do you mean?" Tara said.

Bhutto pointed out the window. "At the horizon," he said, grabbing the wheel again. "That is what they study."

Tremendous billowing storm clouds swept across the plains. In an instant, they converged, surging in mass and spreading out as if someone whipped open a blanket over the land. The storm front soon took command of the upper atmosphere.

"They study clouds?" Ian said.

"No," Bhutto replied. "They study what comes from them."

Lightning's tendrils thrust in all directions, then disappeared in the aftermath of an almost indiscernible pulse on the heels of distant thunder. Before long, it returned, one bolt immediately after another, and several in unison.

"That's some storm," Tara said.

Bhutto chuckled. "Welcome to Africa."

By the time they arrived in a camp at the base of the plateau, the billowing gray extinguished what little sun remained overhead. The camp bustled with activity. A dozen or more people hurried about the compound. A middle-aged gentleman and young woman stood at the center, shouting orders and waving their hands about.

Ian jumped out of the Jeep while the throng of people scattered.

Dr. Willoughsby and, who Ian deduced was his daughter, separated then headed in different directions.

Bhutto stood next to Ian. "This storm was supposed to hit last night, or at least earlier today. They were packing when the recordings indicated it was on its way after all. That's why there's more confusion than typical," the assistant said. "The father can be short-tempered and single-minded about his experiments. The daughter will be more approachable in the midst of all this."

They followed Bhutto between flapping tents and reached the edge of camp, where a towering antenna stood in a clearing. Two tables of instrumentation and cables were attached at its base. Off to the side were three massive cameras encased in plastic, attached to thick tripods and bolted to concrete slabs.

The young Dr. Willoughsby appeared to be in her mid-twenties and dressed like she was ready to lead a jungle expedition.

"Dr. Willoughsby, this is the Pur Heir," Bhutto announced with subtle reverence.

She stopped what she was doing long enough to size Ian up with emerald eyes before turning around and flipping a few more switches on a console. "I believe my father was expecting you, but he's a little busy at the moment."

"I am intrigued by what you do here, Dr. Willoughsby." Ian took in her instrumentation.

"Joule." She turned and extended her hand. "Dr. Willoughsby is my father. It's easier to tell us apart that way." She stepped around him and paused at a nearby console.

"Joule is a measurement of electricity, is it not?" Tara said.

Ian grinned, frequently amazed by Tara's scientific knowledge.

"My father sees everything through a narrow lens. He lives and breathes his passion," Joule said. A strand of her auburn hair had escaped from her ponytail. She blew it from her face. "I'll answer any other questions you have if you'll give me a minute to complete my prep."

Ian watched the storm in the distance and stroked a restless, panting Saxon.

"Is it headed this way?" Tara asked.

"We're counting on it," Joule said. Before long, thunderous echoes collided with each other. A sheet of rain pelted the area. "Shemsu, make sure your view is five degrees to the west. I can't accurately line it up on my screen," Joule shouted over the claps of thunder. A man, poised behind a camera, gave her a thumbs-up.

The electrical energy magnified the closer it crept toward Ian. His core absorbed much more than he was used to and the power ignited nerve endings. It felt exhilarating, but at the same time, uncomfortable. Sparks jumped between his fingers. When he held his hands parallel to each other, they formed an electrical arc. Joule paused and stared at it.

"I'm not used to absorbing this much power," he said.

"Would you consider being a part of my experiment?" she asked with excitement in her voice.

He flashed a tenuous smile. "Depends," he shouted over the thunderclap.

"I'm testing where upward leaders come from," Joule said. "Actually I'm not only trying to gauge where they come from, but from what source."

"I don't know what that is," Ian admitted, leaning in to hear over the deafening strikes.

"Think of it as upward lightning," Joule shouted. "One of nature's greatest mysteries." She grasped his forearm but jerked back, wringing her hand. A look of pure glee sparkled in her eyes. "You're exactly what I need."

Ian, maybe we should just observe, Tara channeled, with a calming hand on Saxon.

My core feels the strongest it has in months, Tara. Something tells me that this is exactly what I need. Wait here. Ian followed the scientist.

Joule led Ian to the center of a small clearing, in the direct path of the cameras. "You control the electromagnetic energy through your core, am I right, Pur Heir?"

He nodded. "Ian, please. I'm not one for formality." Two lightning strikes, one on top of the other, hit the tower. The resulting electricity raced down the metal structure and directly into Ian's core. The intense power surged inside his core and he held his palm up to release the energy through his hand.

She raised his other arm and took several steps back. A series of lightning strikes, one after another, connected with Ian's upturned palm. The impact of the tremendous force broke gravity's hold and it lifted him.

The affect cramped every muscle in Ian's body. Light-headed, Ian feared he might pass out.

"Are you all right?" Joule shouted. "The power isn't too much for you?"

"I'm fine, but is it affecting you?" he asked while hovering a few feet above her.

She spread her arms wide and flexed her fingers. "It's tingling," she exclaimed. "Is this what it feels like to shyft?"

"No, the magnetic field creates a cold, numbing sensation."

"This is incredible!" she screamed at the storm overhead. "Thank you!"

Ian's thoughts whirled and gained speed as if birthing a tornado. He wouldn't be able to tolerate the power flow for much longer and he gave into the strain loosening his pull of the electricity, easing himself downward.

The second he reached the ground, Ian released the remaining electrical energy. When the charged raindrops touched the air, they lit up like glittering sparks.

Joule grabbed Ian around his neck. "Incredible!"

The electricity left his core fully charged and his entire body energized. Joule kissed him hard on the lips, then rushed over to her instruments.

Ian, are you okay? Tara channeled.

"That was amazing," Ian said.

Which part? Tara channeled. He ignored her and studied the storm's fury overhead with renewed eyes as it pelted the Congo Basin. The gradual shift in atmospheric pressure signaled its retreat.

"This is the lightning capital of the world," Bhutto said. "Most storms elicit sixty or fewer strikes in an hour. Here, we can get that many every minute." Bhutto set a canvas chair down for him and another for Tara.

Ian declined, too energized to accept the offered seat. Saxon jumped on it and rested his head across the back canvas.

"What exactly happened?" Tara asked.

From the look on her face, Ian wasn't sure if she was curious, or concerned.

"When lightning reaches down out of the sky it's called a step leader," Joule said. "If it connects with an upward charge from the earth, called a positive streamer, then the lightning touches the ground."

Ian nodded. "I was the positive streamer."

"You charged the ground with tremendous amounts of electricity and concentrated it in the clearing."

"Did you get the footage?" Bhutto asked.

Her smile spread wide. "Come see."

Everyone huddled around the computer console. Bright flashes lit across their faces.

The footage looped back to the beginning. The screen displayed an image of the clearing with Ian and Joule at the center, his outstretched arm reaching upward, and the lightning connecting with it. As the image played, Ian lifted up into the air while the camera followed him.

What was captured on the footage after they left the clearing triggered goose bumps along his arms, in spite of the heat.

Replayed in slow motion, lightning erupted upward from the ground and appeared as an instant leafless tree, branching out in all directions, sizzling white and intense with the earth's power.

"That," Joule said, "is upward lightning."

The pulsating energy trees multiplied like a small forest grove, only to disappear as quickly as they formed. Enthralled, Ian pressed closer and peered over Joule's shoulder, mesmerized by the spectacle on the screen.

"Isn't the earth's power breathtaking?" she said, resting against his chest.

{5}

A throat cleared from behind them. The group separated like the parting sea as a stout, middle-aged, scientist entered the tent. His shirt was drenched. "Please excuse the impertinence of my daughter, Pur Heir." Dr. Willoughsby's British accent was deep and resonant. He threw Joule the reprimanding look. At his approach, Ian caught a whiff of burnt wood mixed with musk aftershave.

"On the contrary Doctor, don't give it another thought. I've been enthralled with her work and what she helped me discover about my core's ability," Ian said.

"I must apologize for her lack of reverence." Willoughsby offered an outstretched hand. Ian was greeted with a firm but brief shake. "You honor us with your cooperation, Highness."

"He wants to be called, Ian, Father." Joule said. "He's not into pomp and circumstance like you." She gestured toward her screen. "We got the most amazing footage."

"Yes, and unfortunately it will have to be destroyed." Willoughsby approached the monitor with his full attention on the images playing in a continuous loop. The scowl on his face deepened.

"You're not erasing any of this!" Joule's expression turned menacing.

"You have video of the Pur Heir that can never be seen by anyone outside of this group. What were you thinking, Joule?"

He's right, Ian thought, the Syndrion would never allow it. "She can cut me out; edit it to keep the upward lightning intact," he suggested.

"With no explanation of how the energy was so concentrated," Willoughsby said.

Joule turned and rushed out of the tent without another word.

"I have taken the responsibility for your safety while you are on this research site, unfortunately, above all else." From Dr. Willoughsby's slumped shoulders and weary eyes, he too, weathered his daughter's sacrifice. "I can vouch for those individuals who observed the experiment firsthand, but the recording is too volatile."

"I'm sorry as well," Ian said.

"Why are we here, Doctor?" Tara asked.

"And you are?" Willoughsby asked, as if recognizing that Tara and Saxon were present for the first time.

"My Channel and companion," Ian offered.

"Let us head to my research site. It will be easier to show you." Willoughsby held the flap of the tent open. An immense arch met Ian when he stepped out as the storm's moisture clung to the sun's energy, creating a brilliant palette.

They ventured around the base of the plateau and came upon a monstrous structure suspended above a large clearing and held in place by a massive crane. The structure resembled enormous white seashells clustered in a tight bud like flower petals.

"What are those petal designs?" Ian asked.

"They're a variation on exedrae," Tara said. "What are they made out of, Dr. Willoughsby?"

"Titanium." The scientist looked impressed. "You have some knowledge of architectural design."

Ian stared at the enormous bolts holding the petal structure together. "What is your research?"

"Channeling the Earth's power," he said. "What you do naturally, I do with geophysics. In fact, I was on the team that designed your—what did Dr. Angus MacBride end up calling it?" He touched a finger to his lip. "Oh, yes. A boost."

"I though he designed it," Tara said.

"He dictated which of the natural elements needed to be drawn from the earth. I designed the structure to collect them. In fact, it's not too dissimilar to the one hanging above us." Dr. Willoughsby stared at his design with nothing less than immense pride.

"What does it do?" Ian asked.

"I've been testing a design theory for harnessing the electricity of the lightning and focusing it elsewhere." Willoughsby pointed overhead. "Do you see that scorch mark?" The scientist indicated a blackened area where the petals converged at a tip. "After capturing the lightning inside the structure, I was able to enhance it and then channel it to a specific location." The scientist gestured to a burnt patch of dirt that rested in the center of the clearing.

"Why harness energy and direct it into the earth's crust?" Ian asked.

"The potential applications are varied," Willoughsby replied. "Mining, in smaller applications farming, excavation for construction, archeology—"

"Purveyor of death and destruction," Joule said. She stepped to the edge of the clearing.

"Again, excuse my daughter. Not only is she precocious, she is dramatic as well."

"It's possible," Joule said.

"But not the intent."

"Considering the amount of energy you pumped into the earth," Ian said. "It could explain—"

"The energy source of my upward lightning!" The spark returned to Joule's eyes.

Willoughsby regarded Ian with an expression that was difficult to read. It turned to dread when Joule threw her arms around Ian.

"Thank you!" she exclaimed and kissed him on his cheek.

It wasn't exactly a peck. Self-conscious of the awkward moment and in full view of her disgruntled father, Ian pushed away. "Minus my screen footage, of course."

"That goes without saying," Willoughsby said.

"I'm still a little vague on where I fit in with your research," Ian said. "Or how this could help stop the earthquakes."

"Now that I have learned how to collect and direct the power, I would like to see if you can."

*

Jaered slipped into Joule's tent. He found the video link and copied the Heir's footage to his flash drive. There was no need to open it. Eve would study it later. Approaching steps. When he lifted the edge of the tent to exit, Bhutto stood in his path.

"What are you doing here?" Bhutto hissed with furtive glances over his shoulder.

"Eve will want a copy."

"I wasn't sure what to do when the Channel and the wolf arrived with the Heir," Bhutto said.

A pit, deep in Jaered's stomach, stirred. "The wolf is always the wild card."

Bhutto nodded. "The climate does not agree with him. He's pretty sluggish."

Jaered wondered what prompted the Heir to bring them. "For the greater good."

"For the greater good," the gentle doctor replied.

Jaered rested the dart rifle against his shoulder. "I need to get the footage to Eve. Make sure the Heir stays here until I return."

Bhutto stopped him with a firm grasp on his forearm. "The Heir is meeting with Dr. Willoughsby."

"It was the scientist's job to lure him here," Jaered said.

The research associate couldn't mask the fear in his voice. "I'm concerned the old scientist is taking liberties and involving the Heir beyond the original plan.

{6}

Heat filled Dr. Willoughsby's tent like an oven. The scientist rose to his feet and set his empty Scotch glass down on his cluttered desk. "The next storm front will be here soon," Dr. Willoughsby announced. "I suggest you get some rest. The test may be quite exhausting for you."

"He can use my tent," Joule said.

The mischievous tone and wry smile prompted Tara to shut the book in her lap. She slid to the edge of the sling-back chair as though about to spring.

The scientist gave his daughter a peck on the top of her head. "Behave." Dr. Willoughsby exited the tent.

"The Heir can rest in here," Tara said.

Joule eyed Tara closely. "Do Channels have a genetic component?"

"A gene marker, yes," Ian said. He got to his feet and stretched. Tara opened a jug of water and refilled Saxon's water bowl. The wolf's eager laps splashed water across the earthen floor.

"Where's your counterpart?" Joule said.

Tara averted her eyes. "Died."

Ian placed a gentle hand on Tara's shoulder. "Protecting all of us."

"Oh." Joule's tone was dismissive. She picked up a pawn from her father's chessboard. "The offer to join me in my tent still stands," she said in a silky voice.

Her boldness kept Ian's guard at full alert. He'd never met anyone quite like her.

If you're not going to slap the bitch, Tara channeled, *I will.* She made to rise from the chair, but Ian kept a firm hand on her shoulder. Tara held onto the book like a weapon and shot a glare full of warning in Joule's direction. If the young scientist noticed, she ignored it.

Joule tossed Ian the pawn. "I give a killer massage."

Ian approached Joule and she turned toward him with an expectant smile, but he leaned down and placed the pawn on the board. "I'm flattered," he said. "But I'm here to find a way to stop the earthquakes that plague our planet. Your father promised that he could help."

"You know where to find me if you change your mind," she said with a raised chin. She took her leave, swiping at the flap to open it.

"You don't have to protect me in all things," Ian gave Tara a sideways glance.

"Says you," Tara settled back in her chair and opened the book.

She sounded so much like Mara. A twang of sorrow struck at how much he missed the identical twins and their unique differences. Tara was adopting more of Mara's personae each day, and in turn, losing some of her own identity. "Did you come to my defense, or Rayne's?" Ian said.

Tara's face lifted from the book. "Mara and I were raised to protect you. Together we were a team. Then I lost her and our ability to channel."

"Saxon completes our triangle." He stroked the wolf. "Our channeling has been restored."

"Yet, you've kept me at a distance. I wanted to believe that it was to protect Rayne."

Ian didn't acknowledge what they both knew to be true.

"But with Rayne on her own, I'm struggling with where I fit in." The wolf snorted. "Saxon *and* I." Tara rose from the chair and he embraced her tight. Saxon wedged himself between their legs.

"Earth is not well, Tara. I've never needed you more," he whispered in her ear. He held on until her sniffles subsided and they kept their sorrow at losing Rayne to themselves.

The power elicited by the late evening storm had Dr. Willoughsby's crew at a distance. Stiflingly humid air made it difficult to draw a breath under a canopy of deafening thunderclaps. Ian fought to contain the sizzling power being filtered through his core.

Willoughsby's test was taking everything Ian had just to remain on his feet.

He stood beneath the suspended exedrae while the structure took a beating from the lightning bolts. Shocked that the cables could withstand the massive weight of the design given the power they conducted, Ian frequently glanced above him. Ian would be crushed if the bolts should fail.

The structure channeled the captured power to his outstretched arms creating an arch that shot several feet into the air. Tingling had turned to pain minutes ago. The searing heat of his core rose to such a degree that his insides felt cooked. Ian clenched his fists and raised his face releasing a tremendous groan.

Just when he didn't know if he could take any more of the power directed into him, Dr. Willoughsby shouted, "Now!"

Ian clasped his hands in front of him and thrust his fists toward the earth, purging the energy trapped in his core in a continuous stream that glowed blindingly white. It took only a few seconds for his core to drain the overload.

Once purged, he collapsed to his knees and bent over struggling for breath. The surrounding air felt as if he'd shyfted to the Arctic Circle. Violent shivers racked his body. Someone threw a heavy blanket around his shoulders.

"Are you all right?" Tara pressed her hand against his cheek and flashed a penlight in his eyes. "You're beet red." She grabbed his wrist. "Oh my god, your pulse."

"Outstanding!" Willoughsby's voice boomed overhead

Ian looked up. There was a wild look in the scientist's eyes.

"You nearly killed him," Joule shouted, running up. "What were you thinking?"

Ian grabbed Tara's shoulder and pushed up on shaky legs. She grabbed him around his waist.

"I'm okay," came out raspy, husky.

"No you're not," Joule said. "Bhutto, get some oxygen."

Ian waved it off. "Really, I'll be fine." His core temperature had returned to normal after the purge, but the chill ravaging his cramped muscles made it difficult to move.

Joule gripped the blanket and pulled it tighter around him. "Your body is reacting like an overheated engine, suddenly thrust into a vat of ice water." Her insistent tone frayed his reluctance. "You could go into shock, Ian. Let me help you."

His legs buckled, but Bhutto caught him and lifted him against his chest. Ian didn't have the strength to protest. They rushed him to a tent at the edge of the site and he collapsed onto a cot. An oxygen mask appeared over his face. He shivered in silence as Joule grabbed some blankets, but before she could throw them over him, Saxon leapt onto the cot and snuggled with Ian. His shivering faded while Tara kept vigil.

A while later, she reached under Saxon's thick coat and pressed her palm against Ian's chest. Her concerned features morphed into relief.

He sat up on the edge of the cot. "What were the results of the test?" he asked.

"I'll show you," Joule said.

He followed the young scientist back to the center of the clearing with Tara and Saxon close on his heels.

A three-foot-wide circular opening lay beneath the suspended structure. Ian dropped to one knee and surveyed the results of his power drain. A tunnel, three feet in diameter, angled downward at a severe slope. It was deep. Ian couldn't make out a bottom.

"A success and then some," Dr. Willoughsby announced, waving a clipboard. "It far exceeded my expectations."

The tunnel's rounded edge was smooth as if drilled by a precision tool.

"I must take my leave to gather and study the results." Dr. Willoughsby thrust a hand toward Ian. "Thank you for your cooperation."

Ian shook the man's hand with unease, and he didn't let go. "What does this have to do with stopping the earthquakes, Doctor?"

"I'll know more after I study the results." Dr. Willoughsby made to pull away, but Ian didn't loosen his grip on the scientist's hand. "That's not an answer."

"If you can pour enough energy into the earth's mantle, perhaps you can prevent the plates from shifting apart."

"Like fusing them together?" Tara asked.

"The energy moving the plates is incredible," Ian said, confused by the scientist's theory. "We couldn't possibly generate that much power by this means."

"And we'd have to predict where the quake is to occur before it happens," Tara added.

"True, but we are one step closer to making that happen, aren't we? Think of this as reverse engineering." The scientist left, barking orders to his crew.

Joule knelt and reached into the hole. "I don't care what he claims," she said in a voice for only their ears. "In the wrong hands, this is beyond scary."

For the first time, Ian wondered if Joule's earlier flirting had an ulterior motive to get him alone. He helped pull her to her feet, then cupped her elbow and headed for a secluded spot at the base of the plateau. "This wasn't about stopping earthquakes," Ian said. "What's this really about?"

"Keep your voice down," Joule hushed.

Ian stopped under an outcropping while Tara stood guard. Saxon lifted his nose into the air and sniffed, then wandered away with silent steps. Ian let go of Joule. "What do you know about your father's experiments?"

"I suspect his funding comes from a private source. Whoever it is has a lot of money. I fight for every cent that I get, but he seems to have unlimited resources."

"But this is a Pur Weir research team," Ian said. "The Syndrion would be backing you."

"Not me, and I don't think my father's funds come from them either." Joule shook her head. "Why did you think that?"

"Because my summons to assist your father today came from the Primary."

"The head of the Syndrion?" The shocked look on Joule's face seemed genuine. "As far as I know, my father's never had any correspondence with him, or them, in years."

Ian stepped back. Who sent the summons? "Tara, who's the Syndrion representative for this region?"

"Quantaro," Tara said without hesitation.

"Is that name familiar?" Ian asked.

"His name was on our permit, and he sanctioned our working in the area. But that was all," Joule said.

Ian and Tara exchanged questioning glances. The message scroll had the Primary's insignia stamped at the bottom of the message. Could it have been forged? If so, Ian knew of only two people who could have been so daring, so bold.

Aeros? Tara channeled as if reading his thoughts. *Or Eve?*

Was it the Duach Weir leader, or the rebel leader? If either of them were involved, why lure him to meet with Dr. Willoughsby? Was this a test of Ian's core?

"I have questions for your father," Ian said and grabbed Tara's shoulder. Saxon returned and Tara grasped the wolf by the scruff of his neck. "Where could he have gone?"

"He would gather and compare the data in his office tent," Joule said.

Ian shyfted Tara and Saxon to Dr. Willoughsby's tent. The cold of the shyft instantly gave way to blistering heat that scorched Ian's face. The trio had reappeared in the midst of an inferno. The tent and everything in it were ablaze. Ian wrapped his arm around Tara, but before he could grab at Saxon, the wolf's fur caught fire. He shyfted them outside the boundaries of the tent and pulled Saxon to the ground, rolling his beloved companion in the dirt and mud. The odor of singed fur, mixed with creosote, filled Ian's nostrils. He got to his feet as burnt scraps of fabric blew about him, carried on a gentle breeze. Saxon rose and shook off mud mixed with scorched fur. Ian couldn't tell how serious it was.

"Did you see a body?" he asked Tara.

She stopped hacking long enough to shake her head. "The smoke."

Shouts filled the camp as workers ran every which way in an attempt to save what was already lost.

A few minutes later, Joule's shrill screams split the air. One of the men successfully held her back.

Bhutto's booming voice took command. His lanky arms directed the clamoring men carrying buckets of water and earthen sand. It was as effective as putting out a bonfire with spit.

{7}

High on the plateau, Jaered kept his rifle scope aimed at the Heir, but there were too many scrambling bodies to guarantee a clear shot. Jaered had only the one dart filled with half the dose, so his aim had to hit his mark on the first try. After several minutes, his patience ran thin. He pulled his face away from the barrel and rolled onto his back with a silent rant.

The injection had to be administered within a very narrow window of time, and that window was shutting fast.

Jaered rolled back onto his stomach and searched for the Heir through the rifle scope, but he wasn't to be found. He rose as high as his knees and held the nightscope binoculars to his face for a wider view of the camp, taking care to avoid the blinding glare coming from the burning tent. He couldn't find the Heir. Jaered had counted on his staying around to help, an easy target backlit by the fire.

An emerald glint on the rifle barrel caused Jaered to freeze. Voices. A whimper from the wolf. The Heir had shyfted his group to the vortex at the center of the rock formation. Jaered was beyond the perimeter, surrounded by the deep shadows of rock and evening. But the wolf was with them—and the wolf knew Jaered's scent.

"Let me help them," Ian said.

"Saxon's injured. The man who lured you here might just have been murdered. It's not safe. We're going," Tara demanded.

Saxon sniffed loud enough for Jaered to hear, then followed up with a determined snort. Had the animal caught wind of Jaered, or was the rising smoke from below thick enough to camouflage his presence? An emerald flash. The Heir's group was gone.

Jaered's heart resumed beating and he gasped to refill his lungs. He pulled out his cell and called Vael.

The recruit answered on the first ring. "Jaered, where are you?"

"Are you still covering the Heir's mansion?" Jaered asked.

"Yeah, but he isn't here," Vael said.

"Keep covering the house, and let me know the second you see him."

"Where are you? Are you coming?"

"Depends on when you spot the Heir." He hung up on the guy. Jaered was taking his frustrations out on the new rebel recruit, and he took a minute to gather his wits. Eve assigned Vael to Jaered in spite of his protests that it complicated his assignment. He was unsure how Vael would react to his killing the Heir.

Vael's father was the Heir's primary protector and a general in the Pur Weir army. There was no love lost between father and son, but it didn't erase that Vael was Pur, right down to his core. "Ahhh!" Jaered kicked a nearby rock, and it tumbled over the cliff. Failing to inject the Heir here in Africa meant that Jaered had to do it there, under Vael's watch.

He ejected the dart and packed it in the case he'd brought, to avoid potential misfire while shyfting back to the Heir's estate. This was all he had with no way to replenish the serum.

Jaered entered the vortex and drew enough energy to shyft halfway across the world—and steeled himself for what he had to do.

{8}

Rayne tugged on the flapping piece of cardboard. The weathered box ripped and she was rewarded with a face full of dust and dirt that stuck to her perspiration like glue. She backed out of the small shed coughing and stole a breath of clean air while wiping her face on her sleeve.

"What happened to dousing it in lighter fluid and tossing a match at it?" Patrick said from across the yard.

"Setting the cul-de-sac on fire wouldn't have earned me any points with the new neighbors."

"But it would have been a spectacular way of introducing yourself." Patrick grinned at her from the back porch and held up a six-pack.

"Hell, it's five o'clock somewhere," Rayne said, eager for an excuse to turn her back on the torch-worthy shed.

The steamy shower was liquid heaven, and she didn't step out until she ran out of hot water. When she opened the bathroom door, the steam rolled down the hall like fog snaking through London streets. Unable to recall which box or crate held her hairdryer, Rayne settled on pulling her long, honey-tinted hair up into a damp ponytail. She found Patrick in the kitchen.

He opened the freezer and tossed her a barely-chilled brew, then removed a generous slice of pizza from a box that hadn't been there when she stepped into her shower. He handed the droopy triangle to her on a brown napkin. "I couldn't find any plates."

"I only own two. One has a Mickey Mouse on it. The other has a hairline crack down the middle. Rayne left him to take a seat in her living room where a lone couch sat. It would probably stay there since it was the only piece of furniture she inherited from her mom that wasn't found in a Dumpster and eventually returned there, two moves back. Their vagabond life never had room for too many comforts, or possessions.

Patrick chose the floor and leaned against the non-functional fireplace that brought a splash of color to the room thanks to its fuchsia paint job. Rayne stared it, imagining a rainbow of shades beneath the current one.

"Ian wanted your address," he said.

"What did you tell him?"

"That you needed your space. Didn't want him shyfting over unexpectedly to check up on you."

"True enough," Rayne said and took a swig from her bottle. She held it in her mouth for a second before swallowing. The beer had already turned room temperature. No air conditioning was going to make for a long summer. "God forbid he should show up and get a peek at my research."

"It looks like that's all you've unpacked." Patrick took a generous bite of pizza and chewed while he flipped through a stack of papers at his knee. "Why isn't this on your laptop?" came out garbled.

"Technology and I have a tenuous relationship." Rayne held up her hands and wiggled her fingers. "I've come to appreciate that my touch does more than drain the energy of Weir Sars."

"Techno bummer," Patrick said. He eyed the piles. "Looks like you're a hell farther along than me."

"It's a mess, is what it is," Rayne said. "I typed in the name Jaered gave you and it opened up this quagmire of other names that don't make sense."

"What do you mean?" Patrick took a swig.

"It was like some kind of code. When I typed it in the search engine, at least two dozen women's names popped up. Some of them were listed as being born within a couple of years apart and others that living around the same time but a world apart."

"I might have failed biology," Patrick said. "Not once, but twice, mind you, but even I know you can't have more than one mother. Genetically speaking, of course."

"I'm beginning to think that Jaered gave us busy work to keep us out of his hair. At this rate, we'll never figure out who Ian's mother was."

"An idea of mine might have paid off." Patrick shoved a cardboard box toward her then opened his mouth wide enough to catch a dripping glob of cheese from the edge of his slice. "I thought about the genetics labs in Oregon," he hesitated, "and your father's experiments. If we're to believe everything

Jaered told me when I was his prisoner, and that Ian's was the first successful artificial core, maybe you weren't the only experiment going on up there. I mean, you were—"

"Created in those labs." She abandoned her pizza slice on the rolling arm of the couch and joined him on the floor. The shipping label on his cardboard box was addressed to the auditorium office. The return address label was Dr. Rulin Orr's. Rayne ran her fingertip over the QualSton logo that stirred memories she'd rather forget, but never could.

"Did he question you wanting some of my father's things?" Rayne asked.

"I went through Allison. She owed us after we kept mum that Saxon was alive. By the way, she was thrilled to hear that the wolf had found a home with Ian. She wasn't optimistic that she'd find much information, since the Pur soldiers took most everything after the raid on the compound."

Rayne bit her lip. From the meager size of the QualSton box, Allison's pessimism was warranted. Patrick removed a framed picture from the box and handed it to her. It held a newspaper photo with a short article below. "Here, I needed a magnifying glass to read the caption under the picture." He removed one from the box and passed it to her.

She studied it. There were four rows of scientists. Each row held ten or more people. "That's definitely my dad in the center."

"I asked Allison if she could find information on just the women," Patrick said. "The photo was taken way before she started working at QualSton, but she checked the company's records against the names in the caption." Patrick grabbed a sheet of paper from the box. "She organized them by projects that each scientist was assigned to. One of the women worked on a genetics team.

"Which one?" Rayne asked.

Patrick tilted the picture and indicated a dark-haired woman standing between two towering scientists. Only the upper two-thirds of her face were visible. It piqued Rayne's curiosity. Why stand in the back? Was she shy, self-assured enough to give her colleagues center stage, or did she want to disappear into the background? Rayne studied the image and her pulse jumped a beat when a vague memory of Rayne's mother carrying her as a toddler through the forest crept into her thoughts. Flashlight signals through the trees. A man and a woman standing next to a car parked behind bushes. Both motioning for her mother to hurry.

But it was the scientist's ebony hair and familiar, dark eyes that cooled the blood in Rayne's veins. She touched the image and peered for a long time at the woman. Could this be Ian's mother?

{9}

Ian remained in the northern vortex structure to connect with the Primary while Tara went ahead to tend to Saxon.

He leaned against the wall as the Primary's image floated at the center of the vortex chamber. Ian swore that the leader of the Syndrion was aging before his eyes.

"You should have known I would never send you into such a dangerous situation," the Primary said.

"Your insignia was on the message scroll. Nothing gave me reason for concern."

"They certainly knew what carrot to dangle." The Primary stuck his hands inside his loose sleeves and the scowl on his face deepened. "This was too manipulative to be Aeros. It had to be Eve who lured you there."

Ian had come to the same conclusion. "Dr. Willoughsby is familiar to you?"

"He had a hand in developing your boost. He left Weir projects soon after that to pursue his own interests. I will look into this. You have more important needs to attend to in your area."

Marcus's floating image suddenly appeared a few yards from the Primary's. "I've connected with Milo," Marcus said. "He's seen no unusual activity at the estate during your absence. I'm bringing a regiment to check things further. We should be there within the hour. Keep the estate energy jam on high."

"Why go to such lengths?" Ian said. "If our enemies were going to attack me, they had ample opportunity when I was halfway across the globe and vulnerable. I'd rather you leave your forces to clean up what they can. The San Francisco area needs them much more than I do."

"Alert me of any changes." The Primary's image snuffed out.

"I don't need reinforcements, Marcus." Ian rubbed his chest. "I returned from Africa with my core stronger than ever. If anything, they did me a favor. I'll assist with the cleanup after I enjoy one full night in my bed. Besides, Milo won't rest until he rams a couple of meals down my throat."

"Very well. But if anything changes, I want to be the first one to hear about it," Marcus said.

Ian yawned and stretched. His stomach growled, and he hoped Milo had planned an ample feast for dinner.

"Ian, I've been looking into the multiple burglaries that Vael and Jaered committed." Marcus lowered his voice in spite of the Primary's absence.

"What'd you find?" Ian pushed away from the wall, stuffed his hands in his pockets, and slowly paced around the circular room to gain control of his temper. The topic of Jaered was a sore that wouldn't heal.

"Xander and Parker——" A throat forcefully cleared in the background. Marcus's geeks were there with him. The Drion grunted. "Xander and *Pacman* have been researching the locations, along with what Vael and Jaered stole. It appears that the burglaries were connected."

Ian's steps came to a halt. "Connected how?"

"Each item gave them access to the next one on the list, like pieces of a puzzle," Marcus said.

"More like earning keys to the next level in a video game." A flaming red head of hair appeared at the edge of Marcus's floating image. Marcus grabbed Pacman by the neck. "You idiot! You'll cause me to parashyft!"

"Sweet!" Pacman said, muffled from under Marcus's arm.

"Can I come?" Xander's hand waved in front of them.

"Stand back or you'll get us all killed!" Marcus's agitation ceased once the boys put some distance between them and the Drion.

"But their final burglary was stealing my medical records," Ian continued.

"That was the ultimate prize," Pacman shouted from somewhere nearby.

When he'd first discovered that Jaered had his medical records, Ian thought the rebels had wanted the info to create artificial Sar cores. Had he been wrong? "Marcus, you never told the Primary about Vael?"

The muscles at Marcus's jaw bulged. "I had hoped to track down my son and deal with his actions without the Primary's knowledge. But it's been several weeks since he took off with Jaered, and I'm no closer to finding him. I don't dare use my typical resources. It could get back to the Primary. But it's like searching for that turd in a haystack.

{10}

It took a few minutes for Jaered to climb the hill overlooking the Heir's estate and join Vael. The young recruit handed off the binoculars.

"Only Tara and Saxon returned. I haven't seen Ian," Vael said.

"Where are they now?" Jaered scanned the inner compound below.

"They went inside a few minutes ago. The wolf limped like it might be hurt."

Jaered lowered the binoculars and settled back against the tree. He set the rifle case on the ground and removed the weapon.

"What's that under the barrel?" Vael asked.

"Pressurized gas."

"What for?"

"You ask too many questions." Jaered tossed the binoculars at Vael's feet. He stared at Vael debating how much he should tell the young recruit. Eve had left his orientation up to Jaered, and he wasn't one for sharing. "The Heir's probably meeting with the Primary." He hesitated. "Maybe your dad."

"Dad always made more time for him than me." Vael twisted the scope's strap between his fingers.

Jaered banked on the Syndrion being too spooked at the Congo events to send the Heir on another assignment. If they did, Jaered's mission would tank. "Hopefully your dad has his hands full with the latest quake and won't interfere."

"Interfere with what? You haven't told me a goddamn thing," Vael snapped. "It's been weeks, Jaered. Suddenly you act like you don't trust me, even after everything I gave up to join you and the rebels."

"Don't smear me with your guilt. I couldn't shake you off, no matter what I tried," Jaered said. Movement in the trees. Rusty hinges. The inner compound's gate swung open.

Jaered grabbed Vael and they ducked down beneath the group of fallen logs. The Heir often took the path that led by Galen and Mara's gravesites whenever he arrived at the estate. Jaered counted on today being no different. It would give him the clearest shot.

Positioning the tip of the rifle on the log, Jaered flipped up the scope then followed the Heir's progression down the path. At the fork, the Heir paused. Jaered held his breath. A second later, the Heir turned in the direction of the graves and Jaered breathed easier. So far, so good. Movement out of the corner of his eye. Vael lowered the binoculars. "Don't move, you're distracting me," Jaered said between clenched teeth.

"What are you going to do?"

"Not now," Jaered hissed.

"What are you going to do?" Vael said, his voice husky, desperate.

"I warned you when you joined the rebels that you might not like our methods." Jaered kept a keen eye on the Heir's progress, but remained acutely aware of Vael beside him.

"You can't kill the Heir. The Prophecy. If he dies, you'll damn Earth for sure," Vael said.

"We have that covered," Jaered said. "Now shut up and let me do my job." The Heir hesitated at the entrance to the gravesite and raised his face to the sun. Jaered prepared to take the shot but a gust of wind kicked up decaying leaves between him and his target. Jaered waited with his finger on the trigger. He applied the slightest of pressure.

Vael grabbed the barrel, blocking Jaered's line of site. "You can't kill him! There's got to be another way." Vael pushed against the log and stood, clutching the rifle barrel as his hand took on a subtle glow.

Jaered swung around on his hip and took out Vael's legs before he could use his power to ruin the gun barrel. The recruit slammed against the log with a moan cut short as the wind was knocked out of him. Jaered kicked the rifle butt and it slipped out of Vael's hand. The weapon bounced off the log and came to a rest on the ground without discharging.

Vael threw himself on top of Jaered. Jaered grabbed him and twisted him onto his back, then straddled Vael's chest and arms, pinning him down with sheer weight. When Vael clawed at Jaered, Jaered smashed the edge of his hand against Vael's throat.

The recruit's eyes widened and he went limp while choking, gasping for air, made all the harder by Jaered sitting on his chest.

Jaered grabbed the rifle and raised it to his face. He swept the tip in all directions until he found the Heir standing stock-still at the graves.

"Can't . . . kill," Vael wheezed.

"Watch me," Jaered snarled, and pulled the trigger.

{11}

A sting at the back of his neck. Ian brushed off what felt like a sizable bee, then rubbed the spot. He turned and looked up the hill. Something, a muffled noise, had caught his attention, but the absence of movement through the trees had him second-guessing himself, and he headed for home. The vibrant colors of dusk peeked above the tree line at the horizon. They'd left Africa in the middle of the night only to appear in Northern California in late afternoon, hours earlier.

By the time he reached the mansion's back patio, his core felt as if it had absorbed the last heat of the day. He pressed a fist against his chest and took a deep breath.

"You okay?" Tara asked. She sat on a patio chair wrapping gauze around Saxon's chest.

"How is he?" Ian said, wiping perspiration from the back of his neck.

"Third-degree blistering but thanks to his thick coat, the burn area wasn't larger than a half-dollar. He can reach it, though, so Mac told me to bandage it." Tara tied off the end and knotted it, then gathered Saxon's snout in her cupped hands. "Now leave it alone and it'll heal faster.

Saxon snorted and ran off.

"Betcha five dollars it's not there when he returns," Ian said.

"Yeah, why did I bother?" Tara rolled up the gauze.

"Is Mac here?" Ian said.

"I got sick of my cooking," Dr. Mac said from the open back door. He held a pitcher of tea in one hand and his old, weathered medical bag in the other.

"When have you ever cooked?" Milo said nudging him out the door. The old caretaker had a plate of fresh fruit in his hand. "This is all the snacking anyone's allowed or you won't eat the meal I've prepared."

Dr. Mac set the pitcher on the patio table and handed his bag to Tara. She stowed the gauze and ointment inside. The old Weir doctor came over and threw an arm around Ian's shoulder. "I've been concerned about how you've been holding up lately. But I have to admit, you look like your old self again."

"I didn't know I could trap and control so much electricity in my core, Doc."

"Tara shared a little with us. Something about lifting off the ground?" Mac said.

"It was easy once I redirected the electricity out my feet." Ian sat on the edge of the chair and released deep breaths in a slow continuous stream. The cool, salty breeze across the back of his neck did nothing to ease the heat emanating from his chest.

"Ian, are you all right?" Tara peered at him.

"My core's been depleted for so long, I'll have to get used to it at full capacity again." He stood. "That iced tea looks good. I think I'll grab a glass."

"Grab one for me," Tara said. "Lots of ice."

Ian stepped into the kitchen and opened the cupboard, removing two glasses. When he turned toward the refrigerator, his thoughts transformed into a tidal pool. One of the glasses slipped out of his hand and rolled to a stop on the counter. Ian grabbed the refrigerator handle to steady himself. He opened the freezer and leaned against the edge, bathing in the frigid air. He closed his eyes and focused on breathing. In. Out. He tried to recall the last time he'd eaten.

"Ian?" Dr. Mac said from the patio doorway. "Are you sure you're okay?"

"I just need a cold shower and to wash off the grime from the Congo." Ian used one of the hand towels to wipe the perspiration off the back of his neck. "Would you mind getting Tara's drink?"

"Of course," Dr. Mac said. He put a gentle hand on Ian's back. "Milo told me about Rayne. I'm sorry."

"Rubber gloves and feathers just got us so far, Doc."

"I wish I could have done more for you both. I should have . . .," his voice trailed off.

"We can't change fate." Ian left and took the stairs slower than usual, using the banister for support up the winding staircase. His core might be at full capacity, he thought, but his body was weighed down by exhaustion thanks to weeks of disaster relief assignments.

The shower's cold setting wasn't cold enough. Ian dialed the faucet as far to the right as possible. Steam rose from the center of his chest when the blast of frigid water slammed against him, and his thoughts turned muddy. The last thing he recalled was sliding down the wall of cool tile.

The intense cold raised goose bumps across Ian's skin, and he shivered beyond control. His jaw ached from teeth jack-hammering together. The scalding heat in his chest made it difficult to breathe. Frantic voices. Ian opened his eyes to find himself naked in his bathtub and submerged up to his neck in mounds of ice.

Tara held her palm against his forehead, and with her other hand, plunged the core thermometer through the chunks of ice and pressed it to his chest. The ice cubes acted like a prism as the thermometer's stones in its handle looked like giant precious jewels. "It's not helping," she announced.

"That's the last of it. He's melting it faster than I can replenish it," Milo said.

"Then shyft and get more," Dr. Mac said. "This is all I know to do until I can figure out what's going on."

"Wh-wh-what," Ian stammered. "Haaaappend?"

"From what we can tell, your core is overheating," Dr. Mac said. Tara pulled the core thermometer away from Ian's chest and handed it to Dr. Mac. He looked at it, then shook and checked it again. "Your core temperature is off my scale."

"The last time we measured it, your body temperature was at one hundred thirty," Tara said.

"If you weren't a Weir Sar, you'd be dead," Milo folded a wet washcloth and dabbed at Ian's forehead. "What the hell is going on, Mac? You told us years ago that the boy could never get sick."

"Not by anything in the natural world," Dr. Mac said.

"Where is everyone?" Patrick's voice came from down the hall.

"In here!" Milo shouted.

Patrick appeared in the bathroom archway. "What's shakin' Houdini?" He chuckled. "Trying out a new illusion?"

"Ian's core is burning up. We need more ice." Milo slipped past Patrick and ran out of the room.

"What?" Patrick fell to one knee and pressed his hand against Ian's forehead. "Whoa!" He pulled it away and rubbed it on his pant leg. "Why?"

"If we knew that, we wouldn't be so scared," Tara said.

"Tara, I'm going to shyft to my clinic and grab some supplies," Dr. Mac said. "I'll need a microscope and other things if I'm to figure out what's going on."

"I'll help," Patrick said.

Dr. Mac shook his head. "Patrick, I'm shyfting."

"I heard you. We better get going." Patrick stood with pursed lips. He rubbed Tara's back. "Dr. Mac will figure it out."

"Call us if you think of something else we need to bring," Dr. Mac said. "Or if his condition drastically changes." Patrick followed the doctor out and they disappeared down the hall.

"It has to be the experiments they did on you." Tara scooped a few of the ice chunks onto Ian's chest and held them there, but they soon melted beneath her hand.

He shook his head. "I was stronger, not weaker."

"You're reacting the same way you did after Willoughsby's exedrae experiment," she said. "Only a hundred times worse."

"This feels . . . different," he said, shocked at how weak his voice came out. He gasped for air as the searing heat in his chest stole his breath. "My core wasn't affected, only my body." With the ice gone, the water temperature rose rapidly. The bath was quickly turning into a hot tub. "Drain the water and fill it with cold."

Tara's face lifted in panic. "Milo isn't back with more ice."

Ian raised his hands and focused on the last time he had visited the Arctic Circle. He'd barely made a dent in the premature ice melt, but was able to rescue hundreds of trapped wildlife and relocate them. The Inuit tribal leader had Ian sleep in an igloo. He closed his eyes and recalled the feel of his icy abode.

A large brick of solid ice appeared in Ian's hand. Too weak to hold onto it, the block plopped in his lap and water splashed everywhere. Tara scooped it up and held it to his chest. A moment later, his shivering returned.

{12}

It took several minutes for Vael to recover. Jaered had come close to crushing his windpipe and he kept a keen ear to the man's labored breathing while dismantling the rifle and storing the pieces in his duffle.

Vael propped himself up on an elbow. "What did you shoot him with?" he rasped.

"A dart," Jaered said.

"Filled with what?" When Jaered didn't answer him, Vael rolled to his side and got up on all fours. He hung his head and coughed. A couple of minutes later, he settled on his knees. "What?" Vael forcefully cleared his throat. "You owe me that much."

"A serum that Eve had made," Jaered said.

Vael wiped his brow on his sleeve. "Do you really want me to torture you with my questions?"

Jaered grabbed Vael by his shirt. "You ever, ever get in my way like that again, I'll kill you!" At the look of terror in Vael's eyes, Jaered let go and backed away. He only had himself to blame. He'd chosen a spot at the maximum distance to avoid the Heir hearing them, but the Heir had knocked the dart away immediately. Jaered wasn't confident that the full injection had been delivered.

A deep breath helped to stifle Jaered's mood. He zipped the duffle closed, then peered over the top of the log. The Heir was gone. "Do you know why your father had your name spelled with a-e instead of the more common a-l-e?" Jaered asked.

"It's the Weir spelling. My old man's sentimental, nauseatingly traditional."

"He honored a culture he knows nothing about," Jaered said through gritted teeth.

"No one knows more about Weir culture than my parents. Well, maybe my grandfather," Vael said.

"The Weir didn't originate on Earth." Jaered paused. "I'm not from Earth."

Vael shrugged. "Your clear corona gave you away."

"I was born on Thrae," Jaered said. "Earth's parallel dimension."

"The Syndrion would have you killed if they knew you were here. Parashyfting is—"

"Punishable by death," Jaered said. "Do you know why?"

"It disrupts the balance between planets, could bring about natural disaster."

Jaered scoffed. "The Primary has fed the Pur Weir lies for centuries." Too late, he caught his blunder, and counted on it slipping past Vael. It didn't.

"*Centuries?* The Primary isn't that much older than my dad."

Jaered needed Vael's unwavering cooperation if he was to complete the rest of his mission. Hell, the guy wouldn't be allowed to leave the rebels, even if he wanted to. Vael knew Eve's true identity. "Johann, the man that you and the rest of Earth's Weir know as the Primary, is one of the original five Ancients," Jaered said. "He's more than two thousand years old. So is Aeros . . . and Eve."

Vael's mouth sagged, and he sat in stunned silence.

Jaered got to his feet and slung the duffle over his shoulder. He offered a hand to Vael. "Come on, we don't have much time to find cover." Vael grabbed his hand and Jaered pulled him to his feet. Jaered turned and maneuvered through the boulders like a mountain goat, pulling well ahead of Vael.

"What's the rush?" Vael called out.

"Mother Nature is about to unleash its fury on a global scale," Jaered shouted from over his shoulder.

"Why?" Vael asked.

Because the Heir is dying, Jaered kept to himself.

{13}

P atrick's teeth wouldn't stop chattering and he focused on collecting the supplies while ignoring the lingering effects of the shyft. He wasn't looking forward to the the return trip. grabbed the box and followed Dr. Mac into the adjoining exam room. "Have you ever seen anything like this before?"

"Never," Dr. Mac said. "As far as I know this is unprecedented."

"But you can stop it, right?" Patrick opened the drawer Mac pointed to and grabbed all the hypodermic needles wrapped in antiseptic bags. "No one understands Sar cores and how they work better than you."

Dr. Mac paused at opening a cupboard and postured as if to say something, but then grabbed IV bags and tubing and tossed them into his medical bag without a word. Patrick was impressed at how quickly the doctor gathered the necessary things, as if he had rehearsed it. It struck Patrick that this wasn't the first time he'd treated Ian in an emergency.

"You've got to save him, Doc," Patrick said.

Dr. Mac gave him a weak smile and patted his hand. The doctor's ragged, soiled bunny slippers made a scuffling noise when he walked to the opposite side of the room and put his hand on top of a machine sitting on the counter. "This is the last thing I'll need. We've got enough to carry as it is. I'll return for this."

A thick tree branch crashed against the window, but it held firm with a croak. The wind howled in the vents, racing through the brownstone medical office. Nature's siege on London intensified the longer they were there.

"This is only the beginning, isn't it?" Patrick said at the overhead billowing clouds.

"The Syndrion will question the Heir's well-being if it gets much worse."

"Is Milo contacting them?" Patrick said.

"I told him to hold off. If this is contagious, we could be exposing the bulk of the Syndrion to the same fate. We need to keep the last remaining Weir Sars safe."

"But they'll come to investigate if you don't at least warn them," Patrick said.

"They might not associate the storms with Ian's health. The increase in volcanic eruptions in Southeast Asia might be blamed." Dr. Mac set the clasp on his bag while Patrick secured the flaps on the box, bulging with the top of the microscope peeking out. Dr. Mac returned to his front office and stepped into the center of his waiting room. An emerald hue formed.

"Must be nice to have a vortex in the middle of your office," Patrick said.

"It forces us to carefully schedule Weir Sar appointments around human ones." He motioned for Patrick to join him. "Text Milo we're on our way."

Patrick punched in the message. A minute later, Milo confirmed. "The power jam is off. We can shyft directly to the foyer." Patrick picked up the heavy box and propped it on his hip. He grabbed the old doctor's shoulder. At the needle-like tingling, he braced himself for the frigid cold and disorientation of the shyft. Molecule baths were his least favorite method of travel.

They appeared next to the mansion's foyer table. The green cloud dispersed. Patrick shuddered. A waiting Milo grabbed the box from him and headed into the kitchen. "I've cleared the center island and table for you. If you need to spread out farther, just say so."

Patrick looked up at the balcony. "Do you need—"

"Go. Send Tara down," Dr. Mac said. "Her medical training will be useful." He left for the kitchen.

Patrick took the stairs up the winding staircase two at a time, and rushed into Ian's room to find Tara sitting on the edge of Ian's bed with her back to the door. "Tara, Dr. Mac wants you."

She wiped her face with her hands and stood without looking at him. Patrick grabbed her and gave her a tight hug. She pressed her face into his chest, but it did nothing to suppress her sob. "It'll be all right," he said softly. "Dr. Mac will figure this out." But Tara pulled away and headed out of the room without a word.

He approached Ian's bed. Milo had placed him in his boost with large bricks of ice piled up around and on top of him. The base of Ian's bed glowed, reminiscent of the Aurora Borealis.

Ian's skin looked sunburned and the center of his chest glowed dull, like a low-watt light bulb through the ice. His eyes were closed and his lips slightly parted. Labored, strident breaths came and went.

Patrick gripped the hand-carved bedpost and felt utterly useless.

Beyond Ian's bedroom balcony, lightning lit up the night's sky with zigzag bolts. Thunder shook the window panes in his balcony door. A sheet of rain drenched the two, cushioned chairs outside.

Patrick had lived through this before and knew the Prophecy to be true. If Ian should die, no living thing on Earth would be spared Mother Nature's wrath.

Tara returned wearing rubber gloves and carrying supplies. She created an IV port in the back of Ian's hand, then tied rubber tubing around his bicep and inserted a needle, withdrawing three vials of blood. As they filled, she alternated holding and letting go of the glass vials as if his blood was too hot to handle. She dropped them into a bag, disposed of the needle in a red plastic biohazard container, and left in silence.

Ian stirred. "Bee," he gasped.

Patrick leaned close. "Ian, what about a bee?"

"Back . . . my neck." His eyes fluttered, then opened under half-closed lids.

"Don't pass out on me." Patrick ran to the balcony and shouted. "Ian's awake. He's trying to tell us something!"

The others soon rushed into the bedroom. Dr. Mac placed his medical bag down on the nearby dresser. "What is it?"

"He said something about a bee stinging him," Patrick said.

"A bee wouldn't sting him," Tara said.

Milo shook his head. "Or have any effect, even if it did."

"He might be delirious." Dr. Mac pulled out a penlight and shone it in Ian's eyes. "What are you trying to say, Ian?"

"Stung me," Ian whispered.

"At the back of his neck," Patrick added.

Dr. Mac felt underneath. "It feels like a raised, tiny welt. Milo, help me." The two men removed some ice blocks and lifted one of Ian's shoulders. Dr. Mac pulled out his headgear and put it on. Half a dozen lenses popped out like spider legs and moved as though they had a mind of their own. The largest one adjusted itself over one of Dr. Mac's eyes and he peered at the back of Ian's neck. "There is a small puncture. But from what I can see, there's no stinger." They settled Ian back on his pillow and arranged fresh ice blocks around him.

"A bee sting wouldn't do this to him," Tara said.

"Not a bee," Ian said so softly, Patrick wasn't sure he'd spoken at all. "No buzz." Ian coughed and gulped in a large amount of air. "A . . . *pop*, came from up the hill."

"Where were you?" Patrick said.

"Graves." Ian closed his eyes.

"Patrick, go. See if you can find something," Dr. Mac said.

Patrick hesitated. "But what am I looking for?"

"I have no idea," Dr. Mac said. "A dart, perhaps."

"It would be very, very small," Tara said. "Otherwise Ian wouldn't have taken it to be a bee sting."

Downstairs, Patrick rummaged around and found a flashlight in the utility room junk drawer. He grabbed Milo's rain slicker and stuffed his bare feet into the old caretaker's galoshes. The hood covered his head and then some. At a tremendous clap of thunder, Patrick paused with his hand on the doorknob then turned and pushed, but the door was held firm by the wind. It took a hearty shove before he could step out into the storm.

He followed the path to Mara and Galen's gravesites, dodging tree branches, trusting that the lightning rod at the top of the mansion was a preferable target over his drenched slicker. When a tall nearby tree took a sizzling hit, his steps quickened.

As he rounded the far corner of Milo's greenhouse, Patrick paused at a blur of white in the distance. Saxon scratched and clawed at the greenhouse door with low, determined growls.

"Come here, Saxon," Patrick shouted, but the wolf ignored him, determined to gain entrance. Patrick cowered at another strike a few yards away. "Saxon, come here," he yelled over the storm.

Saxon left his quest with a growl. Together they reached the gravesite clearing and Patrick stood where he'd seen Ian frequently pause during his vigils. Patrick shone the flashlight toward the graves and mimicked brushing a bee away from the back of his neck and then looked about on the ground. The area was soaked with spindly creeks flowing in all directions before converging into a continuous stream a few feet behind him, carrying the overabundance of rainwater down the gentle slope.

"We're looking for something the size of a bee," he told Saxon, holding two fingers close together, unsure if the animal could hear him over the thunder. "It stung Ian at the back of the neck, then fell away." Patrick tossed in charade-like gestures for good measure. "For all I know, it was washed or blown away as soon as the storm hit."

Undeterred by human doubt, Saxon put his nose to the ground and went in search. Patrick swept the flashlight back and forth but found nothing other than rocks, twigs, pine needles and the occasional pinecone. The visor on the slicker did little good when the wind turned the rain horizontal. He swiped at his wet face and shone the flashlight in the direction of the headstones. Mara's name stared back at him. "Come on, girl. Help us out. It happened on your watch." Patrick blinked back the rain and swiped at his nose with his fist. Saxon returned with his snout close to the ground following an invisible trail but stopped at the edge of Mara's grave. He looked up at Patrick expectedly.

Patrick crouched low and shone the flashlight near the wolf's paws. Something small and bulbous, sat in a cluster of small rocks. Upon closer examination, it had a kind of fuzzy covering—and a short, thin, delicate needle.

He went to grab it, but thought better of it, as if Mara stayed his hand. He found a pile of leaves, separated a thick one from the bunch, and scooped up the dart. He wrapped the leaf around it and stuffed it in the outer pocket of the slicker. The beam from the flashlight lit up Mara's gravestone. "Good job," he whispered. Saxon nudged him so rough that he lost his balance and nearly toppled into the mud. "You, too, Sherlock." Patrick patted the wolf. He shone the light on Galen's headstone. "Now you take over and help the Doc find answers before it's too late."

Energetic steps carried Patrick home, and he was met at the back door by eager faces. He unwrapped the leaf and presented his find. Dr. Mac and Tara scurried off. Patrick discarded the wet gear in the mud room and dried off with a towel from Milo's laundry basket. By the time he returned to the kitchen, Dr. Mac had his face to the microscope, studying whatever was found inside the miniature dart. Patrick paced around the kitchen table but came to a halt when Dr. Mac sat up with a start.

Tara paused from inserting one of the vials of blood into the centrifuge. "What is it?" she said.

"Take a look," Dr. Mac pushed away from the kitchen island and approached the counter. He topped off the coffee in his mug, then stared out the window above the sink without taking a sip.

Tara positioned her eye over the lens. "What are those?"

"Nothing natural," Dr. Mac muttered with his back to them.

"What do you see?" Patrick asked from across the counter.

"It's nanotechnology," Dr. Mac said.

"No shit?" Patrick raked his fingers through his damp hair. "They injected Ian with mini-robots?"

Tara positioned a different lens in place and turned the dial to refocus. "Programmed to do what?" She pulled away and swung the microscope around for Patrick to take a look.

He leaned in. About half a dozen tiny squares floated in the saline solution. Light from the microscope highlighted circuit-like technology on a couple of them. "I thought nanites were active little buggers. These look dead."

"In simplistic terms, once injected, nanites are carried through the bloodstream and then attach to whatever host they were programmed to," Dr. Mac said. "Then they go about their job."

"What did they attach to?" Patrick asked.

"It's got to be something associated with Ian's core," Tara said.

Dr. Mac turned and paced around the kitchen island. "Sar cores are made up of cells that collect and store a specific energy found in the natural world."

"Except in Ian's case, he has a variety of core cells, not just one type like other Sars," Tara said, as though reasoning aloud. "That's what gives him several, different powers."

"If the nanites attack the protein that covers core cells, it could prevent them from purging or spending the energy," Dr. Mac said.

"Which would cause them to overheat." Tara pushed away from the counter. "This has got to be connected to Africa, somehow."

"But why make Ian healthier, stronger than ever if they intended to attack him?" Patrick said.

"If the nanites are preventing his core from purging its energy, the stronger his core—"

"The faster his core would overheat." Dr. Mac grabbed his mug from the counter.

"So if I'm following your science mumbo jumbo," Patrick said. "He's better off if his core is unhealthy."

Dr. Mac and Tara exchanged stunned looks, then rushed out of the kitchen. Dr. Mac shouted up the stairs, "Milo get Ian out of his boost, now!"

Tara ran past him and sprinted up the staircase. "It could be killing him!" she yelled.

They reached the room just as Milo stepped away from the bed with Ian cradled in his arms. The boost's glow ceased and his room was pitched in darkness, lit by intermittent lightning flashes. "If not his boost, where?" Milo said gruffly.

"The bathtub," Tara said, gathering what was left of the ice blocks.

"No," Dr. Mac said. "It may be too close to the energy source of his boost. If we're right, we have to keep him far away from all power sources, even the vortex in the foyer."

"Patrick's wing. The guest room at the end of the hall," Milo said. "And it has a bathroom."

"Put him in that tub." Dr. Mac grabbed his medical bag.

Patrick ran ahead and opened doors, then threw aside the shower curtain. Milo lowered Ian into the bathtub. "I'll grab more ice blocks," the old caretaker said.

"I'll help," Patrick said.

By the time Patrick returned, he didn't have to ask how Ian was. The translucent skin had clouded, and the glow radiating from his chest appeared duller. Ian's breathing wasn't as labored.

"Those sick bastards," Milo muttered.

"Ingenious, really," Tara said. "The thing that heals him, kills him."

"Yeah, well, whoever this is, is one twisted fuck," Patrick said.

"We still don't know for sure what the nanites are attacking, or how to reverse it," Dr. Mac said, measuring Ian's core with the gilded thermometer. "This may only slow down the inevitable."

"But buys us time to figure it out," Patrick said. Tara withdrew her cell from her pocket. "Who are you calling?" Patrick asked.

"Rayne." Tara looked between the men as if daring them to stop her. No one objected. She punched in the number and held the phone to her ear. "If a healthy core is not in Ian's favor—"

"Rayne drain to the rescue," Patrick said.

"The Syndrion!" Ian grabbed Dr. Mac's sleeve. "Gotta . . . keep them away."

"He's right. If they show up, they'll discover Rayne's secret for sure," Dr. Mac said.

"If his condition deteriorates much more, they'll be on our doorstep, invited or not." Milo said.

{14}

Jaered stayed stock-still, listening for signs that the wolf had gained access to the greenhouse and had followed their scent to the tunnel entrance. He'd closed the hatch, but kept his ear to it. The rest of his mission hinged on staying under everyone's radar.

Vael waited in silence at the base of the ladder. When Jaered's boot lowered for the next rung down, Vael released an audible sigh of relief. "That was close," he said.

"The wolf and I have a tolerance hate relationship, that's pretty much stuck in hate." Jaered reached the tunnel floor and slung his duffle off his shoulder. "If it wasn't for the storm, I would have realized he was tracking us a lot sooner."

"How did you know about this tunnel?" Vael asked.

Jaered removed a flashlight from his pack, then picked up the duffle by the handles. He turned on the beam and headed down the tunnel. "Eve has blueprints to the entire estate."

"How'd she get those?" Vael said.

"It was among the items we stole a while back. Now quiet and let me think. I memorized our route, but I have to count off a few steps at each junction."

"Why?" When Jaered flashed the beam in Vael's eyes, he squinted and threw his hands up. "Okay, mums the word."

"That'd be a fucking miracle." At the first intersection, Jaered paused. He took the left tunnel and counted off five paces. When he flipped a switch on the flashlight, the white beam turned to ultraviolet. Crimson streaks crisscrossed at the height of their ankles and ended at each wall. The laser beam alarm system was two steps ahead. "See that?" Jaered said. Vael peered over his shoulder. "Don't trip it."

"Gotcha," Vael said. "Laser beams, bad."

They stepped over the beams and continued. Jaered navigated two more intersections and they came to the base of a ladder. It rose so high that the glow from Jaered's flashlight couldn't find the top. "We're here," he said and dropped the duffle.

"Where's here?" Vael asked, grabbing the flashlight and aiming it up the ladder. "We're under the mansion, but where?"

"Just chill." Jaered slid down to the dirt floor and withdrew the receiver from the pack. He stuck the bud in his ear and dialed the switch until he picked up voices. He leaned against the tunnel wall and took a deep breath. So much could have gone wrong over the past few hours. Nearly did, when he missed taking his shot in Africa, but he hoped that enough of the serum was injected, and that Eve's plan was back on track.

This next phase was entirely up to the Pur doctor.

"Now what?" Vael settled across from him. Jaered ignored the question, focused on the conversation on the other end.

Vael kicked his boot. "Last time I checked, I speak the same language as you, dumbshit."

Jaered whipped out a handgun and pointed it at Vael. It held a fast-acting tranquilizer that Jaered was itching to use on the recruit. "Keep distracting me and you'll get us both killed." Jaered turned down the volume and rested the gun on his lap, but his finger wasn't far from the trigger. "We're waiting for another rebel to follow through on his end. Until then, all we have is time."

"What did you shoot the Heir with?" Vael asked.

"Microscopic robots."

"Why?"

Jaered weighed his words carefully. "They're overheating his core. Once his core temperature reaches four hundred fifty degrees, he'll burn up." Jaered thought back to the human trial that he'd witnessed a few months earlier. "Literally."

"If you want him dead, why didn't you just use a bullet?" Vael said. "Or is torturing a man to death the rebels' way?"

"We couldn't kill him outright," Jaered said. "We had to do it in such a way, that his connection to the earth would disconnect."

Vael stared at Jaered and shook his head. "Earth is already on the road to self-destruction. Why take out the best defense this planet has?"

"Earth's Armageddon has already begun, there's no stopping it. Eve has one goal. To ensure that as many as possible survive what's coming. Sacrifice is inevitable."

Memories of Jaered's wife bubbled to the surface, and he shut that door the second it opened. "Shit happens," he snapped.

"But the Prophecy," Vael muttered.

"Is about to be tweaked." Jaered took his hand off the gun and turned up the volume on the receiver.

{15}

Rayne battled the storm and made it to the estate in record time. She let herself in through the garage but paused at the odor of burnt food and the mansion's silence.

She rushed up the steps, then stopped at voices coming from the east wing. "Tara?" Rayne called out. "Milo?"

Tara stuck her head out of the room at the end of the hall and gestured. "Here."

At the deep creases of concern on Tara's face, Rayne's stomach lurched. "Ian?"

"He's alive, but barely," Tara said. She gripped Rayne's hand and led her past the empty guest bed to the adjoining bathroom.

Dr. Mac, Milo, and Patrick were huddled inside the cramped space.

Rayne took one look at Ian, submerged up to his neck in large chunks of ice, and stopped short. His normally dark-tanned skin was pasty and a bright glow came from his chest, magnified by the ice, lighting up the chunks like massive diamonds. An IV bag filled with a clear liquid hung from the overhead shower rod. It was attached to a port in the back of

Ian's hand. He appeared asleep. Patrick slipped past her to make room.

She dropped to her knees beside the tub. "What happened?"

Ian's eyes fluttered. Heat rose while beads of perspiration dotted every inch of his exposed skin. "Rayne?"

"I'm here, Ian," she said. "I thought he couldn't get sick. Why isn't he in his boost?"

"He was injected with nanites." Dr. Mac sat on the closed toilet seat. He looked like he'd weathered a hurricane.

"They're causing Ian's core to overheat," Tara said.

Rayne took in the mounds of thick chunks. "The ice—"

"Slowing it down, but not stopping it," Patrick said from the bedroom.

"Who did this?" Rayne asked. Was it Aeros, or the rebels? She closed her eyes. Not Jaered, she hoped.

"We don't know for sure," Milo said. "But my money's on that bitch, Eve."

Rayne looked at Patrick. Had they been too trusting of Jaered? "What can I do?"

"We need you to try and drain energy from his core," Dr. Mac said. "Just a little, at first, to test it."

"You *want* me to touch him?" She shook her head at the thought of something so forbidden.

"Here," Dr. Mac said. He grabbed a towel, then removed Ian's hand from under the ice and dried it.

Touching Ian wasn't just dangerous, it caused him incredible pain. Rayne gently cupped Ian's hand in hers and whispered, "I'm sorry."

Ian's jaw tensed at the same time his breaths grew shallow and quick. His back arched and his chest rose above the water. His energy flowed through her, then dissipated where she knelt as if the floor sucked it out of her. A couple of seconds later, Rayne let go. Ian's body relaxed and settled. She joined Tara at the doorway, making room for Dr. Mac, fearful she'd brush against the old doctor and drain him, too.

A minute later, Dr. Mac pulled back and shook out the thermometer. "It made a dent," he announced.

"How much of a dent," Milo growled.

"Along with the ice, it'll help buy us some time," Dr. Mac said. "We'll need to repeat it."

Rayne shook her head.

"Better than the alternative." Tara threw an arm around Rayne's shoulders and led her away.

Rayne stepped from the window and left Patrick to watch the storm's wrath. She navigated around Saxon, sprawled on the bathroom floor like a rug, and then sat on the edge of the tub. A twinge of peace set in as she stroked the wolf's coat while the whirring fan blew her hair across her face.

It had been more than two hours and Ian wasn't improving; he just wasn't getting much worse. The holding pattern had frayed everyone's nerves. Milo had come up with the idea of using dry ice and had shyfted to a nearby industrial gas plant to bring back sixty-pound blocks. The carbon dioxide gas from its melting forced them to use powerful fans. They had to leave the window open in the bedroom beyond, and the humidity had everyone dripping wet.

Voices. The others had returned. "We may have a solution," Dr. Mac announced.

"There's nothing we about it. It's your idea. I want no part of it," Milo barked. "There's got to be something else."

"There isn't," Dr. Mac said. "I can't treat what I don't understand."

"If we can't treat the cause, then we focus on stopping the symptom, Milo," Tara said.

"The dry ice is better than the regular ice," Patrick said from the window.

"The boy is dehydrating faster than I can pump fluids into him," Dr. Mac said. "His body won't be able to tolerate this holding pattern much longer."

"What's your solution?" Rayne called out the open bathroom door.

Tara stuck her head in. "We want you to drain Ian's core."

"That's what I've been doing," Rayne said. "My torturing him isn't getting us anywhere."

"We want you to drain . . . *all* of it," Tara said.

Rayne shot to her feet. "You can't be serious."

"No!" Ian gasped. The icy water sloshed and the ice chunks clinked together. He made to sit up but in his weakened state, he slipped and collapsed back against the tub. His breaths came rapid, labored.

"The nanites are winning," Dr. Mac said. "Time is on their side."

"There's got to be someone who knows more about these bugs than you," Milo snapped.

"I've reached out to the best scientific minds I know." Dr. Mac growled. "I've been told that nanites are designed with a purpose. These are obviously attacking his core."

"Ian, in theory, if we shut your core off, they'll die," Tara said from beside the tub.

Rayne shook her head. Her greatest fear was taking shape. Never, in her wildest nightmares, had she imagined it would be these people to ask this of her.

"They left out the best part," Milo muttered. "There's no guarantee they can restart your core."

"It would take a tremendous energy source," Dr. Mac said. "Perhaps, if we could modify his boost."

"What's to stop the little buggers from resurrecting when Ian's core is restarted?" Patrick asked.

"We're counting on them dying along with his core," Dr. Mac said.

"This is hogwash," Milo said. "Nothing but theories." He pointed a finger at Dr. Mac. "Have you ever known a core to be restarted?"

Dr. Mac slowly shook his head. Milo stormed out of the bedroom.

Sweat carved a path down Ian's cheek at the same time a tear fell from Rayne's. She leaned over the edge of the tub. "I won't be the one that kills you," she whispered. "I won't."

Rayne stepped up to the balcony and listened to the argument coming from the foyer, below. She'd never known Tara and Milo to fight, much less disagree, about anything.

Ian had said once, that desperation transforms people. How desperate would Rayne have to become, to kill the man she loved?

Tara grabbed Milo's sleeve. "Dr. Mac can't leave Ian. Patrick can't take me. I need you," she yelled.

He growled in her face, but Tara didn't back down. A second later, he pulled back. "Don't make me a part of this," he said so soft that Rayne barely made out his words.

"He's dying, Milo. It's the scumbag who shot him. He's the one who's killing Ian. Not us." She let go of his shirt. "But you can help us save him."

Rayne sniffed and blew her nose with a tissue.

Milo looked up. "Are you going to be a part of this?"

"I don't want him to die," Rayne said.

"That's not an answer." Milo grunted

"It's the only thing I know for certain." Rayne looked down at Tara. "If you convince me that you can bring Ian back, then I'll help you."

Tara waved a slip of paper at Milo. "Then it looks like you're taking me to Africa."

The caretaker grabbed the paper from her and read what was written on it. With a low, drawn-out growl, he grabbed her hand. An emerald burst. They were gone.

Rayne returned to the guest bathroom and sat on the floor next to Saxon. She pulled her knees to her chest and rested her head against the tub. The cold of the porcelain bit into her cheek, but she ignored it as the fan whirred about the cramped room. Ian stirred.

"Who shot you?" Rayne asked, fearful of the answer, but needing to wrap her head around the madness.

Ian inhaled deep. "This reeks of Eve." He took another deep breath. "And Jaered does her bidding." Immeasurable pain and misery flowed from his dark eyes. From his physical torture, or the emotional toll, Rayne couldn't guess.

"I don't know if I can do it," she said. Tears dampened her cheeks and she didn't wipe them, wanting Ian to see what she was unable to convey through words. How she ached to hold him and stop his pain, but was even more tortured at the thought of hurting him. "Ian, what should I do? But he closed his eyes, and didn't respond.

{16}

Jaered's knee wouldn't stop bouncing. He scrambled to his feet with a tight hold on the receiver while his emotions ran amuck. Rayne's nuances, pitch and inflection, everything about her voice was identical to Kyre's. The last few hours were as if Jaered's dead wife had been whispering in his ear.

"What is it?" Vael asked, opening his eyes.

"I can't sit any longer. I'll be back," Jaered said.

"What am I supposed to do?"

"Just what you're doing," Jaered tossed over his shoulder. He followed the curvature of the tunnel until Vael was out of sight then turned on the ball of his foot and paced within the narrow confines. He'd forgotten to bring the flashlight and didn't trust tripping the alarm if he wandered too far away. Pent-up energy fueled his limbs and his steps picked up speed, but soon built into a frenzy. About to explode, Jaered spun around and rammed his fist against the dirt wall. Between throbs he focused on the pain, the only thing that kept Kyre's memories at bay.

A few minutes later, Jaered returned to his spot and plopped down.

Vael kept his attention riveted on Jaered's bloody knuckles. "Thanks for not taking that out on me."

The corner of Jaered's mouth twitched. "I've been tempted."

"I used to drive my mom nuts. She said if she could survive my," Vael made quote marks in the air, "'why-stage' of development, then she could survive anything."

Jaered pressed his back against the wall. "You've been quiet for a while."

"I've been trying to wrap my head around the fact that the Primary's hundreds—"

"Thousands," Jaered corrected.

"Goddamn, frickin', blow-my-mind old," Vael said. "Everything I was raised to believe, my dad, my grandfather and countless other ancestors . . . we were fed nothing but lies. That's a lot to swallow, Jaered." Vael paused. "Is my dad in danger?"

"If he learns that the Primary rewrote Weir lore, then the answer would be, yeah."

"But the Primary, my dad, and the Syndrion, they've done a lot of good. Their conservation projects have spanned the globe for decades." Vael caught himself. "Probably longer."

"The man has a dark side, Vael."

"How dark?"

"He has his elite guard hunt down anyone who won't follow his agenda. If the unlucky soul is a shyftor, they're murdered. The others are displaced. The remaining few who get away hide among the billions of people on Earth. The Primary refers to them as—"

"Duach," Vael said. "But they're evil."

"That's what he would have the Pur believe to keep everyone separated." Swelling had transformed the throbs in Jaered's hand to a pounding ache. He cradled it under his arm.

"What do you mean, displaced?"

"I've spent much of my adult life helping Thraens escape our dying planet, while at the same time, your Primary has condemned his enemies from Earth, to live there."

Vael's lips parted with an audible breath. He didn't inhale.

"Your Primary secretly defies his own law and parashyfts his enemies to Thrae."

{17}

At the sound of voices and commotion, Rayne ran to the balcony. A young woman, not much older than her, stood between Tara and Milo. The old caretaker had a firm hand on the woman's upper arm. She bumped into the foyer table, knocking the silver platter on the floor. Several, tinny wobbles later, it came to a rest.

"Let go of me!" she shouted.

"Joule, please calm down," Tara said.

"I demanded that you leave my research site. How did I end up in that equation?"

"What's going on?" Rayne asked.

The girl locked a hateful glare on Rayne. "Was kidnapping me your idea?"

"You kidnapped her?" Rayne quickly descended the stairs.

"How's Ian?" Tara and Milo asked in unison.

"His core temperature was at three hundred twenty degrees the last we checked," Rayne said.

"Whoa." The young woman stilled. "That's way too hot. His body won't be able to tolerate that kind of heat." When her temper didn't rear its head again, Milo let go of her arm.

"That's why we needed you," Tara said. "But you wouldn't let me explain."

"Since you and Ian showed up at our site, my life went from near perfect to fucked in a nanosecond. My dad's work has been destroyed, he's missing, and asshole marauders raided our site and stole most of our equipment. They sent four of my team to the hospital, including my assistant. They got away with my laptop and all my research notes." At her pause, Rayne wondered if it was to take a breath, or to gear up for round two. "Who did you tell about our experiments?" Joule demanded.

"What do you mean?" Milo said.

"It's as if someone deliberately shut us down," Joule said.

"It didn't come from us," Tara said. "We never really trusted you."

Joule thrust out her chin. "Then why kidnap me?"

"Because Ian is dying," Rayne snapped. The young woman quieted. "Armageddon is about to rain down on us all."

"Literally." Milo grunted. "Thanks to your experiments."

Joule shook her head. "It couldn't have been a result of our tests."

"He was ambushed soon after we returned," Tara said. "Whoever it was, injected him with nanites. Whatever they're doing, it's elevating his core temperature."

"That's not my area of expertise," Joule said. "My father worked with the other core doctors and scientists, not me."

"But you live and breathe electricity. We're going to drain Ian's core—"

Panic widened her eyes. "That'll kill him for sure."

"That's what I've been trying to tell them," Milo said and crossed his arms over his chest.

"Ian retains oxygen as efficiently as amphibians," Dr. Mac said from the balcony. "After his core drains, his oxygen reserves will feed his brain and major organs for up to five minutes, probably longer. We may be able to gain a few more if we can successfully lower his body temperature below ninety degrees."

"How?" Rayne asked.

"I'm thinking liquid nitrogen," Dr. Mac said.

"Even if you could drain his core, how did you plan on restarting it?" Joule climbed a few stairs then turned and sat down. "It would take a tremendous amount of energy. A standard defibrillator would be no more than a tickle." The girl had morphed from an off-her-meds psych-ward inmate to an intrigued scientist before Rayne's eyes.

"We're counting on you having some knowledge of your father's exedrae designs," Dr. Mac said. "I still have copies of his original blueprints. With your help, we may be able to modify the Heir's boost, to no longer draw minerals and proteins, but to pull and trap energy from lightning."

Tara took a couple of steps toward Joule. "If the Prophecy holds true, the storm that Ian's death unleashes will be unbelievably violent."

"We intend to use that to our advantage, and bring his core back to life," Dr. Mac said.

"Like Frankenstein's monster," Milo snarled. "And look how that ended up."

Joule stood. "If I help you with this, you've got to help me. I need to know what happened to my father."

"Deal," Tara said.

Dr. Mac, Joule and Tara gathered in Ian's bedroom. They slid his mattress back, unscrewed the panels and exposed the guts that made up his boost. Tara asked a barrage of questions while they dismantled much of it. Some, Joule patiently answered, while others caused her to become animated and slide into mini lectures. Every time she asked, Dr. Mac and Tara skirted the topic about draining Ian's core.

From comments Joule made, it was obvious to Rayne that the young woman had a complicated relationship with her father. Her admiration for his brilliant designs and discoveries about the natural world seemed to eclipse an emotional disconnect. Rayne wondered if her father cared more for his science than for his family. The topic scraped open old wounds of her own.

She left them to their work and returned to the guest bedroom. Patrick sat on the closed toilet, keeping vigil while Saxon slumbered on the rug.

Ian's skin had turned translucent. Arteries ran the course of his body, branching out into lesser capillaries, a vast river system that nurtured muscles and bone. Sometime earlier, Dr.

Mac had placed an oxygen mask over his nose and mouth. Rayne wondered if it was to help build up his reserves in preparation for the event, or if his vitals were fading faster than the old doctor would admit.

"Not much longer, one way or the other." Patrick looked like he'd awakened after an all-night frat party.

Rayne gazed at her hands. "I don't know if I have what it takes to do this."

"You're saving more than just Ian, Rayne," he said.

"Am I? There's no guarantee that this will work. Not only could I end up murdering Ian, but billions of people."

"It's going to work. It has to," Patrick said.

"Let's say it does, and they revive him." She pressed a fist to her chest. "I'm the result of a science experiment that didn't turn out the way it was supposed to!" She dialed back her anger, grabbed Patrick's arm and pulled him out of the bathroom, leaving the door ajar. She then closed the bedroom door leading to the hall. Rayne glanced in the direction of the bathroom, and lowered her voice. "Jaered told you that Ian was the first successful artificial core. If that is true, when he wakes up, will he still have his powers?" She gulped, but the constriction in her throat remained, making it difficult to swallow her emotions along with her words. "If by some miracle he survives this, will Ian be the same?"

{18}

Rayne stood at the foot of the configured boost and stared at an opened flower with massive steel-gray petals, that waited to cradle a dying Ian. Gone were the standard comforts of Ian's bedroom, giving it the appearance of a science lab, instead of a place of retreat. They'd left Ian's mattress upended and resting against the wall. His pillows were stacked next to it. Joule had opened the door leading to the balcony, and gusts of rain swept into the room while she secured a lightning rod at the edge of the patio. The thunder had grown deafening, and the winds were at hurricane intensity. Rayne grabbed the bedpost to stay steady on her feet.

Milo had received a couple of messages from Marcus, inquiring about the Heir's well-being. The old caretaker responded that he was fine, just exhausted. They kept the estate's security jam to maximum so no one could make a surprise appearance. If anyone tried to shyft there, they'd have to use the two outlying vortex fields—and be faced with a very soggy and tedious journey.

Dr. Mac stepped up next to her. "Are you ready?"

She closed her eyes. "Promise me he'll live through this."

Dr. Mac glanced in the direction of the master bedroom door. The others were in the east wing with Ian, and yet, he lowered his voice. Rayne had to strain to hear him. "I wouldn't ask this of you if we had any options left."

"I wouldn't be doing this if *I* had any," Rayne shouted over the thunder.

"Only through sacrifice will others live," he said. "For the greater good."

Rayne had spent most of the night torturing a man whose only crime was his devotion to the world. She was about to murder the only man she'd ever loved. What was sacrifice, if not that?

A tremendous clap of thunder. Sparks burst at the edge of the patio. "The rods are working!" Joule shouted.

Rayne walked to the guest bedroom with Dr. Mac.

Milo had laid Ian in the guest bed but had left his chest exposed. The outer triangle of Ian's Seal glowed amber as the sun inside the image pulsated, lit up by the intense energy trapped in Ian's core. If it wasn't for the oxygen mask and translucent skin, Rayne might have taken him to be sleeping. Saxon lay next to Ian. The wolf's snout brushed Ian's fingertips.

"The liquid nitrogen lowered his body temperature," Dr. Mac said. "But it won't stay that way for long."

Ian hadn't uttered a word for more than an hour, yet Rayne lingered in the doorway, willing him to wake up and spare her of this burden.

"It's time, Ian," Tara said. She leaned over and kissed him on the forehead. Her tears wet his cheek. Saxon licked his hand, then leapt off the bed and followed Tara out with a whimper.

Milo stepped up and squeezed Ian's arm. The old caretaker postured as if to say something, but instead raised his face in an emotional battle, and took a minute to compose himself. He leaned close and muttered, "Survive this or I'll kick your ass for all eternity." He bumped shoulders with Dr. Mac as he charged out of the room.

Patrick stood looking out the window. When Rayne placed her hand on his back, he shook his head. "This isn't goodbye."

"There must be something you want to say?" Rayne said softly. Her show of empathy had more to do with selfishness, seeking any delay possible.

A second later, Patrick tore away from the window and walked up to the bed. He leaned next to Ian's ear. "You're a hard act to follow, Ian," Patrick whispered. "Since the day we met, you were more than a client." He turned his face to the side and wiped his nose on his sleeve. "You're my best friend—brother. You're going to make it, and not because it's what's best for the earth," Patrick said. "You've got to live through this because I can't go after the sons-of-bitches without you! Survive this, goddamn it!" He backed up and stood next to Rayne. "Dr. Mac gave me the honor of carrying him to his resurrection."

"Patrick is the only one strong enough," Dr. Mac said. "The power from our cores might be felt in Ian's. We can't take that chance. Once you drain Ian's core, it must stay that way for the first few minutes. You may need to keep the connection all the way to his bedroom."

"Long enough to make those nasty bugs believe he's dead." Patrick locked his fingers and cracked his knuckles.

"Once Patrick gets him in the boost, Joule will take it from there," Dr. Mac said. "Any questions?"

Rayne stepped up next to the bed. She shook her head.

"Hurry Patrick. I don't know how long it will take Joule to direct a bolt into the room and into the boost. Every second will count."

"I got this Doc," he said.

"Then it's time," Dr. Mac said.

Rayne cringed. Dr. Mac had raised his voice as if announcing a man's execution to a crowd. The Weir doctor left them, closing the door behind him. The click rang like a death toll in her ears.

*

Jaered sprang to his feet and stuck the tranquilizer gun into his belt. He withdrew another one from the duffle, then kicked Vael's boot. The recruit snorted and opened his eyes. "Get up, it's time," Jaered said.

"Now will you tell me what we're doing here?" Vael rubbed his eyes and stood.

Jaered handed Vael one of the tranquilizer guns. "There's two rounds. Use them to take down the caretaker, then the doctor, in that order. Don't let the doctor touch you, or you'll wake up in a Pur prison."

"What are you going to do?" Vael asked.

"I'll take care of the others, and if need be, the wolf. Stay behind me until we get to the room, and don't improvise." Jaered got in Vael's face. "If you even remotely interfere with what I'm going to do, you won't walk out of there."

Jaered started up the ladder. Shooting pain erupted from his hand, but he fought past it and kept going. He had three stories to climb in a matter of seconds. For this next part, timing was everything.

{19}

Ian's lips parted, and he gulped air. "Rayne," he said barely above a whisper. He opened his eyes and looked at her with such compassion that it was impossible for Rayne to keep the tears away. She gave into their flow and stared back at those incredible dark eyes full of depth and emotion, unwilling to lose even a blink of a moment to gaze upon them for what might be the last time.

"Don't speak, Ian," she said. "Please." Disheartened that he had awakened, she had convinced herself that killing him would be easier if he didn't know what she was doing. If he couldn't feel anything. But she had only been kidding herself.

His chest rose as he filled his lungs. "If I am to leave this world," he gasped, "know that I want it to be with your lips upon mine."

She collapsed next to him on the bed. Sobs racked her chest and denied her breath. "Forgive me," she whimpered.

Ian moved his hand toward her. "I love—"

"No!" Rayne screamed as anger rushed in like a tsunami. "Don't you dare say it! Not now, not like this."

"I do," Ian whispered. His voice rose above her sobs. "I always—"

Rayne grabbed his head and kissed him. Hard. Rough. Forcing herself to carry out what was demanded of her, emptying her mind and not thinking about why, but only focusing on who. Ian returned her kiss with incredible tenderness, in spite of the pain his body must have endured. She felt his hands on her back, pulling her closer until she pressed against his chest. Her kiss transformed into a hunger to savor as much of this moment as she could, giving into what had been denied them both for so long. The energy drain intensified, and Rayne found herself in a battle, resisting the instinct to let go as his energy, his very life force flowed into her, through her—and out.

Within seconds, his skin cooled, and their kisses became one-sided. His heartbeat slowed. Rayne made to pull back, but Ian had locked his arms around her and with the last of his strength, wouldn't release her from her duty—no longer for his sake, but for the sake of the Earth.

Rayne pulled her lips away. His eyes were closed. As she gazed upon him, the muscles in his face relaxed and he appeared at peace for the first time in hours. A final breath escaped his blue, parted lips. His arms slipped away.

A blinding flash and the bedroom window splintered into the room, making way for a deafening thunderclap that shook the mansion like an earthquake.

Patrick grabbed Rayne and held her tight until her screams subsided and turned to sobs. "It's not the end," he shouted.

Rayne threw back the covers and Patrick grabbed Ian's hands, then hoisted him up and over his shoulder. She opened the door and as Patrick rushed by, she gripped Ian's hand in hers and they hurried down the hall. An icy chill snaked up her arm, but she didn't let go. His lips had turned from blue to deep purple. His skin was opaque, pasty, and lifeless. Ian was dead. It was up to Rayne to make sure his core stayed that way for the next few minutes.

The house shook with Mother Nature's thunderous retaliation. The lightning came, one on top of the other, turning the mansion into a scene from a horror movie. They made it to the intersection and turned into the west wing, but a large body stood directly in their path. A flash of lightning. It was Drion Marcus.

Marcus's clothes were drenched. He wiped his face with his hand. "I knew Milo's reports about Ian were crap. What happened? How bad is it?"

"Out of our way!" Patrick sidestepped him and rushed onward.

Rayne glanced over her shoulder. Drion Marcus fell in close behind. "We have to get Ian in his boost and restart his core, or he'll stay dead," she yelled over the thunder.

"He's what?" Marcus shouted, and froze in his tracks.

They made it to Ian's bedroom. Dr. Mac held his arm out, stopping Milo from getting close. "Milo, you can't help him!"

Tara lifted Ian's head and bit her lip at his deathly pallor. "Hurry, Joule!" she screamed through the open bedroom door. "They're here!"

The group in the hall blocked Marcus from entering. Shouts rose as the Drion wouldn't stop his questions long enough for Dr. Mac to explain. Tara and Milo helped hold him back.

Patrick paused next to the bed, and then laid Ian gently in his boost. Once Ian was nestled in his giant titanium flower petals, Rayne lingered a couple of seconds, then let go of his icy hand.

The rain had turned to hail the size of softballs, which pummeled the balcony patio. Joule had taken cover just inside the open door. The hurricane storm drenched everything in Ian's room unlucky enough to be within several feet of the open door. A bolt of lightning struck the rod Joule had secured at the edge of the balcony. It connected with the second rod she held in her thick, rubber-gloved hands. Milo's fishing waders, reached her upper chest, held in place by his suspenders. "Get to the hall. I can't protect you in here!" she shouted at Rayne. Another strike and an electrical arch formed high above her head, and then another, and another. She held the rod out in front of her and slowly backed her way toward the bed.

Patrick grabbed Rayne's shoulder. "We've got to go!"

Rayne could hardly make out his words above the thunder and sizzling energy in the room. She sensed, as much as heard someone behind them just as Patrick took a header and landed on top of Ian.

Stunned, Rayne blinked back her shock. Jaered had pushed Patrick into the boost.

The panel leading to Ian's escape tunnel stood wide open and Vael rushed out. Rayne screamed but a jolt of thunderous lightning muffled her shriek with a resounding clap.

The rebel pulled back and punched Patrick when he rose. Patrick went limp.

A blur of white. Saxon leapt at Jaered, but Vael tackled the airborne wolf, knocking him into the tunnel, then slammed the panel shut. Jaered pulled the upright dresser from the wall and sent it crashing to the floor, trapping the wolf inside.

Rayne lunged at Jaered but he sidestepped and she crashed headlong into the toppled dresser.

Jaered fired a gun toward the open bedroom door. A dart hit Tara in her chest and she slumped to the floor, blocking the doorway.

A second dart hit Marcus in the neck and he wobbled then landed in a slump on top of Tara.

Joule stumbled toward the bed, but she battled to hold onto the rod with the connecting electrical strikes.

Rayne ignored the tornado in her head and crawled toward Jaered, but he put some distance between them and raised his hand. A lightning bolt from Joule's rod connected with the tip of his middle finger and he whipped it at Rayne.

A tendril of lightning struck her squarely in the chest. The jolt sent her skidding across the rug, and she crashed into the far wall. The energy ignited every pore, every cell of her body. Paralyzed by the most energy she'd ever absorbed, Rayne lay immobilized. Movement in the room turned to slow motion, voices and noises garbled.

Vael fired his gun, taking out Milo in the hall. Dr. Mac waved, "No, stop!" A dart in his shoulder dropped him on top of his friend.

The room turned stark white when a massive bolt of electricity shot from Joule's rod and connected with Jaered's hand. He bent over the boost and spread his hands apart. A cloud of energy formed and grew wider and wider, turning brighter than the sun.

"No!" Rayne screamed, but she couldn't hear her own voice.

A hand grasped the edge of the boost, and the top half of Patrick's face appeared. He looked at Rayne, and then his eyes widened at the hovering ball of energy. He screamed and threw his arms over his face just as Jaered dropped the sizzling cloud on top of him.

Once inside the modified container, the energy fed upon itself and quickly expanded like a balloon, reaching toward the ceiling. Patrick's screams were cut short.

Jaered took a couple of steps back, then turned toward Rayne. The satisfaction on his face pierced her soul. He had just murdered the two men closest to her.

{20}

Patrick was heavier than Jaered had judged. He now understood why Eve had insisted that Vael come. It took both of them to keep him upright and drag him through the trees toward the eastern vortex field.

"How long until the dart wears off?" Vael puffed.

"A while. Just keep moving." Jaered glanced over his shoulder. The rain had eased into a steady drizzle, but the thunder overhead told him that lightning remained a threat, especially once they'd reach the clearing.

Jaered went over the events in his head. Vael's two darts took out the caretaker and doctor. Jaered's were to take out the Channel and the wolf.

But he didn't drugged the wolf, couldn't with Vael's dad there. Jaered glanced over his shoulder. No movement from behind. He hung on tighter to Patrick whose arm was, at the moment, slung across Jaered's shoulders.

"What the fuck was your dad doing there?" Jaered said.

"How am I supposed to know?" Vael slowed his steps, and then stopped. "Hold up, I'm losing him." He shifted Patrick's arm higher across the back of his neck. They continued through the trees.

Patrick's head bobbed between moans. They came every few seconds like ticktocks from a clock. "What . . ." Patrick mumbled, but any further attempt to talk morphed into a groan.

Jaered picked up their pace. The last thing he needed was Patrick coming to his senses and fighting back.

"What'd you do to him?" Vael asked.

"Need-to-know only, and right now, you don't." Jaered stared through the trees. He swore there was a white blur on a parallel path to theirs, but the lightning flashes made it difficult to distinguish boulders from animal, and he counted on it being paranoia.

The low hum of an engine. Jaered stopped short. Vael's momentum pulled Patrick from Jaered's grasp, and their prisoner swung toward Vael. The recruit grabbed Patrick around the waist and managed to keep him upright.

"What?" Vael said.

"A car." Jaered slung Patrick's arm across his shoulders and pulled him up higher by his waist. "Someone woke up."

The wolf wasn't Jaered's only concern.

*

Rayne's fury fed her splitting headache, yet she appreciated that her ability to drain kept the electrocution from knocking her out completely. The moment she had control of her faculties, she rushed to the boost. Convinced that Jaered's intrusion had cost Ian his life, Rayne felt his neck with trembling fingers. She gasped and let go when she found a weak, but steady, pulse. She didn't hold back the tears, and they dampened her cheeks.

"Did it . . . work?" When Jaered became his own lightning rod, Joule had taken some of the voltage and had landed next to the open patio door. She sat in a daze with her hair upended. Rain puddles sloshed around her, and smoky fumes rose from her shoulders.

"He's alive," Rayne said. Joule gave her a weak nod.

It took some effort to drag the dresser away from the tunnel, but when Rayne got it open, Saxon wasn't there.

She ran out of the room, and then paused at the upstairs balcony. The front door to the mansion stood wide open. She rushed down the stairs and outside into the weakening storm. Time had become skewed after she was hit with the bolt, and she had no idea how much of a head start Jaered and Vael had.

Rayne took off for her car, fighting to keep her thoughts coherent. If they drove there, they would have stashed their car farther away and hiked to the security gates. So for now, their exit had to be on foot, she reasoned.

Jaered and Vael had lifted Patrick's body out of the boost and carried him out of the room. Why? The question burned at the back of her thoughts.

Certain where they were headed, she kept one eye on the road and the other on movement through the trees, driving toward the eastern vortex, the only one Jaered could access. Stashed car or not, Jaered would shyft without a trail they could follow.

He'd done it before.

She reached the clearing and slowed the car to a crawl. Jaered and Vael were dragging Patrick toward the center of the field.

Rayne gunned the engine and left the dirt road, entered the field at top speed, and swerved straight for them. She navigated ruts and the occasional rocks, but reached her quarry before they could make it to the vortex at the center. The car slid sideways in the mud when she slammed on the brake, then came to a stop, blocking their path. She jumped out but remained behind the open door, using it like a shield.

Vael grunted. "You didn't zap her very good."

"She drains energy," Jaered said.

When they didn't point a dart gun at her or draw lightning from the overhead storm, Rayne stepped away from the car. "What the hell are you doing?" she screamed.

"We don't have time for this," Jaered snapped. "Get back in your car and don't interfere."

She looked at Patrick when he moaned. He had survived. "Why did you kill Ian?"

The corner of Jaered's mouth pulled into a smirk. What Rayne would have given to have had a gun within reach.

"I revived him," Jaered said. "You were the one who killed him. What made you think that your destiny would be a cakewalk?"

"Stop with your double-talk and bullshit!" she screamed. "I want a straight answer."

"Welcome to my world," Vael mumbled. He avoided Jaered's glare.

"We are here by design. Everything, everyone has a purpose in this universe," Jaered said. "All exist for the greater good."

The same reference that Dr. Mac had used earlier gave her pause. "Why are you doing this to Ian?" she said. "What do the rebels have against the Pur?"

The smirk vanished. Jaered's eyes grew dark, ominous. "Don't believe for one second that this has ever been about *him.*" Jaered let go of Patrick and took a few steps toward her.

"Ugh!" Vael caught the slumping Patrick in his arms.

"Your boyfriend will be fine. I saw to it. Go back to him and leave us to save his life." Jaered pointed at Patrick.

Rayne's thoughts raced to make sense of this nightmare, and she stared at Patrick while the throbs at her temples took their time to ease. "What did you do to him? Where are you taking him?"

"To fulfill *his* destiny," Jaered said. "And unless you want him to die, you won't try to stop us." He turned his back on Rayne, grabbed Patrick, and together Jaered and Vael dragged him into the center of the vortex.

The air shimmered and lit up their faces with a brilliant glow. Rayne stood just beyond the edge of the field, at a loss about what to do. Was Patrick really going to die if she stopped them? Wet leaves lifted, swirling around them. Her hands pulled into tight fists. "I need answers!" she shouted. "You owe me that much."

Jaered pursed his lips and peered past her as if mulling it over. "Be here when I return, and I'll take you to someone who can answer your questions."

She shook her head. "You can't shyft me. I'll drain you."

"I'm not from Earth—"

"You're from Thrae," Rayne said and tossed him a smug expression. "Ian figured that much out."

If Jaered was shocked that she knew, he didn't show it. "I can draw greater amounts of energy than your boyfriend. I've done the calculations. We'll have eleven seconds. I won't need nearly that much to take you where you'll be going."

Lightning struck the ground within a few feet of Rayne. The flash blinded her and by the time she recovered, they were gone.

{21}

Jaered shyfted the three of them to the vortex stream in Eve's basement where the rebel leader stood in wait. The second they fully materialized, her gaze fell to her son. Patrick moaned and shuddered violently in their arms. Eve's shoulders relaxed, and she gave into a tremendous sigh. "Oh, thank God."

"He's really weak," Jaered said.

"And heavy as hell," Vael griped. "Cut back on the carbs, buddy."

"In here." Eve crossed the room, reached up and tilted a sconce on the wall. The sound of stone scraping stone filled the small room as a portion of the concrete wall slid out of view to expose a pitch-black space beyond. She stepped in and darkness engulfed her. A second later, a low-watt light bulb lit up the room in a dull glow. She stood next to a rectangular titanium tub.

Jaered grabbed Patrick under his arms and Vael scooped him up by his ankles. They carried him over and lowered him inside.

"Vael, go upstairs to the kitchen. There's a meal waiting. We'll join you in a few minutes," Eve said.

"Is someone finally going to tell me what this is all about over donuts?" he asked.

"That depends on what happens in the next few seconds," she said. Vael's footsteps faded in the direction of the stairs. Eve leaned in and unbuttoned Patrick's shirt.

"Moment of truth," Jaered said.

Eve gently pressed her palm to her son's exposed chest. An amber glow appeared beneath her hand. A second later, it pulsed as if in rhythm with Patrick's heartbeat. When she lifted her hand, a triangle had formed—with a sun trapped inside.

The boost lit up the room in a ruby glow that danced across the stone surface like a smoldering fire. Patrick's emerged Seal pulsated in an amber outline.

"Behold, the true Heir of Earth," Eve said softly. She stumbled back, but Jaered caught her.

"It worked," he said. "All your planning—"

"So much sacrifice. So much death." Eve said. She shivered with emotion.

Jaered tightened his arm around her and guided her out of the room. She reached up and righted the sconce. The stone wall closed. "How long?" he asked.

"A few hours, most of the day, maybe more. This is virgin territory, even for me." Eve pulled away and headed toward the stairs. "Come. Beatrice has prepared quite the feast for us."

Jaered didn't follow, but stepped into the vortex stream at the center of the room. "I'll be back in a minute. Add one more place setting."

She turned on him. Confusion crimped her face. "Who?"

"I promised her answers," he said. The air lit up in sparkles as he drew on the magnetic field. "I'm bringing her to you."

"No!" Eve screamed and rushed at him. "You can't go back!"

Jaered shyfted.

{22}

Rayne sat on the hood of her car, welcoming the gentle drizzle of rain on her face to quench the knots in her stomach.

Countless unknowns and great risk faced her if she went with Jaered. The only certainty was that she'd alienate herself from the man she loved and the family that had embraced her, and loved her enough to keep her darkest secret.

An emerald glow flashed across the hood of her car. Ian appeared in the vortex. The second he materialized, he dropped to all fours.

Her elation gave way to fear, and she stood by helpless as he rose and stumbled toward her. She opened the car door and Ian slumped down in the passenger seat. She crouched next to him. "You're all right."

Ian's chest rose and fell with each breath. "When I woke up . . . Joule told me." He gulped in air. "You went after the Sars that attacked us."

"It was Jaered and Vael. They took Patrick," Rayne said.

He stilled. "Why?"

"I don't know. But I'm going to find out." It struck her that she'd made up her mind. Rayne stood. "I'm going to get answers, or die trying."

"Come back with me," he said. "We'll figure it out." He raised his face toward her, but a bright light in her rearview mirror reflected on his face.

Jaered stood in the vortex field.

"I have to go," Rayne said gently. Her nostrils flared, and she suppressed a sob that she couldn't throw her arms around him.

Ian gave her a perplexed stare as his confusion gave way to awareness. "Don't," he said.

"They took Patrick. I have to find out what this is all about."

"You can't trust him." Ian reached for her. "I need you."

"What we need," she said and backed away, "are answers." She turned and ran toward Jaered.

"I didn't know if you'd be here," he said at her approach.

"I still don't trust you." She stepped next to him. "It's going to take a lot on your part to earn that."

"That works both ways." He offered his hand.

Rayne hesitated as her psyche made a last-ditch argument for her to back out. A second later, she placed her hand in his. A shimmering cloud formed around them.

"Stop!" Ian shouted. He fell out of the car. "You aren't taking her!" Ian made it as far as the headlights, then leaned on the hood.

Saxon came charging out of the tree line heading straight for the vortex. At the same time, Ian pulled his arm back, and a weak core blast formed in his hand. He flung it at Jaered.

Jaered threw his arms around Rayne with a crushing embrace, and her face smashed into his chest. He fell into a crouch, pulling her down with him.

The entire vortex field was ablaze. A frigid tingling mixed with blistering heat. Unable to breathe, Rayne couldn't cry out.

Jaered's horrific scream rose above a tremendous clap of thunder and carried them into oblivion.

{23}

A dead weight pressed upon Rayne. She reached up and tried to push Jaered off, but he didn't budge. She managed to wiggle out from underneath him and rolled away as fast as she could. How long had they been lying there? Had she drained his core? He lay chest down on the cement floor with his face turned away from her. She didn't dare feel for a pulse.

"Jaered," she whispered. No response. She raised her voice. "Jaered." Nothing.

The back of her hand stung. A nauseating burnt odor hung in the air. It took a full minute for her eyes to adjust to the darkness. Jaered had shyfted them to what looked like a storage room. Wooden crates with narrow slats were arranged along one wall. Rectangular containers, made of a dark metal and the size of coffins, were stacked behind her. A lone, small square window sat just below the ceiling. Wide silver tape held a piece of cardboard in place, covering it. The door looked to be metal with massive bolts securing it to the wall. It didn't have a knob, at least not on the inside. At the bottom, a dim orange light reached into the room. It blinked on and off.

A moan.

Rayne swallowed her relief and crawled over to Jaered, but an overwhelming whiff of burnt flesh stopped her cold. Bile rose in her throat, and she covered her mouth and nose with her hand. Charred and peeling skin could be seen between scraps of burnt cloth that had once been his shirt. Jaered's entire back and upper arms had shielded her from the fiery vortex. Everything below his belt looked untouched.

"Jaered, if you can hear me, I'm going to find help." Rayne got to her feet but paused until the spinning in her head righted itself along with the room. When she couldn't find a way to open the door, she climbed up the metal containers to the window and ignored the shooting pain that came from the back of her hand.

The window didn't have a latch or hinges, and there was no way to open it other than breaking it. Rayne peeled away an edge of the tape and gripped the corner of the cardboard. She ripped it from the window.

Rayne froze at a brilliant red sky beyond.

Running footsteps. From the sound of it, several people converged on the other side of the door. Someone barked an order to wait. Scraping metal. The door flung open.

A flashing beam of amber light reached into the center of the room, far enough that Jaered's body was caught in its path.

The bird's-eye view exposed the extent of his injuries. Rayne swallowed her gasp. She lay down on the uppermost container and drew her legs against her chest, trying to wedge herself deeper into the narrow space at the ceiling. Where was she? Who were these people?

"Who is it?" a voice from outside the room asked.

A man entered the room and knelt beside Jaered. "I can't tell, he's too severely burned." Another man joined him and they lifted Jaered enough to see his face and upper chest. "Dear god, it's the Heir!"

Rayne's racing pulse slammed to a halt. The Heir?

"Get him in his boost, stat!" commanded the voice from the hallway. A handful of men dressed in simple, loose garments rushed in and encircled Jaered. They gently picked him up in unison and carried him facedown, out of the room.

A short, stout gentleman stepped inside. His groomed, thick beard had abundant streaks of varying shades of gray. The top of his head was bald except for white patches of hair over both ears. He gave a short wave just outside the door. A dangling bulb a few feet from Rayne lit up the room, and she squinted from the glare.

The bearded man glanced around. "I know he brought someone with him. Otherwise the alarm would not have been triggered."

Something was familiar about the voice. Rayne didn't move as she tried to sort out why.

"Really, there's not that many places to conceal a person in here." He looked up and stared at Rayne. She slipped out of her hiding spot and climbed down the containers. When she reached the floor, she turned toward him, but held back.

Shock swept across his features, then disappeared just as quickly. "Did you come through unscathed?"

The familiar morphed into recognition. "Dr. Mac?" she said, knowing it wasn't him, couldn't be, unless he'd grown a full beard in the past couple of hours.

He stiffened in spite of giving her a tight-lipped smile. "You are of Earth. You know my paral." He drank her in from head to toe with sad eyes. The corners of his mouth drooped. "You're the mirror image of her. It will be quite unnerving for the others to meet you. Don't be surprised if you receive a great many stares. They mean no disrespect."

"I don't understand," Rayne said. She glanced over her shoulder at the red sky beyond the window. "Where the hell am I?"

"Here, I am known as Angus," he said. "Welcome to Thrae."

{24}

Angus led Rayne down a winding, windowless corridor that gave her the impression of being in a tunnel. Walking felt odd, like she was light on her feet. The sensation was coupled with an intense, chilled tremor that had racked her body since first appearing in the room. It was difficult to catch her breath. Blisters had appeared on the back of her burnt hand, but that was nothing compared to what Jaered had endured.

What had happened? She'd never heard of a vortex catching fire.

The walls looked to be made of adobe, and their texture looked rough. The overhead lights were motion activated, turning on at their approach, only to turn off a few feet behind them. The air was stale, but cool.

Angus paused at the first door they came to. "What do I call you?" he asked.

"Rayne," she said. "Where's Jaered? Are you taking me to him?"

Angus opened the door and gestured for her to go inside. She stepped into what appeared to be a simple apartment. A couch and a couple of chairs were set around a rectangular coffee table. The cushions were lumpy and worn, the material thinning from much use. A kitchen sat at the end of the long room. A handful of chairs were scattered around a table in between.

Angus walked across the apartment and knocked on a door at the opposite side of the room. It was opened by a middle-aged woman. A breath caught in Rayne's throat. It was the woman from the QualSton picture that Allison had shipped to Patrick. She'd grown out her thick, ebony hair since the picture was taken almost three decades ago. Full of body with a hint of curl, it cascaded below her shoulders. Although her face showed signs of middle age, her eyes were as dark as Ian's. If this wasn't Ian's mother, they were closely related.

"How bad?" Angus entered the room while Rayne hesitated in the doorway.

"Serious, but by the miracle of his core, he's still breathing," she said. The woman regarded Rayne with a concerned, tight-lipped smile.

"This is Rayne," Angus said from over his shoulder.

If she was shocked by Rayne's appearance, as Angus had predicted, the woman didn't show it. "Come." She stepped to the side and gestured for Rayne to enter the room. "I'm Gwynn."

The windowless room was small with an upright dresser next to one wall. A narrow mattress leaned against another wall. Its sheets were in a pile at the floor, as if someone had pulled everything off in a hurry. A large vat, like the ones Rayne had seen in the vortex room, extended into the middle of the bedroom. They had placed Jaered inside and he floated faceup in a purple substance that reminded Rayne of the gel her mother used in her hair when she was a child. Rayne might have taken him to be slumbering peacefully in a tub, if not for the almost iridescent gel.

Angus leaned over him and pulled out a core thermometer that wasn't as ornate as Dr. Mac's. He pressed it against Jaered's bare chest, checked the results, then shook it out. "It's damn serious. His core is almost entirely drained."

Her head threatened to explode from the tornado of questions.

"You were burned." Gwynn lifted Rayne's injured hand and gently examined it. "Angus, we need to attend to her as well."

"Why didn't you say something?" he said gruffly. He opened one of the dresser drawers and removed a roll of gauze, then grabbed a squirt bottle from on top.

"Let's go to the other room. You must be light-headed and weak," Gwynn said. "Thrae's gravity is not as great as Earth's. Our oxygen levels are also different. You'll eventually adjust, but it will take a few days."

Days? An overwhelming compulsion to call Ian struck and Rayne grabbed the cell phone out of her pocket. A nervous chuckle at her predicament gave way to giddiness.

Gwynn took Rayne's elbow and guided her to the kitchen table in the other room, then set about putting a kettle on the stove that she had to light with a match. The appliances and fixtures resembled something from the first half of the twentieth century on Earth. None of the furniture in the sparse room looked modern, but was simple, heavy, and bulky.

Gwynn stuffed a generous pinch of tea leaves into a metal strainer the size of a large walnut, then dropped it into the handmade, lopsided ceramic mug.

Angus scooted a chair across from Rayne and sat down. He squirted a dollop of purple goo on her hand, but as he went to spread it with his finger, Rayne jerked her hand away. Back on Earth, Dr. Mac was a Sar. Was Angus? Would she drain him?

He gave her a perplexed look. "I won't hurt you."

"Sorry," Rayne said. "I'm just a little unnerved, by everything." She spread the goop across the burned area. The sting vanished. Angus scraped his chair back and sat at the head of the table while she wrapped the gauze around her hand, then tucked the flap underneath. He fidgeted with the button on his sleeve cuff. "It won't take more than a few minutes, but keep it wrapped until then."

"Minutes?" Rayne said.

"Angus's special recipe," Gwynn said. She set a steaming cup down next to Rayne and handed one to Angus, then settled in a chair across the narrow table from her. She blew across its surface while she studied Rayne. "You must have lots of questions."

A grunt came from Angus. "So do we." He wrapped his hands around his mug, but didn't take a sip.

"Angus, where are your manners?" Gwynn said. "It isn't the poor girl's fault that she ended up here."

"No, it's his," Angus thrust a finger in the direction of the bedroom. "What was he thinking?" He shot to his feet. "Aeros won't ignore this. The Heir has gotten someone else killed!"

Gwynn turned to Rayne. "Where was he taking you?"

"I don't know." She shook her head. "To someone who could answer my questions."

"What caused the fire?" Angus asked.

"I don't know. It's the first time I've ever shyfted," Rayne said.

"Angus, sit down. The damage is done," Gwynn said calmly. "The boy was either too injured to keep his concentration during the shyft, or it was deliberate."

"He came to the only person who could save his life." Angus settled in the chair.

Gwynn grabbed Angus's hand and squeezed it. "I'm sure that's it," she said and gave him a pained smile.

"Is he going to survive?" Rayne said.

"How is your hand?" Angus asked in a tone tinged with pride.

Rayne flexed her fingers. She didn't feel numb, yet there wasn't any pain. She had full use of her hand.

"The Heir's injuries are too great to heal as fast as your hand, but in a couple of days, he'll be back to normal," Gwynn said.

"Two minutes, two hours, two days, what does it matter? It's forbidden for the Heir to set foot on Thrae. Aeros will come for him, and god knows what else." Angus left them and disappeared into the bedroom, slamming the door.

"Forgive him. He's the only doctor our colony has left. Whenever Aeros comes to Thrae, it's Angus who has to deal with the aftermath."

"The aftermath of what?" Rayne said.

"Aeros returns for one reason only." Gwynn got to her feet and stepped up to the kitchen counter. She set her partially emptied mug in the sink. "To hunt."

Rayne grabbed her mug tight and relished the warmth. The lingering cold of the parashyft faded. Her thoughts were clearing, and she wondered what animals were here that would bring the Duach leader to Earth's sister world. "Hunt what?"

"Not what, whom." Gwynn turned to Rayne. Weariness filled her eyes that hadn't been there a second earlier. "He hunts us."

{25}

A voice shouted Ian's name, and it took him a few seconds to recognize that it was in his head. He opened his eyes to discover Saxon sitting erect next to him, as if standing guard over Rayne's executioner.

Here, the wolf channeled and added an image of Ian lying in the eastern vortex field, splattered in mud and shivering. Saxon was trying to communicate with Tara, to let her know where Ian was.

Leave me, he channeled. *I don't want to be found.* He turned his face to the puddle and succumbed to his anguish as his sorrow mixed with the rainwater and splashed into his nose and mouth with every sob. He tasted mud and bits of grass, but didn't have the will to spit.

"Ian!" Tara was beside him. Fingers pressed against his neck, a hand on his back. "Oh my god, you're freezing cold."

Ian coughed, unable to lift his head.

"Here!" Tara shouted and waved, then she bent close. "Ian, where is Rayne?"

She-wolf—fire—gone, Saxon channeled.

Tara paused. *What do you mean, gone?* she channeled back.

Saxon didn't respond, but lay down on the burnt grass next to Ian and nudged him with his snout.

The truck skidded to a stop, splattering clumps of mud across Ian's bare legs and onto his briefs. Doors opened, but didn't slam shut. "How bad?" Dr. Mac said from close by.

"The boy's kissin' mud. What do you think, you old coot?" Milo barked. "He can't even move." Strong hands grabbed him and lifted him from the damp earth. Milo carried Ian toward the bright headlights. "I've gotcha boy," the old caretaker said. "You'll be okay, we just need to get you to your boost. That scientist gal is trying to fix it."

Ian's head bobbed, and he fought to keep his eyes open. Incoherent sounds escaped when he tried to scream that it wasn't okay. Rayne was dead. In trying to stop Jaered, he had killed her. Nothing would ever be okay again. But his confession came out as rambling moans and Milo hesitated.

"What are you trying to say, Ian?" the old caretaker said.

Dr. Mac crouched down next to the ground and rubbed his palm across the field. "The ground, it's scorched."

"What could have burned it like that?" Tara asked.

Milo laid Ian in the back of the truck. A moment later, Dr. Mac climbed in and pressed the core thermometer against Ian's chest. He shuddered at the icy cold of the metal and his teeth chattered. Dr. Mac grabbed a blanket with his free hand and covered Ian. He removed the thermometer and looked at it. "Hurry, Milo!" Dr. Mac yelled. "His core is barely registering."

The engine turned over.

Tara climbed in with them. "Come on, Saxon, get in," she called out.

"Why isn't he coming?" Dr. Mac said.

Tara tucked the blanket around Ian. "I don't know. He channeled something about a fire, and Rayne being gone." She banged against the back of the cab. "Go, Milo!"

The truck lurched and started moving. Dr. Mac stuck his thermometer in his jacket pocket. "Tara, let Marcus know we found him and he can call off the search." She pulled out her cell and bent over, punching in a message. "Ian, did you catch up to them?" Dr. Mac leaned close to Ian's ear. "Did you summon a core blast?"

Ian's chest heaved. "Rayne."

Dr. Mac stiffened. "Oh, no," he said under his breath.

"What?" Tara asked, but her attention fell to her cell when a text message came through.

"Catastrophe," Dr. Mac whispered.

Earth's energy circulated throughout Ian's body. It fed his core and carried essential nutrients to replenish what Ian had lost while burning up from the inside out. With a touch to Ian's forehead, Dr. Mac had put him under with his Somex power, but Ian was resisting it and lay in a semiconscious state. He ached to tell them what happened—what he saw— what he'd done. But a part of him wasn't ready to face it and welcomed the drugless sleep.

Soon after returning to the mansion and putting Ian in the boost, Dr. Mac had told everyone what he'd figured out: that

Ian had somehow conjured a core blast and had flung it at someone shyfting in the field. They feared that Rayne had been caught in the fire. Shocked, the group didn't have it in them to leave Ian's bedroom. Instead they worked through their grief, and the events of the past twelve hours, together.

"How could a core blast ignite a shyft?" Tara asked.

"Perhaps from gases trapped in the conjured energy. Many are flammable," Dr. Mac said.

"But there weren't any bodies," Milo said. "She could still be alive."

"If the shyft was far enough along, their bodies might be at the intended destination," Dr. Mac said. "Or somewhere in between."

"She's not dead," Tara said, from the edge of the bed. She sniffled. "Neither is Patrick. They can't be."

Ian tried to shout that Patrick wasn't there, but it couldn't penetrate the darkness that engulfed him. Where was Saxon? Ian reached out to the wolf to come, that he needed to channel with Tara. If Saxon had stayed at the eastern vortex, he was out of range and couldn't hear Ian's plea.

"What was the girl thinking?" Milo said. "Going after two Sars by herself."

"She wasn't drugged like everyone else. But she took a massive jolt, worse than mine," Joule said. "How could she just get up and run after them, after something like that?"

"What is she talking about?" Marcus said.

"We need to concentrate on our missing," Dr. Mac said. "And sort out who might have perished. Your son included, Marcus."

"Saxon and Ian only mentioned Rayne and the fire," Tara said.

Marcus grunted. "One of them might have shyfted away with Patrick, while the other remained to confront her."

The Drion's tone dripped with concern, not anger. Ian needed to wake up. He clawed to bring his consciousness to the surface, to let Marcus know that it was Jaered standing in the vortex, not his son, when it caught fire.

"I need you to tell me everything that happened, from the moment that Ian shyfted to Africa, all the way to the part where I woke up on this floor!" Marcus roared. "And if I find out later that you leave *anything* out, I'll see to it that you are reassigned where the sun don't shine."

"You can't—" Tara blurted.

"I can, I will, and I'll make it stick. I've had it up to here with this group taking on our enemies by themselves. The Heir is my responsibility, not yours. I can't do my job with my hands tied and functioning most of the time in the dark!" Marcus's voice came from next to the bed. "And someone better own up about Rayne and what she can do."

Ian stood still in the middle of the eastern vortex, staring at the burnt grass. Shudders ravaged his body, the price for breaking Dr. Mac's Somex power over him and leaving the boost after everyone deserted his room.

Marcus had brought in his troops to protect the grounds from further infiltration. Several stood guard at the field. The second Ian shyfted there, he commanded them to keep their distance and they took up positions at the tree line.

He didn't move from the vortex, as if he couldn't bring himself to leave what, in the space between heartbeats, may have become Rayne's gravesite. Saxon hadn't budged from his resting spot. The wolf barely acknowledged Ian when he shyfted there.

She's not coming back, Ian channeled with clenched fists deep in his pockets. Saxon whimpered, then stood and shook as much of the rain from his thick coat as he could. Ian's beloved companion leaned against his leg, ready to forgive what Ian could not.

The Jeep pulled up. Tara found him. From what he could see through the windshield, she was alone. She killed the engine but sat in the car. He didn't raise his face to her, unrepentant for leaving his boost and sneaking out of the mansion. She got out a few minutes later, then leaned against the Jeep and stood vigil at the edge of the field, giving him his space.

The storm eased into a steady downpour. Too riddled with guilt to mourn, Mother Earth mourned for him.

An idea struck and fired his thoughts into action. *We're going to find Patrick,* he channeled. *Whatever it takes.*

And make those bastards pay, Tara channeled. *Promise me that much.*

Saxon snorted and nudged him. Ian set out, and headed for Tara as Saxon ran ahead. With each step, Ian's anguish transformed into a fury that ignited his core, and the afterburn cleared his head.

{26}

Gwynn pressed at the top left corner, lower right, and lower left on the panel. The wall at the back of the narrow pantry popped open. She gestured for Rayne to enter what appeared to be a dark tunnel, then pushed the panel shut behind them. Gwynn grabbed something off a hook on the earthen wall. "Here, put this on," she said.

It covered Rayne like a cloak. Made of straw-like fibers, it smelled like mown grass and another odor that she didn't recognize, but was quite pungent. "What is this?" she asked.

"It's made from a plant that grows in our fields," Gwynn said. From the swish-like sound, the woman had tossed another cloak around her shoulders. "There's no light, but I know the way. Stay close."

The cool tunnel sent a shiver across Rayne's back. Back home, it was summer and had been unusually hot. Her clothing consisted of shorts and a thin, sleeveless shirt. Dirt kicked up at her feet and small pebbles got stuck in her sandals. The straw cloak didn't offer much warmth.

The series of twists and turns seemed to go on forever, and it felt as if they were gradually descending. Gwynn never hesitated whenever they reached a fork in their path, and remained silent as she navigated their trek. At one point, a sound came from the other side of the earthen wall.

"Is that water?" Rayne asked.

"We have a massive underground river system," Gwynn said. She grabbed Rayne's arm and stopped. "Are you doing okay? Am I going too fast for you?"

"I'm okay," Rayne said, but took a deep breath. "Where are we?"

"Much of Thrae's surface is uninhabitable, but over the past several decades, we've managed to create an underground home," she said. "It's not much farther." Gwynn took Rayne's hand and walked at a slower pace, as if they were two friends taking a stroll.

"Angus said that I look like someone from Thrae. He called me a paral. Said people might stare," Rayne said.

Gwynn didn't respond. "There are infinite combinations of genes in the universe. Two sister dimensions, like Earth and Thrae, narrow down that number. It is rare, but not impossible, for two individuals to share the same mix of genetics. They are often mirror images of each other. One might be left-handed, the other right."

"So the paral on Thrae is someone a lot like me?" Rayne asked.

"Not a lot," Gwynn said. "Identical, from the number of hair follicles, to your skin pigmentation, to many other genetic traits."

"What's her name?" Rayne asked. She'd never had a sister, much less a sibling, and had always been fascinated at Tara and Mara being identical twins. "Can I meet her?"

Gwynn slowed her steps, then stopped at a wide door. A dim light peered out from beneath. The moisture in the underground tunnel system made it slimy to the touch and from what she could tell, it looked to be thick planked.

The woman knocked with rhythmic taps. Rayne listened but heard no return from the other side. A muted metallic scrape. A second later, the door opened silently and stood ajar as if it had opened itself. Gwynn hesitated.

Rayne reached toward the door, but Gwynn grabbed her wrist. "Rayne, they will stare. Some might even attempt to touch you. There will be a great many whispers. Please, understand that your paral was loved by everyone."

"Was?" Rayne said.

"Her name was Kyre. Aeros murdered her to punish Jaered." Gwynn pushed the door open. "She was his wife."

A bright light blinded Rayne, and it took several seconds for her eyes to adjust.

Gwynn led her into a massive underground cavern. Giant stalagmites rose from the uneven floor while stalactites hung from the ceiling overhead. An intense light as bright as the sun came from the center of the cavern. A column of what appeared to be pure energy pulsated in a rhythmic beat. It grew from the floor of the cavern and disappeared into the ceiling above. Rayne couldn't tell how wide it was because the column had no clear edge to it, but she imagined the column holding up a skyscraper single-handedly.

"Welcome," Gwynn said under her breath. Rayne's sight slowly recovered from the glare and she stood aghast at the number of people in the cavern. The rock ledges embedded in its curved walls looked to be painted with minerals in a palate of earth-toned colors. Bodies lined the ledges like books on a shelf. Others had settled on the floor of the cavern. Young, old, couples and their offspring, all gathered together.

What must have been close to a hundred faces focused on Gwynn and Rayne.

It was their silence that struck her. The only sounds in the enormous cavern came from intermittent drips of moisture falling from the cavern ceiling into pools scattered along the floor. Some pools looked to be deeper than others. The column of energy emitted a low hum, like a buzz from fluorescent lights.

Gwynn closed the door behind them. A nearby man stepped up and helped her lift a heavy iron bar. They secured it across the door. She gestured for Rayne to sit on a nearby rock and then sat next to her. The woman grabbed Rayne's hand and rested it in her lap.

A horde of eyes stared at Rayne. Fingers pointed. Chins jutted her way. Many sat in stunned disbelief while others looked at her with sadness. A few tossed her disgruntled glares.

Rayne didn't know how to return the attention and dropped her gaze to her lap. Gwynn stroked her back like a mother reassuring a child. But Rayne was a stranger on a strange planet and no amount of comforting could change that.

The longer Gwynn stroked Rayne's back, the more her muscles unwound and her shoulders relaxed. She looked around the cavern where a hundred people had gathered and sat as still as mice. In spite of their collective calm, fear was palpable in their expressions.

{27}

Jaered focused on the ooze tickling his ear while forcing himself to climb out of the darkness. He made to swallow, but a parched mouth and throat had nothing to purge and the taste of smoke lingered. He shivered from intense cold. Familiar smells of chamomile, lavender, and calendula stroked memories, which in turn brought images of a life, long ago.

He'd made it to Thrae, but what of Rayne? Had he protected her from the worst of the flames? Jaered fought to open his eyes, but the weights tugging at his lids made it a chore. Between blinks, he discovered a dimly lit room with a pulsating violet glow coming from beneath him.

A shallow cough brought Angus's disgruntled face into view, and the old doctor peered down at Jaered. Angus's beard was peppered with more gray since Jaered had seen him last. "Don't start," Jaered said, but it came out raspy. "The girl."

The old doctor's perturbed glare made Jaered feel right at home. "Shocked, confused, disoriented, but otherwise fine." Angus said, and gave into a deep sigh. "Gwynn sounded the alarm. Everyone headed for the tunnels." He put a couple of fingers to Jaered's throat. "If we're lucky, Aeros won't have too many to choose from."

Jaered closed his eyes. In saving Rayne, he'd condemned someone else. "Please, protect her."

"Gwynn's taken charge of that. Your sorry buttocks are my job."

A door banged open in the apartment beyond. A shout of Jaered's name. The bedroom door opened.

"Sophenna, you should be seeking refuge with the others," Angus said.

Jaered's mother leaned over the vat. Relief brightened her face. A curtain of moisture filled her crystal blue eyes. She took Jaered's hand and squeezed it tight. Angus's goo squirted between their fingers. "Liem told me that they found you in the vortex room." She pressed her palm on Jaered's Seal and stilled. "Your core, it's so weak. Liem said you were badly burned, but it doesn't look that serious."

"You haven't seen his backside." Angus grunted.

"You need to go with the others," Jaered said. "Be safe."

"What more can he do to me, that hasn't already been done?" She placed a gentle hand on Jaered's cheek. "He finds more pleasure from hurting the ones I love."

The tender moment crumbled Jaered's defenses that were keeping the emotions in check. They erupted, and he held his breath until the pain subsided. He'd lost Kyre and their unborn child at the hands of the monster that was his father. And then Aeros had, in turn, punished his mother for bearing a son he couldn't command.

"He brought someone through with him," Angus whispered. "Gwynn will need help concealing her."

Jaered squeezed his mother's hand. "Aeros will catch scent of her for sure," he said. "Please, Mother, go and help Gwynn. Do it for me."

Tears moistened her cheeks. "There's been no time," she whimpered. "He's seen to that."

"I've given him cause," Jaered said without a lick of remorse.

When she shook her head, her golden hair cascaded across one side of her face. "No, my beloved son, I am to blame. My crime has been everyone else's to bear."

"Your only crime was rejecting a monster," Angus said.

"Mother, Eve's plan. It worked," Jaered hushed. Angus and Sophenna exchanged stunned glances. "The third Heir has risen."

"What of Ian?" Sophenna said.

"Survived," Jaered said. "He should be at full power. He just doesn't know it, not yet."

"The triangle is complete," Angus said and straightened his back. "Sophenna. Go, tell Gwynn the good news."

"Please." Jaered let go of her hand. She gave him a lingering kiss on his forehead as her tears carved a path down his temple. "I love you more than there are stars in the universe," she whispered.

Jaered's chest heaved, and he pushed the sorrow to the back of his thoughts. "And I you," he said.

His mother slowly backed up and turned—but froze.

Aeros stood in the bedroom doorway. "Our son has been quite naughty, Sophenna."

"He didn't defy your order," she said. "He's injured."

"Don't waste your breath," Jaered raised his voice, counting on sounding stronger than he felt. "When has reason ever mattered to him?"

"You still don't know when to keep your mouth shut," Angus muttered out of the corner of his mouth.

Aeros grabbed Sophenna by the arm. His father's silver-gray hair was trimmed and smoothed back. Gone was his custom suit and tie. He had taken the time to dress in a polo shirt and khakis for his hunt. There was no need for weapons. "We must savor this family reunion!" he said with sickening exuberance. "It's been two, no, three years?"

"He was shyfting. There was a fire," Angus said.

"Silence!" Aeros roared. Unbridled fury darkened his eyes and flames appeared in his irises. Brilliant core blasts extinguished in his open palms as quickly as they had formed. He regained control. Jaered's father strolled around the vat; his gaze never wavered from his son's face. "You were banned," he said in a steeled voice.

"You caused the devastation that hit Northern California, didn't you?" Jaered said. His father's smug expression was answer enough. "You've been sending Earth's Heir all over the globe, playing with him. I knew he'd go home, so I checked in on him," Jaered said.

"Why?" Aeros sneered. "Would you even care?"

"I wanted to see if his measly powers had developed," Jaered said.

"How does that justify this insolence?" Aeros asked, as if more amused than curious.

"During my exit, he caught up to me." Jaered hesitated and looked at his mother. "He used a core blast."

"Ian, did this?" Sophenna whispered.

"And ignited the methane that your power draws," Aeros said under his breath.

Jaered caught his blunder and chastised himself for sharing too much. "I tried to shyft home, but lost consciousness."

"We found him, barely alive," Angus said.

Aeros stopped pacing. He dipped his finger into the gel and brought it to his nose. "Who knows that Thrae's Heir has returned?"

"Just us." Angus looked at Sophenna. "Not even Gwynn."

A snarl lifted the edge of Aeros's lip. "You and an aging woman carried my son in here, Angus?"

"You've always underestimated me," Sophenna said. "Always."

Angus puffed up his chest. "As you underestimate the worlds you strive to dominate."

It was one thing for Jaered to talk that way to his father, but to hear Angus be so bold caused Jaered's pulse to pound.

"Seems I may have underestimated *you*, Doctor." Aeros gave Angus a relaxed smile and waved his hand. Jaered's father's power gripped his core and lifted his body from the gel. Jaered winced as the thick solution sucked at his injured tissue before it broke free and he hovered over the vat.

"Aeros, stop!" Sophenna shouted.

Without breaking his gaze on Angus, Aeros flicked his fingers. Jaered flipped over and floated facedown, staring at the tub of iridescent gel. His mother pressed a fist to her mouth to stifle her shriek. Aeros looked at Jaered's back. "It appears that this, is at least true."

Jaered clenched his jaw. His nostrils flared as the gel dripped down his sides and, with one plop after another, found their way back to the gel bath below. Exposed nerve endings sent searing needles coursing across his back, turning what skin was left into a jigsaw puzzle of unimaginable agony. He willed himself not to pass out, not to appear weak, anything to rob his father of the moment, and ease his mother's heartache.

Aeros walked around the vat, keeping Jaered suspended, relishing in his injuries. He hesitated when he reached the opposite side. "Were you alone?"

"We only found him," Angus said.

The muscles bulged in his father's jaw. "It's time to go," Aeros announced, as if they had just enjoyed a day at the park. "Say your good-byes, my dear. Who knows when you'll see your son again."

"Jaered," Sophenna said and reached toward him.

A frigid blast. Air sucked out of Jaered's lungs as Aeros shyfted them to a dim room. His father released the power over his core and Jaered dropped, facedown on the cement floor. He wailed and dragged an elbow to support himself then looked up. His father had shyfted them to the vortex storage room. The odor of his burnt flesh still lingered in the closed space.

Aeros stood still and sniffed the air. "Such a pleasant bouquet. My little pyro Ning would have enjoyed it so." He exhaled and brought a fist to his chest. "I do miss the old Thrae," he said with contrived regret. "In spite of her showing her age, your mother is still a ravishing beauty in her own way." He grabbed Jaered by the hair and lifted his head, then bent down and got in Jaered's face. "I know you brought someone with you." With a sneer, he gazed into Jaered's eyes with seething hatred. "How do I repay such insolence?"

A sonic boom deafened Jaered's thoughts. Suffocating, he closed his eyes and gave into the void of the parashyft.

They reappeared in a basement. With a wave of his father's hand, Jaered lifted from the concrete floor and crashed into the wall. He slumped down, robbed of breath and unable to cry out.

"What is this?" Eve demanded while running down the stairs.

"He made a side trip to Thrae," Aeros said. "I had to retrieve him."

She paused at the bottom step. "What did you do to him?"

"Keep him alive until I get back," Aeros said.

"Where are you going?" Eve scoffed. "I want nothing to do with your bastard son."

"I didn't say to make him comfortable." The room brightened as Aeros made to shyft. "I have a hunt."

"No!" Jaered made to rise but collapsed at Eve's feet. A sonic boom, and the room darkened. His father was gone.

Eve crouched down. "Oh, Jaered."

"He's going after Rayne," Jaered said.

"She's alive?" Eve closed her eyes. "Oh, thank God."

He leaned against the wall and tried to straighten his legs to stand, but didn't get very far. Eve threw his arm over her shoulders and hung onto his belt, hoisting him up the rest of the way. He clenched his jaw at the unbearable pain. "How could he know? They hid her before he got there."

Eve leaned him against the wall to examine his back. She stilled. "There's a mark on your side, in the shape of a handprint."

"The second he lays eyes on her, he'll know she's the one. He'll kill her, just like he did Kyre."

"Right now, you're my concern." Eve adjusted the sconce on the wall. "I waited for you after you left. Then flames burst from the vortex on this end and snuffed out. I'd never seen anything like it. Mac called about an hour later, told me what happened. I've been frantic, not knowing where you ended up or if you were both even alive."

"We've got to do something," he said.

"Is she with Gwynn and Sophenna?" Eve asked. Jaered nodded. "Then we trust that my sisters will keep her safe."

{28}

The people shuffled toward the various doors that led out of the cavern. For the third time, the column of energy shimmered bright. Everyone froze. After a couple of seconds, it returned to its rhythmic, low hum.

A sea of panicked faces turned toward Gwynn. She gestured for everyone to sit.

"What's wrong," Rayne whispered.

"He came back," Gwynn said with unease and squeezed Rayne's hand. They sat on their rock. "Remain very still."

Rayne stared at a young family across from her. When the wife met her gaze, Rayne smiled and the woman gave Rayne a subtle nod. The couple wasn't much older than Rayne. The boy in their lap looked to be about three. The child had been resting against his mother's chest for what had to be half an hour, without stirring.

No one in the room moved. The Thraens' patience and self-control was astounding. Had most of the Thraen populace grown up living in fear? It struck Rayne that people from war-torn countries back on Earth would have more in common with the Thraens than she did.

The longer Rayne sat, the more she saw Jaered through a different lens. She was the mirror image of his murdered wife. It explained his strange drive to protect her over the past several months—and his tortured eyes whenever he looked at her. What had Jaered done that drove Aeros to kill his wife? Was Jaered's hatred for Aeros his motivation to join Eve and her rebels? He had told Rayne once that the rebels' fight was with Aeros. She thought back to the events of the previous night. What had they done to Patrick? Why force her to drain Ian's core, only for Jaered to restart it? The unanswered questions brought on a headache and restlessness set in. She shifted her weight on the rock to combat the numbing sensation in her buttocks, but at the sound of her shuffling, fearful glances shot her way.

Rayne studied the faces. An entire world's population had been reduced to this? Jaered was their Heir. These were his people. Gradually, Rayne grew to understand the source of his rage.

After what felt like an eternity, the column shimmered, then drew still. A collective sigh filled the cavern.

"He's gone," Gwynn said.

The dread in her voice stilled Rayne's heart. "Maybe he didn't—"

"He never leaves without taking a life." Gwynn slowly rose from the rock like it pained her to stand. The floor and walls of the cavern came alive with rising bodies.

"Two coming, two going," rang through the gathering crowd.

"Gwynn, why two?" a woman asked. "Did he take two lives this time?"

"Is she why?" A man pointed at Rayne and gave her an irritated look. "Cause she's no ghost."

"We'll convene and share what we know later, I promise. Meet back here at dusk," Gwynn said. "In the meantime, let us bury our fallen and embrace those who are left"

They removed the iron bar from the thick, planked door. Those closest held back, with downcast eyes, allowing Gwynn and Rayne to exit first. The Pur Weir back on Earth treated Ian with similar solemn reverence.

She took Rayne's hand, and they led the procession out of the tunnel. From over her shoulder, Rayne noticed that some groups separated at the various forks in the path, and their numbers thinned to just a handful by the time they reached the pantry door.

Gwynn paused before opening it. "Liem, we need to locate Sophenna as soon as possible. Bring her to my apartment when you find her. Trae, you and the others check on the control room, and then make a sweep of the perimeter wall." She pulled a lever next to the door and it popped open. The tall, wiry man she called Liem hung their straw cloaks on the hooks.

The pantry's pungent assortment of cinnamon, onions, garlic, and basil sent Rayne's stomach gurgling.

Gwynn stood at the bedroom doorway, gripped the edge of the jam, and hung her head.

"What is it?" Rayne looked inside. Jaered was gone and the vat sat empty. "Did Angus move him to a safer place?"

"No," Gwynn said. She approached and ran her finger along the inside of the vat. "The Lavolae, it's gone."

The vat didn't have a drain. "Why would Angus remove it?"

"He wouldn't." Gwynn left Rayne and set the kettle on the stove but when she went to light a match, her hand shook and she couldn't strike it. She bent over the counter and her chest rose and fell with heartbreaking sobs.

"Two coming, two going," Rayne whispered. "He took Jaered—"

"And then came back for Angus," Gwynn said.

"Is he going to kill them?" Rayne hugged herself at the thought of losing Jaered. Her concern wasn't only for her return trip to Earth.

"Aeros can't kill Jaered. He needs him."

"Then he must have realized Jaered's injuries were too severe, and came back for the doctor," Rayne said.

Gwynn composed herself enough to light the match. When she turned the knob, flames flickered like a blue flower. "Aeros took the Lavaloe for Jaered." She stared at the fire. "He took my husband as retribution."

A knock at the outer door. Liem poked his head in. "I found her." His voice softened. "She's in a bad way."

"That sadistic animal," Gwynn said under her breath. She gripped the edge of the stove with white knuckles.

Liem glanced around. "Gwynn, where's Angus?" When she didn't respond, he looked at Rayne. She slowly shook her head.

The cruel reality left the man visibly shaken, and he stared at a worn, overstuffed chair at one end of the room, as if waiting for the old doctor to materialize in what must have been his favorite seat.

Rayne brushed at a tear, not for a man she barely knew, but as if Dr. Mac were suddenly struck down. Angus was clearly respected and loved. He didn't deserve to be murdered, not when he'd devoted his life to so many.

"How do you want me to announce this?" Liem asked gently.

Gwynn swiped at her face and placed the kettle on the stove. She set about rinsing out the mugs from the sink, keeping her back to the rest of the room. "When I address everyone tonight, I'll let them know."

He looked stricken. "I can meet with them, Gwynn. Under the circumstances."

"Help Trae and the others." Gwynn held a hearty pinch of tea leaves between her fingers and stuffed them into the walnut strainer.

"I wouldn't leave it past that bastard to damage our life supports," Liem said.

"Aeros isn't stupid enough to kill his bargaining chips," Gwynn said. "We're the only thing keeping the Heir under his thumb."

He turned to leave, but he paused with his hand on the doorknob. "I'll be back to escort you to the meeting."

"Liem." Gwynn looked at him from over her shoulder. "Thank you."

He walked out and closed the door behind him.

A moment later, the kettle whistled with a burst of steam. Rayne startled. Gwynn filled two thermoses with the hot tea. She screwed tops back on that looked like they could do double duty as cups, then handed the thermoses to Rayne. She opened a cupboard and pulled out a blanket and medical bag from the closet. The weathered appearance told Rayne it had made thousands of house calls.

Gwynn paused at the door to the apartment. "Come, Rayne. My sister needs us."

Any remnants of lingering doubt vanished. Rayne knew Gwynn was indeed Ian's mother.

{29}

Gwynn led Rayne through the winding tunnel. They passed the door of the storage vortex room. Someone had secured it with an iron bar. The light bulb above the door emitted a steady amber glow.

They soon came to another door and Gwynn paused. She let herself in without knocking. The apartment layout was identical to Gwynn and Angus's, but unlike their sparse and simple furnishings, Sophenna's apartment was filled with antiques. It felt as if she'd stepped into a museum. Ancient furniture, paintings, sculptures and trinkets littered every inch of space; a few were kept on display in glass cabinets.

Gwynn gently knocked on the bedroom door and a second later, a plump woman opened it.

"Catherine, thank you for coming," Gwynn said.

"That tyrant," Catherine hissed. She stepped out into the living room and closed the bedroom door behind her. "He's sick and twisted. Why does he target her?"

"Because she is the one thing he can't have in this universe." Gwynn patted her arm. Go home to your family. We'll meet in the cavern at dusk.

Catherine nodded and grabbed a sweater from the back of an intricately carved chair. When she turned, she caught sight of Rayne and paused with parted lips. "Oh, lordy."

"This is Rayne," Gwynn said. "She's from—"

"Earth. Has to be, right? Unless I'm dead and don't know it," Catherine said. "Welcome." The woman dropped her face and scurried by Rayne, exiting the apartment.

Gwynn hesitated and gave Rayne a pained smile. "Sophenna will be shocked to see you. But I'm hoping you will also bring her some comfort."

"How?" Rayne said.

"Because she is Jaered's mother," Gwynn said. They entered the bedroom with quiet steps, but Rayne held back near the doorway. Unlike Angus and Gwynn's apartment, this didn't have a vat full of Lavolae. The bed had pillows and a thick, lacy comforter that had seen better days.

A woman was nestled in the covers. Her long, golden hair had streaks of honey and gray. When she opened her eyes, they were the most beautiful shade of blue she'd ever seen. The woman was striking. She gave Gwynn a weak smile and raised her arms to her sister.

Gwynn set her supplies down at the foot of the bed and embraced Sophenna. They hugged tight for several minutes, not speaking.

Pictures on the dresser caught Rayne's eye and she wandered closer but drew back with her hand to her mouth. The photos were of Jaered and her, but it wasn't her. Rayne stared at a life that she had never lived.

It struck her that she'd never seen Jaered smile, not once. Rayne picked up one of the frames and drank in a side of the man he'd never revealed. Happy, loving, content, and carefree. The black-and-white photos ranged from his childhood all the way up to a wedding that looked simple and intimate. Jaered and Kyre stood in a field, a ring of woven flowers in her hair with a darkened sky as a backdrop. The couple held hands and gazed into each other's eyes. A scattering of people flanked them with Sophenna, Gwynn, and Angus among them. Rayne's stomach twisted at the sight of Dr. Mac's paral. What was Aeros doing to them? Were they even still alive? Rayne pressed the thermoses against her chest, but their warmth couldn't stave off a shudder.

A shared sigh and the two sisters separated a moment later, but pressed foreheads as if unwilling to break their bond just yet.

"Jaered brought someone with him," Gwynn said.

"He begged me to help hide them, but it had been so long." Sophenna whimpered. "I couldn't leave him."

"Shuuush," Gwynn hushed. "As injured as he was, he looked good," she said, but chuckled at her own oxymoron.

Jaered's mother nodded and laughed. "He did. A little weathered." She leaned back. A curtain of tears clouded her eyes. "He never could stay out of the thick of things."

Gwynn cupped her sister's face in her hands and kissed her forehead. "He's fighting the good fight for all of us."

Sophenna's tears dampened her stained ringlet bedspread. When Jaered's mother turned to swipe at her face, she caught sight of Rayne across the room.

Gwynn tucked her sister's hair behind her ear. "This is Rayne."

Sophenna's gaze fell to the photo in Rayne's hand. Self-conscious, Rayne placed the picture back where she'd found it. Jaered's mother slipped out of bed, but cringed and pressed a fist to her lower abdomen. She bent over and grabbed her comforter. It took a couple of seconds for her to stand upright. Bright-red splotches dotted her loose-fitting nightgown.

Gwynn rose from the bed. "Let me check—"

"It's nothing I haven't lived through before." Sophenna approached Rayne with unsteady steps and held out her hand. "Welcome," she said softly, gently. Rayne took her hand. Sophenna stepped close and pressed Rayne's hand to her chest. The woman's heartbeat was rapid and strong. "In another life, I adored you, loved you as if my own child."

Rayne swallowed as words escaped her. The lines of a hard life were etched as shallow curves in Sophenna's features. None of this was familiar. There wasn't a history between them, yet Rayne felt at ease.

"I'm sorry for your loss," Rayne said with more emotion than she would have guessed.

Sophenna gave her a radiant smile. "The universe is nothing but fluid. We can all take comfort in that."

Gwynn took her sister by the shoulders and guided her back to bed. "Rayne, why don't you give us a few minutes, so I can attend to my sister."

Rayne left the bedroom, but leaned against the closed door, at a loss for how to help. She had been thrust into an unfamiliar world that needed more than she could give.

A sword with a gilded handle caught her eye and she made her way through the apartment, peering at the museum-quality artifacts. Some items looked to be hundreds of years old, others from the early fifties, at least back on Earth. She glanced about the room and it dawned on her what was missing. No color photos. There wasn't anything modern about the things she'd seen thus far, other than Angus's miraculous Lavolae. Thrae was a parallel world to Earth, yet their differences extended way beyond the color of the sky. It felt as if Thrae had stalled in time, by fifty, sixty years or more.

Rayne rubbed her arms to ease the jitters. Claustrophobia had set in the longer she moved about windowless dwellings. She wondered if she'd ever see a blue sky, or feel the warmth of the sun on her face again.

{30}

Jaered stood at the edge of the path focused on the upright door nestled in a field of crimson poppies. Invisible walls held it up with a blue sky as its backdrop. A bright ray of sunshine beckoned him from the keyhole in the six-paneled door. Warmth churned inside him and peace embraced him like a glove.

He took a step toward the door, and then another. More than anything, he wanted to find Kyre inside and leave the path that surely someone else could walk in his absence.

An invisible force stilled his hand as he reached for the knob. At that moment, Jaered knew he couldn't—shouldn't enter. He retraced his steps, each one agonizing and strenuous, taxing his muscles and his sheer will, but he persevered and returned to the trail. One final glance at the door, then he turned down the path and headed for the distant void and its unknown.

Jaered rubbed his face back and forth across the bed, erasing the image and blocking out the inviting door, pitching his world into darkness. The physical world returned with an ache and buried Kyre's memories under a pile of agonizing pain.

Someone placed an icy compress on his back, and then another across the back of his arm. The pain eased and then vanished. A hand patted the back of his leg. "He'll heal, thanks to the Lavolae," Angus's gravelly voice announced. "But his burns were quite severe. It takes a tremendous toll on the body. He would recover better, faster in his boost."

"That's not going to happen," Aeros snapped.

"He can't use the boosts on Earth," Eve said. "If he was placed in one, he would be susceptible to the Curse."

"We need him to be able to move freely among both the Pur and Duach." Aeros' voice grew closer as he approached the bed. Jaered's father fingered the pillowcase next to his head. "I'm shocked at how comfortable you made him," Aeros said.

"That's what makes us such effective partners," Eve said. "What little humanity I still possess, cancels out what you lost centuries ago."

"Still, he's not in your favor," Aeros said. "At least that's what you would have me believe."

"We need him alive and cooperative," Eve said. "Honey is much more effective than vinegar."

Aeros scoffed. "A surprising analogy coming from someone who's never cooked a meal in her life." His father's voice grew distant. "But you are cooking up something, on the side, aren't you, my dear?"

"You are the master of two worlds. How could I, or anyone else on Earth, be a threat to you?"

"How indeed." A bright flash. His father was gone.

"Any news from Thrae?" Eve said. "My sisters?"

"They are as well as can be expected," Angus said. "Our numbers are dwindling. Those he hasn't murdered for sport are growing weak. Our crops are not as plentiful and lack essential nutrition. Absence of natural sunlight will do that."

"The third Heir—" Eve said.

"Jaered told us that it worked," Angus said. "And what of Gwynn's son?"

"Ian's core is strengthening by the hour," she said. "It will still take some effort to enlighten him that his powers are fully available. The poor boy has lived his whole life believing he was inadequate. It will take a major jolt to awaken his potential."

"What kind of jolt?" Angus asked tentatively.

"I'm working on it." A moment of silence passed between them. Eve sighed. "Ian believes that Rayne and Jaered are dead."

"Are you going to tell him the truth?" Angus asked.

"I'm weighing the lesser of two evils," Eve said. "I'll either have a self-destructive Pur Heir to contend with, or a vengeful one."

"You've lived too long by the code of secrets and deception," Angus said. "Why not tell the poor boy the truth."

"What is the truth, Angus?" Eve growled. "She might as well be dead. I have no idea how to get her back to Earth without condemning us to the full extent of Aeros's wrath." Footsteps drew closer. "Damn you, Jaered," she whispered in

177

his ear. "Your single act of free will has warped centuries of planning, and likely condemned more people to death."

I know! Jaered shouted, but the words only echoed in his head. I know.

Sounds awakened Jaered. He felt stronger, and for the first time able to open his lids with minimal effort. The bedroom was dark. The covers beneath his face were damp from drool that pooled during his dreamless sleep. He turned his face toward noises coming from the bathroom and stared at the steady stream of light from under the door, trying to break Angus's Somex-induced sleep. Distant music. Eve was home. A classical melody floated toward his bedroom from down the hall. Bach? Beethoven? Jaered couldn't tell the Earthly composers apart.

Jaered's eyes adjusted to the dim light. Aeros sat in the chair across from Jaered's bed. His heart skipped a beat at the murderous expression on his father's face. He fought the Somex.

A running faucet turned off and a moment later, the bathroom door opened. Angus stiffened at seeing Aeros.

"Your holistic knowledge is to be commended, Doctor" Aeros said. "If allowed to be shared, it would end so much suffering here on Earth."

The compresses were heavy. His body's heat had warmed the Lavolae and it weighed him down like cement. He pulled an elbow up under his chest and pushed, lifting one shoulder. The compresses slipped off his arms, but the bulkier one on his back took more effort to shed. "Ahhh," Jaered swallowed any further gasp as the newborn skin protested with lightning jabs at the scraping, sliding compress. It landed on the floor beside the bed with a thud. He rolled onto his back and pressed against the bedspread to ease the worst of the sting.

"Your patient has aroused just in time to say good-bye." Aeros flicked a finger. Angus was dragged out the bathroom doorway by an invisible hand. Aeros closed his fist and the man who helped raise Jaered, the only father he'd ever known, fell to his knees at the center of the room. Angus looked up at Jaered. "I knew my time was up the second he returned for me," Angus said. "He only waited until I healed you enough."

"That, and you amuse me." Aeros stood.

"Stop!" Jaered shouted, but it came out like a croak. "I'll do whatever you want from now on, no resistance, I swear. Just spare him."

"Resisting me is who you are. I'd rather miss our sparring." Aeros slowly paced around the condemned man. "He must pay for his sins. He lied about you coming alone."

"Word spreads fast." Angus gave Aeros a smug look. "By now, everyone knows their Heir is alive and well."

Aeros gave Jaered a murderous stare. "Do you know the damage you've done by going to Thrae?" he said through clenched teeth.

"You've given them back their hope," Angus said, his voice gushing with pride. His voice adopted a husky, desperate tone. "But if you need a reminder of how strong you are, just look in the mirror, boy."

Aeros paused and flexed his neck. "I'll return and hunt down whoever you took." With a wave of his father's hand, Jaered was slammed up against the headboard, pinned by a crushing pressure that denied him air. With one hand thrust at Jaered, Aeros flicked his other at Angus.

The old doctor's hands whipped behind as if secured with invisible handcuffs. "You lost your ability to feel centuries ago, Aeros," Angus said as though rushed to purge what he'd kept to himself. "You feed off of other's emotions." He gagged, then coughed. Purple spittle spurted from his mouth when he looked up at Jaered. "You torture the boy because he has what you'll never possess." Amethyst streams flowed from both nostrils and dripped to his chest, staining his shirt like a bib. "His mother's love," Angus rasped. Gagging, he teetered on his knees and coughed, spraying Lavolae on Aeros's pants. "Look . . . in the mirror . . . Jaered." His uncle's eyes rolled back into his head and he collapsed onto the floor.

"His Lavolae is quite the legacy." Aeros's lip curled. "It's only fitting he's buried with it." His father dropped his hand and Jaered slipped to the bed, sucking air between moans.

Eve appeared in the doorway. How long had she stood, just outside in the hall? She looked at Angus's body with cold indifference. "Well, that's a mess," she said as if coming across dog poop on a rug.

"I never did like honey," Aeros said, and wiped a drop of Lavolae off his hand using the back of Angus's shirt. "Too sweet for my taste."

Jaered screamed. He leapt off the bed, but in his weakened state, landed in a slump at his father's feet.

Aeros stepped away from Jaered and gestured toward Angus. "Get rid of it." A blinding flash. He shyfted.

Eve's stoic demeanor bled into despair and brought her to her knees.

Jaered gathered Angus up and buried his face against his uncle's neck. He rocked in rhythm to his penance. "I'm sorry . . . I'm sorry . . . I'm sorry . . ."

{31}

Rayne sliced a loaf of unleavened bread and spread a jam that she found in the old upright refrigerator. The jam tasted of blueberries. Once she'd finished her snack, Trae brought her to the cavern in time for the assembly.

Whispers fell silent as Gwynn stepped into the cavern and stood, waiting at the door for the crowd to settle. Liem and Trae set the iron bar across the planked door, and then helped Gwynn onto the rock that she and Rayne had sat on a few hours earlier. When she stood tall and ready to address them, the group sat and grew quiet.

Gwynn gestured for Rayne to remain standing.

"Thraens, we were blessed with the presence of our Heir earlier today," Gwynn said. "He is alive and has brought us good news in their fight against our oppressors." She cleared her throat. "But Aeros came, and the Heir was forced to return to Earth before he could meet with you and tell you himself."

"Who was it this time?" a man said from the front row.

"Angus," Gwynn paused as she blinked back tears. Denied the opportunity to mourn the loss of her husband, yet found the strength to carry on in his absence. So much like her son, Rayne thought. "He took my husband." Grumbling, disbelief, and outrage rang throughout the crowd. Many gazed upon her with pity.

"But he's the only doctor we had left," an old woman cried out.

"Anyone who needs help has always been welcomed at my home," Gwynn said. "Nothing has changed. My husband shared much of his knowledge with me. I am now asking for volunteers to assist and learn from me. We will make do, as we always have."

"Is the Heir coming back?" a man shouted from the uppermost ledge.

"He is fighting Aeros on Earth," Gwynn said. "If and when he returns next, let us pray that he brings news of victory."

Fists shot into the air with a resounding cry. Many stood and waved, others clapped. Many remained seated and didn't join in the impromptu rally. From their creased faces, they failed to share their brethren's optimism. Gwynn gestured for the crowd to quiet. It took a couple of minutes for them to settle down.

"What's Kyre's paral doing here?" a man shouted.

Gwynn placed a hand on Rayne's shoulder. "The Heir brought her from Earth."

"When Aeros finds out, he will return!" a woman shrieked. "We can't hide down here forever!"

Gwynn shook her head. "We must do everything we can to protect her, if and when Aeros returns."

"She will draw his wrath and doom us all!" came from the upper ledges.

"She isn't one of us!" another man shouted. "What does Earth know of our struggles? They haven't come to our aid. Why should we risk what little we have left to protect one of theirs?"

Liem stepped forward and waved his arms. "Quiet!" he yelled. "Have you lost everything, including your respect? If you want answers, allow our Mother to share what she can."

Mother? The reference piqued Rayne's curiosity, and she added it to the swelling list of unanswered questions.

"Her name is Rayne, and she is a threat to Aeros, key to the rebels' plan," Gwynn said. "We must protect her, and if needed, be prepared to sacrifice our lives to do so." Rayne stared at Gwynn in stunned silence. The woman cast a gentle smile at Rayne, then looked about the room. "The Heir brought news that the third Heir has risen. The prophesied triangle of power is complete. Their very existence dictates that the Prophecy and all that it claims will come true." Gwynn raised her voice and pointed at the cavern wall behind her. "Why do we protect this young woman who stands before you? It is because, she is the sun."

Rayne looked where Gwynn pointed. A giant replica of Ian's Seal, a triangle with a sun inside, had been carved into the rock. Her legs turned to mush. Liem went to grab her, but pulled back with a grimace when his core's draining energy tickled every nerve of her body. She sat down on the rock as Liem gave her a puzzled stare. He was a Sar. Were there others left on Thrae?

Gwynn continued to address the crowd like a prophet.

Ian had suspected he wasn't the only Heir. Was Jaered the second? But who rose last night? Who was the third? She looked up at Gwynn, who had paused, waiting for the crowd to quiet.

Rayne went over the events of the previous evening—and stilled. Patrick.

Liem and Trae stood guard just outside Gwynn's apartment. The woman insisted that she and Rayne not be disturbed.

Gwynn handed Rayne a steaming mug of tea and chose a chair at the tip of the coffee table. She took a sip from her mug and leaned back in the chair.

"You're Ian's mother," Rayne said, foregoing any pretense as if the bottled-up questions had popped the lid off and were gushing out. "You didn't die in a car accident when he was a baby."

Gwynn looked weary, the lines in her face deeper than ever. "My pregnancy was hidden from everyone. I gave birth to him on a stormy night." A relaxed smile gave her cheeks a rosy glow. "It was as if Mother Earth proclaimed his arrival across the universe." Her voice took on an edge, "but my elation was short-lived."

"Why?" Rayne asked.

"Because Johann, the man you know as the Primary—"

"The head honcho of the Syndrion council?" Rayne said.

"He was determined that the Earth's Heir would be Pur, not Duach. For years, his spies were everywhere. Within minutes of Weir births, the Primary would appear and press his hand to the newborns' chests."

Gwynn looked down at the mug resting in her lap, but she didn't take a sip. "When the time came, I planned to deliver in secret, but I was betrayed. As I was giving birth to Ian, Johann and his men broke in and ripped my newborn from my arms." Gwynn closed her eyes as if she couldn't help but relive it. "Johann pressed his power to Ian's chest, and knew the second he lifted his hand, he'd found Earth's Heir." Her eyes darkened and her lips drew tight. She looked at Rayne. "But more than that, he made him a Pur."

"But was that a bad thing?" Rayne said. "Better a Pur, than Duach."

"The Heir was supposed to be neither," Gwynn said. "He was free to serve Mother Earth, and no one else."

"Jaered told us that Ian," Rayne hesitated, unsure how to ask. "That his core wasn't—"

"Natural?" Gwynn nodded. "He was conceived in a test tube, but I carried him to term."

Rayne had suspected. Allison's list from QualSton indicated that Gwynn was a researcher in the genetics lab. "Is that why Ian didn't have his full range of powers?" Rayne asked.

"He always has, but I made sure that they were stifled," Gwynn said.

Rayne shook her head. "Why?"

SUE DUFF

"The Primary feared Earth's Heir. Such a being, more powerful than he could imagine, might be too much to handle. I was frightened that he would find a way to kill Ian."

"The Primary didn't just want to make the Heir a Pur," Rayne reasoned aloud. "He wanted control over him." She scooted to the edge of the couch. "But they tortured Ian as a child, trying to bring his powers to the surface."

Darkness clouded Gwynn's expression. "To test him. When he failed, he didn't pose a threat to the Primary. They cared for him, but no longer feared him."

"The Earth is vulnerable, the Sars are dying out," Rayne said. "Ian hasn't been able to help because his powers are too weak."

"The Earth is dying because, for the past thirty years, Aeros has been draining its power, like he did for centuries here on Thrae. Only, he found the perfect battleground on Earth."

"The Pur and Duach civil war," Rayne said.

"Aeros fed the hatred, prompting both sides to kill each other. Fewer Sars made it easier for him to drain Earth's sustenance at a faster rate."

"Why would Aeros do such a thing?" Rayne asked.

"Because shyfting across dimensions isn't enough for him. He wants to travel and conquer the universe." Gwynn took a sip of her tea. "But my son has full use of his powers now. Jaered saw to it the other night."

Rayne stared ahead, deep in thought. Jaered had summoned the tremendous cloud of energy and dropped it

188

into the reconfigured boost, modified to trap and increase the energy even further. But Ian hadn't been alone in the boost. "The third Heir, I think I know who it is," Rayne said, as incredible as it seemed. "But what does this have to do with me?"

"Your mother and I were close friends at QualSton. When your father was determined to turn you into the first female Sar, it was an opportunity . . ." Gwynn took Rayne's hand. "To create a weapon."

Rayne pulled her hand out of Gwynn's grasp and bolted to her feet. She stormed around to the back of the couch and stared at the woman who had condemned her to a life of isolation among the Weir. "I can't touch Sars, the people I love the most in the world, because of you?"

"This isn't about you, or my son. This is about saving two worlds." Gwynn stood. She looked more alive than Rayne had seen her all day, as if energized by sheer will. "What happens in the next few days on Earth is critical to a plan that was hatched by three sisters, over a hundred years ago.

"What plan?" Rayne asked.

"To bring down two tyrants and set our worlds back on an evolutionary track that should never have been tampered with. If the three Heirs don't join forces and form their connection before Aeros and his brother Johann discover what we've done, Earth and Thrae will no longer be able to sustain life.

Part Two

The most powerful of lessons is self-discovery

{32}

A rumbling hum filled Patrick's ears while a not-too-subtle vibration shook him into consciousness. It eventually pulled him out of the hangover from hell that kept his eyes glued shut. He rubbed his eyelids, but the effort it took to lift his hands left him exhausted. When he managed to open his eyes, he found himself in a small cabin with a curved ceiling and rectangular windows. The surroundings felt somehow familiar.

He rolled to his side, and fell off the narrow couch he'd been lying on. "Ugh," he moaned when his head connected with the floor. He pressed his palm to his forehead then sat up, leaning his back against the cushion.

"It's about time you woke up." The woman's voice stirred a memory. She was obscured by an opened newspaper at the back of the otherwise empty cabin. A glass of iced tea sat on the small table in front of her, with a half-eaten croissant sandwich beside it. "You've been asleep for most of the day."

Patrick stared at a window across from him. Beyond, a few of the brightest night's stars poked through the last rays of the day, making their appearance before their duller siblings.

"Are you hungry?" she asked, not lowering her paper. "I can have Willow put something together for you. We have a long flight."

Something about the voice. He couldn't remember how he got there. Attempts to play back events yielded nothing, like a video that had been erased. Patrick stared at the fading light coming from the window, and the setting sun drew the shades on his eyelids closed.

Bleating car horns. Squealing brakes. People yelling. Patrick's head wobbled, propped against a car window. He opened his eyes, but grimaced and squinted at the bright sun in his face. He moaned and pushed to right himself.

He was in the backseat of an SUV sitting still in traffic. From the bright pink and coral stucco-looking buildings, he wasn't in Northern California. The car lurched and took off when an opening presented itself.

"He's going to wake up before we get him to the house." A woman's voice came from the front seat.

Acid burned Patrick's throat as stomach contents pushed upward in a slow migration. He bent over and grabbed his stomach. "Sick," he moaned.

A large bag was opened up at his knees as if they were anticipating it. He gagged and coughed, but nothing came out.

A stranger's face appeared between the front bucket seats. "You'll feel better once you purge it," she said.

"What . . . happened?" Patrick groaned. The car took a corner fast. Thrown against the door, Patrick retched and spewed beyond his control. The proffered bag flailed about, trying to catch Patrick's bile with each twist and turn of the wheel. He grabbed the seat belt across his chest and hung on.

"Fuck! It's getting all over," a man said from beside Patrick.

Having purged the last of it, Patrick leaned his head back against the headrest.

"Clean him up," the woman said.

Someone wiped Patrick's face with a towel, then swiped at his shirt.

"Get us to the house," the disgruntled woman said. "Or we'll all be sharing his pain."

Sunlight flickered on and off as the car sped by a row of buildings. Patrick fought to keep conscious, but whatever they'd given him made him woozy.

Where was he? The salty air and squawk of birds could have been outside his bedroom window at home, but the simple town and décor was undeniably foreign, unless he was on an elaborate movie set.

The car soon left the simple town behind and green fields stretched as far as Patrick could see, at least out of the one eye that cooperated and stayed open. Trees dotted the landscape in neatly formed rows that rushed by like elongated stripes. Migrant workers with wide straw hats were harvesting what came from the trees, stuffing their bounty into cloth bags slung across their chests.

Every few minutes the car passed bent-backed wrinkled men in loose pants and shirts leading donkeys pulling carts filled with stacks of baskets down the dirt road. His surroundings didn't slow down enough for Patrick to catch a glimpse of what they were harvesting.

Dogs ran alongside the SUV until the vehicle left them in the dust, only to pick up another one or two farther down the dirt road. The car slowed and Patrick's vomit-coated chin slid back and forth across the window as the ruts in the road deepened and tested all four shocks at varying times. The man seated beside Patrick bumped into him thanks to a particularly violent bounce, and he released his seat belt to scoot over to the opposite side of the seat.

Patrick pushed to sit up. "Where are we?"

"Shit! You didn't give him enough," the man next to Patrick said. "He needs more."

"I can't or we could have a corpse on our hands," the woman said from the front. Her face turned to the driver. "How much farther?"

"Barring no more delays, fifteen minutes," he said. "Maybe twenty."

"Damn it, that's too long. At this rate he'll be wide awake for sure." The woman's head disappeared below the seat. When she reappeared a minute later, she held a hypodermic. She thrust the needle into a small vial and filled the syringe with a clear liquid, then turned toward Patrick. "Give me his arm, and hold him down," she said.

"No," Patrick groaned and batted at the guy.

One of Patrick's swings hit the driver on the back of the head. The SUV swerved, then corrected. The driver looked over his shoulder. "Take care of him or I'll pull over and do it myself!"

There was a thunderous bang as the windshield shattered. The door Patrick had been resting against flew open and he took flight. In an instant the setting sun turned Patrick's world to midnight.

{33}

*S*lurp. Something slimy scraped across his cheek. The rough tongue caused his head to rock back and forth with each lick. Patrick opened his eyes to a night's sky, and it took a second for him to make out a mangy dog standing over him with its drool clinging to matted fur. The dog's drool flicked with a plop on Patrick with every turn of the animal's head.

"Ewww." Patrick brought his arm up to shove the animal away, but pain shot through his forearm and he couldn't offset the animal's resuscitation efforts. "Go, get out of here." Patrick rolled onto his side and propped himself up by an elbow. An odd sensation, like the onset of numb that never quite makes it to numbness, coursed through his body. He got as high as his knees. The smell of gasoline gagged him, and he held his breath until the nausea passed.

The car had rammed into a huge boulder at a curve in the road. The bumper lay a few feet away and the hood had folded up like an accordion halfway to the windshield wipers. Something dark, that Patrick surmised to be blood, smeared one half of the driver's face, and from the angle that his head rested, it looked like he'd suffered a broken neck. Why hadn't the airbags deployed?

Unable to see the woman in the front seat and the man who had been sitting next to him from where he knelt, Patrick waited for the spinning in his head to stop and for the jackhammer at the back of his skull to throttle down. He reached back and felt something wet and sticky. The dog whined and tugged at Patrick's back.

"No, you can't lick it and make it feel better," Patrick said. "Shoo!"

A small hand connected with Patrick's as he waved off the mutt from over his shoulder. When he turned, a child no more than four stared at him with dark brown eyes the size of ping-pong balls. His black hair glistened in the moonlight. It was cut short and hugged his skull. He gave Patrick the widest smile he'd ever seen with crooked teeth dotted in dark splotches as if already rotting from poor oral hygiene.

"Who are you?" Patrick said and got to his feet. "Where am I?"

The child didn't respond and stared up at Patrick.

"Does that fur-ball belong to you?" Patrick said. He pointed between the dog and the child.

The boy smiled and said something, but Patrick didn't recognize the language, much less understand. He shook his head and shrugged. "Sorry, kid, that's all Greek to me." The boy looked over his shoulder and gestured to the wreck.

Patrick leaned against the boulder until he could catch a deep breath and work past the throb in his head. The child giggled when the dog licked Patrick's pant leg.

He left the two companions and peered inside the car. The woman was slumped over. The man from the backseat was pinned between the front bucket seats. Both lay unmoving. A walkie- talkie crackled. A man's voice spoke in the strange language.

Patrick leaned through the open back door to check on the guy and to search for a cell phone, but the child squealed and tugged on his belt.

"What?" Patrick said.

The child pointed toward oncoming headlights. The boy climbed into the car and retrieved the walkie-talkie from under the seat, held it up, and shook his head. Whatever the man on the other end was saying, it frightened the child.

A moan came from the front of the car. The woman was alive. The child tugged on Patrick's shirt. A spike in Patrick's adrenaline ignited his limbs. He followed the child into a nearby grove of trees.

For having such short legs, the kid was fast. Still groggy, Patrick struggled to keep track of the boy in the dark grove. When he caught up with him, he grabbed the child to stop and leaned over to catch his breath. A foggy memory took shape at remembering a hypodermic needle.

He glanced about. The tightly packed orchard obliterated any surrounding landscape. If there was a farm house in the distance, the lights were off. Where had the boy come from?

Was he part of the migrant-workers group Patrick had seen earlier, or was that imagined? His thoughts took their time to clear, like sludge draining while someone filled his brain with fresh water.

Shouts and angry voices came from behind. The child took Patrick's hand and turned down a narrow path that cut between the trees. This section of the grove appeared more mature than where they had entered near the wreck. He had to give the child credit. The thicker branches would conceal them better.

Flashlights flickered in and out of the trees. The voices grew more distant. Whoever the child was afraid of, he was leading Patrick in the opposite direction.

"Hey, thanks, kid," he said. Patrick rubbed the child's head. The boy stopped and giggled, then smoothed down his hair with spit. Patrick wiped his hand on his shirt. He touched his chest. "Patrick," he said.

The child slapped his own chest. "Epifanio."

"Well, Epi, thanks for the save back there, or whatever it was." Patrick patted his pockets. They were empty. "I need a phone," he said to the child, and gestured as if talking with one held to his ear. "I don't suppose you can point me in the direction of the nearest town?" The child imitated Patrick. He threw the kid a disgruntled look that was wasted in the dark. "You're mocking me, aren't you?"

A shout, followed by what sounded like a gunshot. Yelling. The child hugged Patrick's legs. The dog dropped to the ground and covered its eyes with its paws.

"Shit!" Patrick grabbed the boy and crouched down. Once the echoing gunshot faded, only the shrill cry of the insects could be heard. He pulled the child away and grabbed him by his shoulders. "Where can we hide?"

The boy pulled out of Patrick's grasp and took off at top speed down a nearby path. Patrick scrambled to his feet and followed. The child soon veered off the path and navigated in and out of the trees. It was everything Patrick could do to keep up with one eye on the child and another on the lowest limbs. Just when Patrick's lungs threatened to explode, the child came to a halt at the edge of the orchard and held onto the trunk of a small sapling. He stared into the distance.

Patrick caught up and bent over to suck in air. When he righted, a smile touched his lips and he scooped the boy up into his arms. Dull dots of light were scattered at the horizon. The town didn't look very dense, but surely someone there would have a phone.

There didn't appear to be much cover between the orchard and the town. Unwilling to put the child in any more danger, Patrick set him back down and stuck his hand out.

"Thanks, Epi," Patrick said and gave the child an exaggerated handshake. "Now scamper away and stay away from bad guys." The child smiled and giggled, but his face fell when Patrick backed up, leaving him standing there alone. "Go, find your family." Patrick gestured for him to leave, then started out across the field at a quick pace, putting some distance between him and the grove.

At a bark, Patrick glanced over his shoulder, then stopped. The child and dog were following a couple of yards behind him. "Go home," Patrick hissed and waved.

Epi stopped and tossed him that infectious smile from behind a returned wave. The dog whined and rose on its back legs, hopping about like a circus performer. It landed on its front paws, kicking up dust from the field.

He couldn't endanger the child. "You need to go home," Patrick whispered.

The child didn't budge. Lights in the trees. Patrick walked up and gathered the child in his arms. Epi patted Patrick's face. "Come on, I'll drop you off with the first people I find. Someone who speaks your language." He took off for the distant town under the veil of darkness, thankful for there was nothing more than a crescent moon overhead.

What the hell had happened? Who was after him? Why?

{34}

Ian leaned forward between the seats and stared at the address Marcus's geeks had found. "This one," Xander said from the driver's seat. "I bet you a year's worth of Red Bull."

"Game over!" Pacman said as his licorice stick swerved to the corner of his mouth. The boys slapped hands and rapped knuckles at their self-proclaimed victory.

"Are you sure this time?" Tara said.

"It fits. Look." Pacman held up his tablet to show Ian and Tara a rental listing. The photo depicted a small bungalow at the end of a cul-de-sac.

"Simple and nondescript, that's something Rayne would have chosen," Tara said.

Ian had Marcus's geeks pull up Patrick's GPS history in his car. They'd tracked his movements over the few days leading up to his kidnapping and found what they believed was Rayne's new address.

Pacman turned around and gave Tara a conspirator's grin. "How are you going to sneak away?"

"We haven't gotten that far," Tara said.

Pacman waved his tablet. "We could try and jam the jam."

"I'm thinking of coming clean and telling Marcus," Ian said.

"What, exactly?" Tara asked.

"That's the part I'm still working on." He leaned between the bucket seats. "Thanks, guys. I owe you one."

"Anything for the Heir," Pacman said.

"We're at your beck and call, oh commandant!" Xander gave Ian a two-finger salute.

Ian stuck out his fists. The boys bumped and slapped their ritual hand gestures, then everyone exited Patrick's car.

Marcus stood next to the driveway with crossed arms and a scowl that rammed his bushy eyebrows together. "What are you cooking up?"

"Let's take a walk," Ian said. The others scattered. He led Marcus down the north path. "I want to find Patrick."

"So do I," Marcus said, sticking his hands in his pockets. "For a multitude of reasons," he said with an edge in his voice that put Ian on the alert.

"We have to assume he's alive," Ian said.

"Agreed." Marcus stopped. "But what I want to know is, how could he have survived being electrocuted like that?"

"I don't know. Joule was confident that her modifications to my boost were correct. If that's true, Patrick had to have endured an astronomical amount of energy." Ian rubbed his chest and gazed at the sun's texture across the ocean's surface. What would he uncover if he pursued this? He'd already lost Rayne. He wasn't about to lose Patrick.

"What did you find in his GPS?" Marcus asked. When Ian looked surprised, the old general grunted. "Give me some credit."

"There were his typical haunts, and he made a couple of stops at the auditorium." Ian wondered why. For the past few months, Patrick had managed the auditorium from his laptop. "He also made more than one visit to Rayne's new place."

Marcus pulled a cell phone out of his pocket. It was Patrick's. "I found this in his room. Dr. Mac said he left it behind when they shyfted to London to gather supplies."

"It's not shielded against the magnetic effects of shyfting, like ours," Ian said.

"I'm going to have the boys get contact info and anything else they can off of it," Marcus said. "They took Patrick for a reason, Ian, and I don't think it's because of his association with you."

Ian nodded. If that were the case, Jaered would have interrogated Patrick the first time he kidnapped him. But Patrick swore that didn't happen. Had his friend held something back from the first kidnapping? Ever since that incident, Patrick had been distant, evasive. The more Ian thought back to the past few weeks, so had Rayne. Why didn't they want Ian to know Rayne's new address?

"What is it?" Marcus said, staring at Ian. "Your gears are cranking out something."

"I know where to start," Ian said.

Ian shyfted Marcus and Tara to Rayne's house. He'd chosen a spot behind a large bush that he'd seen in the real-estate listing that the boys had shown him. Tara led them through a side gate. They stepped up to the back screen door, then in unison, peered inside. It was the kitchen. An emptied cardboard box sat on the floor with crumpled newspaper scattered around it. Another one, its flaps still folded upon each other, rested on the small kitchenette table. A pizza box stuck out of the trash can.

Tara looked over her shoulder. "Tall, plentiful trees. No bodies in the few windows I can see." Marcus shyfted inside and unlocked the door.

Tara opened it, but at Ian's hesitation, she paused and lowered her voice. "Ian, if you want, Marcus and I can check things out. You don't have to do this."

Ian hadn't prepared himself for the emotional upheaval that had swept over him, but he didn't hesitate, and pushed the door wider. "This is about Patrick, not me." He entered the kitchen.

Odors of bacon, sausage, and barbecued chicken came from the direction of the pizza box. That and the empty beer bottles confirmed that Patrick had made a recent visit. Tara opened the fridge and found a loaf of bread, an unopened carton of milk, and a small tub of butter with its shrink wrap still attached.

Ian wandered into the front room. Rayne had kept her mother's couch, but not much else from her old apartment.

Marcus was seated on the edge of the lone piece of furniture, flipping through sheets from one of the many stacks of papers.

Tara sat on the floor and grabbed a sheet from the top of another one. "What is all this?"

Ian stared at the QualSton logo on a cardboard box. It had been addressed to Patrick at the auditorium. Why the secrecy? He opened the carton and found a framed picture, a magnifying glass, and other miscellaneous papers.

Marcus held up a sheet. "This is a list of scientists at QualSton. What would she want with this?"

"Maybe she was curious about her background," Tara said.

Ian looked at the framed news article and photo. Dr. Benjamin Harcourt was listed in the caption along with a few dozen other names. "I wouldn't be surprised if she was researching her father," he said.

"Or someone else." Tara grabbed another sheet from her pile. "There's a woman's name that keeps coming up in my stack. Each entry is highlighted."

Marcus gathered his pile in his arms and stood. "I want to take all of this back and have the boys analyze the info."

Tara got up from the floor. "I'll grab the unpacked box from the kitchen."

Ian wandered down a short hall and discovered a spare bedroom. Other than a cardboard box with Rayne's laptop sitting on top and charging, the room was empty. He grabbed the laptop and the charger. When he poked his head into the cramped bathroom, he caught a whiff of vanilla. His stomach lurched at the scent of her hair, and he took a deep breath to stave off the threatening melancholy. Any resolve he had left crumbled the moment Ian reached her bedroom threshold. The knickknacks on her dresser stopped the beat of his heart.

Rayne had saved a memento from almost everything that the two of them had shared. Her visitor pass from QualSton hung from one of the knobs on her garage-sale dresser. The napkin from their dinner in Rogue Basin stuck out of its plastic Ziploc pouch. She had pressed a delicate wildflower she'd picked next to the outdoor patio of their favorite pizza café. He picked up a small seashell he'd given her on a walk along the beach one moonlit evening and clenched it in his fist. Each souvenir that caught his eye drove a spike into his heart and he backed up, bumping into the bed and sliding to the floor. He hung his head while his shoulders heaved with every suppressed ache.

Tara knelt beside him and gathered him in her arms. A few minutes later, drained, he lifted his face. "Where's Marcus," Ian choked.

"He shyfted the box to the mansion." She wiped her face and left him on the bedroom floor. When she returned, she had a handful of toilet paper. Tara tore some off for herself and handed him the rest of the wad. They blew their noses until the toilet paper was spent, and then sat in silence. Ian focused on steadying the beat of his heart, and the blessed numb gradually returned. "Patrick," he whispered.

"Patrick," Tara said with conviction. She stuffed the laptop into the Faraday case she'd brought, then grabbed Ian's hand. He shyfted them home.

{35}

By the time Ian joined the others in the great room, the techno geniuses had set up a virtual roadmap of information they'd gleaned from Rayne's research.

Pacman was seated cross-legged on the couch with his laptop propped on his knees. Xander stood in the middle of the room with extended index fingers controlling free-floating data.

Joule was in a heated debate with Tara at the far end of the room. Ian cocked his ear and eavesdropped on the girls while bits of data floated in the air around him. Every few seconds, Pacman punched the keys on his laptop, adding another new word or term from a fresh sheet off a stack on the coffee table. The info popped up in midair and, with the swish of his finger, Xander added it to an already existing group.

Fascinated by the technology laid out before him, Ian's attention drifted from the girls, and he didn't refocus until the tail end of their conversation. From what he could decipher, Joule was upset no one had offered to locate her father. "You promised," came out in repeated hisses along with strings of expletives that if Ian uttered, would have Milo reaching for a bar of soap.

"Joule, let us get a handle on this, and then if we can, we'll split up our efforts and help you, too," Ian said.

Marcus wandered in with one of Milo's rolls in his hand and a steaming mug in the other. The smell of freshly brewed coffee made Ian rethink his earlier decline of the beverage. "How much longer?" Milo asked.

Pacman tapped the short stack in front of him. "This is the last of it."

"Preliminary report," Marcus barked, then took a generous bite of his roll.

"It appears that she was researching a woman," Xander said. He added what looked to be a German car company logo to a new column.

"I don't need your fan-dangled tech to tell me what a highlighter already did," Marcus said with a bulge in his cheek. He took a sip of coffee and the bulge disappeared.

"A lot of the info dates back more than forty years," Xander said. He stopped chewing his gum and stood back, staring at the virtual board. "Some, longer than that."

"It can't be one woman, or she'd have to be older than dirt," Pacman said without lifting his face from his screen.

"My money says it's more than one person." Xander blew a bubble and popped it.

"I betcha next year's ComicCon tickets it's two," Pacman said. He grabbed another red licorice stick, then gnawed on it and stared at his screen.

The overwhelming data had Ian's head swimming. The international companies varied from a custom-built German car to an Irish, hundred-year-old whiskey company. The only one he recognized from the first column was QualSton genetics. If not her father, who the hell had Rayne been tracking—why the secrecy?

Pacman's laptop keys fell silent. "Some of these companies are over a hundred years old but I also found some newbies. The most recent has only been in business for three years.

Joule walked up and bobbed a finger at one of the entries. "That's my father's favorite whiskey."

Her comment prompted Ian to rescan the lists, looking for anything familiar other than QualSton.

"Has anyone ever heard of a car by this name?" Tara indicated the word Osera.

"It's an anagram." The gruff voice came from the direction of the foyer.

The Primary stood in the archway. Ian couldn't remember when he'd ever seen the man so angry. Dr. Mac was with him and was staring at the virtual board with wide eyes and a slack jaw. Ian wasn't the only one impressed by the boys' toys.

"An anagram for what?" Joule said.

"Aeros." The name came out like a hissing snake. The Primary approached the virtual board and tapped Osera with his finger. Its pixels scattered but then corrected, the Primary unable to erase the Duach Leader. He gave the group a sweeping scowl, and turned back to the board. "Where did this information come from?"

"Rayne," Marcus said.

"The Duach had this?" the Primary snarled.

Heat rose in Ian's core and traveled to his tightly clenched fists. Tara shot a look of warning at him. "We found it in her house," she said.

"We're sorting the mess out." Marcus set his mug on the coffee table and sat on the edge of the couch.

"I thought I made it clear a few months ago." Heat emanated from every pore of the Primary's face." You were to stay away from her!"

Ian had only seen the Primary this angry once before, when his arch enemy had surfaced. The Pur leader gazed at the virtual board in fuming silence. When he picked up the framed picture of the QualSton researchers, his knuckles turned ghostly white. Marcus threw Ian a look chock-full of questions. Was Rayne searching for Eve?

Ian recalled the night in the vortex field. Ian forced himself to recall every detail. Jaered wasn't kidnapping her. She was going with him willingly, in search of answers.

Milo wandered in from the kitchen, carrying a large silver tray piled with assorted snacks. "Mac, what are you doing here?" he said on his way past his old friend.

"I brought him to reexamine the Heir," the Primary said. "I want to know what the rebels did to Ian."

"I've given you my report, I found nothing other than a strong, healthy core," Dr. Mac said. "This is a waste of my time and resources. I have other patients."

The Primary glared at Dr. Mac. "I want everything confirmed."

The front door to the mansion flew open and the Primary's elite guard filed in, one after another, carrying what looked to be medical equipment. They towered over scrawny Henrick, the Primary's personal assistant, who brought up the rear.

"Henrick will be monitoring your examination, Doctor," the Primary said.

"Then let's get this hogwash over with so I can get back to people who actually need me. Milo, I'm commandeering the kitchen." Dr. Mac led the five guards away. Henrick stood next to the table. His watchful eyes never straying from the Primary.

"I want the guards to confiscate all of this," the Primary gestured at the stacks of paper. "Don't leave anything behind." Henrick nodded.

Pacman's licorice fell from his mouth. "Bullshit! You're not taking my stuff, Pops."

The Primary took a step toward him with murder in his eyes. Pacman shied away, melting into the couch. "Make sure they get it all," the Primary snarled.

"Whatever," Pacman muttered under his breath.

"I'll return with you and help," Marcus said.

"Tell me, Marcus. What is your son up to these days?" The Primary glared at Marcus as if a lie would be the death of him.

Marcus's jaw clenched. "I have no idea. We haven't spoken in months."

"You are now confined to the estate with the others," ordered the Primary. Marcus made to protest, but the Primary raised his hand. "Or would you rather be incarcerated?"

Marcus sobered. The Primary approached the foyer table and, without missing a beat in his step, shyfted in an emerald cloud. Henrick stood in front of Pacman and stuck out his hand.

"It you're going to hack off my right arm, at least let me back up my stuff," he whined.

"Perhaps you'd rather one of the guards intervene." Henrick thrust his hand closer.

"Give it up, bro," Xander said.

Pacman hit a key and the floating virtual board vanished. He slammed the computer lid shut, then shoved it onto the coffee table. Henrick picked it up and headed for the kitchen.

"I better get all my data back, or I'll hack your credit cards," Pacman yelled to his retreating back.

A drawn-out exhale came from Xander and he deflated, slouching on the coffee table. "Fuck me. For being a runt, that's one scary dude."

"There goes what may be our chance to find Patrick," Tara said.

Marcus shook his head. "And Vael."

"Oh ye of little faith," Pacman said, but swallowed his snicker the second Marcus turned on him.

"What'd you do?" Marcus hushed under his breath.

"I'd already pushed everything to the Cloud," Pacman said.

Xander reached out and they bumped knuckles. "We had a bet as to who'd be the first to crack Rayne's puzzle."

"We just need a computer and WiFi, and we're set to go," Pacman said. He rubbed his hands and sprang to his feet. "So, the way I see it, someone owes me a new computer and a year's worth of licorice."

"I could kiss you," Tara said, but when Pacman licked his lips, she rolled her eyes in regret.

"If it leads us to Vael," Marcus said, glanced in the direction of the foyer, then lowered his voice, "I'll buy you the goddamn licorice factory."

Ian put a hand on Pacman's shoulder. "I'm sorry about your laptop. We'll get it back for you."

"Nah, it'll be fried by then," Pacman said, pulling the last licorice stick out of the cellophane package and crinkling it up into a ball.

"My man Pac has the most gnarly security system," Xander said, gushing with pride.

"A work of art, am I right?" Pacman said. They bumped chests, then leaned back and wiggled their fingers.

"Sweet and geek!" Xander said, but in an instant, sobered and slapped his friend's arm. "Eulogy, bro." He placed his hand over his heart. Pacman did the same.

Ian pressed a fist to his Seal and stood across from the boys while they paid homage to their sacrificed equipment. If they found Patrick, would they also find Eve?

{36}

Thick, salty air and a distant foghorn told Patrick that an ocean was nearby. Unsure of anything he saw or heard in the dark, he kept pinching himself, hoping to wake up and find out this was nothing but a bad dream.

He reached what looked to be a main street and turned onto it with the soft plops of the mongrel following at his heels. The boy rested his head on Patrick's shoulder and was snoring before they'd made it to the edge of town.

Why the hell would anyone kidnap him? Was this about his family? The questions burned a hole in his thoughts while he navigated the field headed toward the town. He'd been estranged from his billionaire father for as long as he could remember, and contact with his society-minded mother was nothing more than a couple text messages a month.

The unknown continued to plague Patrick as he wandered the dirt street between simple, single and two-story rural structures. Handmade bricks peeked out from beneath crumbling plaster exteriors, while some of their verandas were held up with rotting timber rails. Absence of street lamps made it difficult to see the brightly colored buildings he vaguely remembered from his earlier drug-induced fog.

Everything now appeared as a gray palate lining the moonlit streets. The scattering of lights he'd seen from the edge of the orchard at nightfall had slowly extinguished on his trek toward town. By the time he reached the first building, only a few were visible in upper stories. From the flickering, he guessed that the light either came from candles or oil lamps. His hope that modern technology would come to his rescue faded the more his thoughts cleared.

Epi stirred in his arms, turned his head, and settled once again into a deep slumber. Patrick reached a crossroads and stopped to assess his options. The dog whined and looked up at him. "Sorry, I don't speak dog," Patrick muttered.

The mangy mutt lifted his back leg and peed in one long, continuous stream that landed directly in front of Patrick's shoes. Splatters of pee mixed with the dirt landed on the bottom of his pants, and he did an Irish jig to get out of the way. "Oh, for the love of . . ." His voice trailed off as his focus turned to sounds one street over. From the noise of their engines, the high-powered vehicles were picking up speed.

Adrenaline kicked in and Patrick frantically searched for a hiding place. He ran toward a rug that was suspended from a second story window, and long enough that it nearly touched the ground. Slipping behind it, he pressed his hand over Epi's mouth when the jostled child awakened in his arms. The mutt barked from the other side, but Patrick coaxed it to join them, and it quieted as long as the animal licked his face.

The child squirmed, then pulled back and rubbed his eyes. "Bad men," Patrick said, counting on the tone of his voice to break the language barrier and make the child understand.

Epi hugged Patrick around the neck and leaned in, staying very still. A few heartbeats later, Patrick felt the tiny hand rubbing his back shoulder. It brought instant comfort and Patrick slowly released an exhale, then breathed deep.

Tires skidded to a gravel-spitting stop farther down the street. Car doors opened and slammed shut. Hushed voices. Scuffles on the dirt road quickly spread out in different directions. Patrick peered out of the slit between him and the thick rug, which smelled of mildew and damp wool. A glint of moonlight on metal confirmed the men came bearing guns.

Footsteps approached. Patrick tightened his hold on Epi, pushed back against the solid wall, and then crouched down, shielding the boy. His pulse revved the closer the steps. Heat rose in the center of his chest, simmering, then blistering with each passing second. A gentle breeze passed between the building and the rug, and Patrick shuddered.

He loosed his grip on Epi and pressed a fist to his chest. Goddamn it! He'd picked a hell of a time for a heart attack. The child whimpered softly. Patrick ignored the searing pressure and tuned into the noises on the other side of the rug.

The surrounding shadows melted into pitch, as if someone turned off the moon. A muffled rustle and the rug quivered behind him. The blistering internal heat burned Patrick's throat as adrenaline exacerbated whatever was happening in his chest. He parted his lips and swore a heated plume escaped. Shouts from farther down the street. The edge of the rug fell still. Voices faded along with their hurried footsteps.

Every one of Patrick's strained muscles released at once and Epi stretched from beneath Patrick's loosened hold. The mutt licked its butt then settled back down at Patrick's knee. The heated pressure in Patrick's chest eased but failed to completely vanish as if it left a scorch mark to remember it by. He pressed his back against the wall and took deep, silent breaths, trying to erase the lingering sensation.No matter what he did, the reaction had left its imprint.

Whack! Whack!

Dust filled Patrick's lungs and he let go of Epi, hacking on the surrounding cloud. He opened his eyes to discover that the sun's rays peeked through the slit and contributed to the sweltering heat in the cramped space.

Whack!

His racking coughs woke up the boy and the child sneezed then rubbed his face. The mutt stretched its front paws with a yelp of a yawn. A dirt cloud filled the cramped space between the wall and the hung rug, and Patrick made to stand but stiff, unforgiving muscles screamed in protest. He grabbed at his back.

Whop! Whop! Whop! Patrick covered his nose and mouth with his hand and, choking and gagging, emerged from their hiding spot. He covered his eyes at the brilliant sun overhead.

When Epi went to step out into the street, Patrick restrained him while scanning for trouble. The vehicles from the previous night were gone along with the gunmen. Patrick stepped out from under the veranda and sneezed, wiping his nose on his sleeve. He stretched until the kink in his back popped.

Shrill, staccato speech came from overhead. A middle-aged woman in a loose, flowery dress with her hair tied back in a ponytail stood on the upstairs balcony. Her sun-kissed skin enhanced the light-colored shift. She gripped a long-handled straw broom in one hand and leaned over the railing, addressing him below. Patrick lifted his hands and shook his head to indicate he didn't understand what she was saying. She continued her diatribe anyway. When he didn't answer her, she shook a fist, then waved her arm about. Patrick motioned to Epi. The child stepped out and stood next to Patrick, staring up at the woman. He blinked then rubbed one eye, the other one not leaving the woman overhead. Patrick marveled at the woman's breath support as she carried on about something. Epi just blinked, shook his head a couple of times, then pointed to the rug. The woman's tone grew terse, and she glared at Patrick during her relentless tirade.

Patrick brushed off as much dirt as he could and didn't mask his indifference to her scolding. He patted Epi's shoulder, gestured toward the end of the block, and together they went their merry way. The woman shrieked at their turned backs and the mutt stood its ground, barked in their defense, then ran and caught up. Unsure what had upset the woman, Patrick left his curiosity in the street. He had more pressing things to deal with.

The village that had appeared so uninviting in the middle of the night bustled with activity as men and women of all ages headed out of town on foot. Everyone had loose canvas bags slung across their chests, and most wore wide, floppy straw hats. They chatted among themselves as if off to another typical day in the fields. The cloudless, blue sky overhead promised that the sweltering heat was there to stay. It had already triggered sweat across Patrick's brow and the back of his neck. The pressure and sharp pain in the center of his chest from the previous night had left a dull ache and he massaged his sternum through his shirt. The edge of his fist felt something like a scab over his left breast. Patrick slowed his steps while catching up to the group and let go of Epi's hand. He made to lift the edge of his button-down shirt, but froze at a tap on his shoulder.

Patrick turned and faced a kid, an older teen, giving Patrick a sly grin. The teen said something to Epi, and the child clung to Patrick's leg as if fearing for his life. Epi shook his head at the teenager, then looked up at Patrick with wide, fearful eyes.

"Do you know him?" Patrick said, pressing the child's head against his thigh.

The teen's face lifted in amusement. "You're, English? American?" He gushed, much like a con man finding an unexpected mark. "Good, good. I speak English." He hesitated and his face contorted in contemplation. "We don't get many Americans on our small island."

Patrick glanced about. "What's the name of your island?"

The teenager laughed. It wasn't an easygoing laugh, but exaggerated and drawn-out. Instant dislike ruffled Patrick's patience, but he didn't dare turn his back on the only person who held a promise of salvation. "Do you know him?" Patrick asked and patted Epi's shoulder. At the renewed attention, the child wrapped himself tighter around Patrick's leg and slipped behind, keeping one terrified eye directed at the teen.

The teen flashed a sly grin and arched one eyebrow higher than the other. He said something to Epi and the young boy turned his face away without responding. Fury filled the teen's face, he raised his hand and looked about to strike the child. Patrick sidestepped and put himself in between. "Argh," the teen yelled and threw Patrick a ferocious glare. "He no give me," the teen said and rubbed his fingers together then hissed. "Money."

Patrick regarded Epi. "Seems he doesn't have it. But if you can get me to a phone, I'll pay you what he owes you." Patrick wasn't sure he'd spoken slow enough, or used simple enough English for the teen to understand, but a second later, the teen smiled a polished, dental-hygiene grin and slapped a hand around the back of Patrick's neck.

The young man mimicked holding a phone to his ear. "Phone? I have phone!" His grasp grew tighter across Patrick's neck. A revved engine. An SUV barreled down on them, its tires kicking up dirt and spreading it in a parted wave behind the vehicle. "But it's gonna cost you," the teen sneered in Patrick's ear.

Epi screamed and took off for a nearby alley with the growling mutt close at his heels. The child fell to the ground and disappeared under a low-lying deck. The teen grabbed Patrick and twisted him around to face the oncoming vehicle. The tip of a knife jabbed against Patrick's throat.

He struggled, but the teen was incredibly strong, and the knife drew a few drops of blood. The SUV skidded to a halt inches from Patrick's knees, spitting gravel against his pants. All four doors flew open and men scrambled out.

"Welcome to Greece, Heir," the teen snarled near Patrick's ear.

His chaotic thoughts slammed to a halt. Heir? What the hell? Had they mistaken him for Ian?

{37}

The needle marks made Ian feel like a drug addict. He slipped off the kitchen stool and rubbed his inner elbow, but it didn't erase the reddened dots. "Now, can I go?" Ian asked.

Dr. Mac added the latest vial to the stack. "That's up to them," he snapped.

The Pur guard across the room didn't respond. He hadn't moved since Ian entered the room and underwent the most thorough examination he'd ever been subjected to. Ian knew very little about the Primary's elite guards, and even less of their special training or skills. The guards never carried weapons, and it was rumored that they were all Sars, each one capable of lethal power. Curious, Ian had stolen several glances during his exam.

Tension filled the room more than air. The guard's stoic demeanor was offset by his unwavering gaze on Dr. Mac. Henrick had peered over Dr. Mac's shoulder every few seconds and constantly questioned the physician.

Dr. Mac's simmering anger had rubbed off on Ian, and it became a challenge to regulate his core's heat.

Henrick checked a list in his hand. "You have enough samples to do these tests?" the Primary's assistant asked.

"And then some," Dr. Mac muttered in his gruff, gravelly voice.

"You may go, Sire," Henrick said. "But don't leave the mansion."

Ian took off before they changed their mind. Earlier, he had caught Milo and Tara walking down the hall in the direction of the back stairs. Ian opened the basement door and turned his keen hearing to the darkened room below. Muffled voices. He stepped onto the staircase and closed the door behind him. The voices fell silent, and Ian descended the stairs.

"It's Ian," Milo announced from the bottom-most stair. The group was scattered about the downstairs gym. When Ian paused next to Milo, a dim, amber glow lit up the room. It came from the geeks' virtual data board.

"What have you found?" Ian approached the floating data.

"It's definitely two women, using various aliases," Pacman said.

"Their lives intersect up until about fifteen or more years ago," Joules said.

"That's when one drops out, and from what we can tell, only one is left," Xander added. "But we don't think she died."

"No obituaries were found under any of the aliases," Xander said.

"It's like she fell off the face of the earth," Joules said, leaning against the weapons cabinet.

"Did you download photographs?" Ian asked. Xander swiped his finger and a picture of a young woman appeared. "Where's the other one?"

"No driver's licenses were ever issued to any of them," Pacman said. He nodded at Xander. "This is the only photo we could find of the second woman."

Xander swiped his finger and a photo appeared beside the first. It was the QualSton photo Ian had seen at Rayne's apartment. Her father was dead center in the group of scientists. Pacman tapped a woman's face in the back row. It blurred for a second, then corrected.

There was something familiar about the first woman's photo, but he couldn't tag a memory to it. The QualSton scientist was difficult to make out. She was shadowed by the tall scientist beside her.

Tara stood and stretched. "We have about two dozen products and companies that they were associated with."

"Organized by regions." Milo yawned.

"They've narrowed down dates, when the women were connected to the companies," Marcus said.

Ian walked around the data, committing it to memory. Eve's identity was somewhere in this jumbled mess. The Primary was already a few steps ahead of them. Time wasn't on their side. "We have to figure out who Eve is and find her before the Primary."

229

"Why the race?" Joule said. "Why not let him do our work for us?"

"The Primary has a history with Eve," Ian said. "If he kills her—"

"—we might never locate Patrick," Tara said.

"Did Mac find anything?" Marcus asked. Ian shook his head. "If we're to beat the Primary to Eve, we need a safer location for this data."

"The northern vortex building," Ian said. "I'm the only one who can access it." At soft footsteps on the stairs, Ian brought a finger to his lips then took the stairs two at a time and intercepted Henrick midway down.

"What are you doing?" Henrick asked, looking past Ian.

"I found Tara. Milo's giving her a massage," Ian said. When Henrick made to continue down, Ian blocked him. "She's partially naked."

"Where is Drion Marcus?" Henrick asked.

"I don't know."

From the look on Henrick's face, Ian wasn't sure the Primary's assistant believed him. "I need to talk to the Drion. Help me find him," Henrick said, but then tilted his head as though in afterthought. "Your Majesty."

"Of course." Ian followed Henrick and they split their efforts between the upper floors. As soon as he was clear of Henrick's watchful eyes, Ian texted Marcus to make an appearance. A few minutes later, he heard voices in the great room downstairs. Ian texted a plan to Tara, and then changed into his running gear. He met up with the two men in the foyer. "I need to go for a run."

Henrick shook his head. "You're to stay here."

"The boy gets antsy," Marcus said.

"I promise to stay on the grounds," Ian said. He waved his cell phone. "If you need me before I return, just call."

Henrick whistled. One of the Primary's elite guards let himself into the house from the front stoop and stood at attention. "Falcon, accompany the Heir on his run," Henrick ordered. The guard gave a curt nod.

Ian's voice rose in a half-hearted protest. "He's not exactly dressed for this." A smug twitch at the corner of Falcon's mouth gave Ian concern that he wouldn't easily out-distance the man. He left with his escort and set out along the north cliff path. Falcon kept abreast for the first half of the jog and when Ian increased his pace, the guard fell into sync with Ian's speed.

Saxon met up with them and ran alongside Ian, stealing frequent glances at Falcon from over his shoulder. When the Primary's guards first arrived, the wolf's obvious agitation had baffled Ian. He tried to channel with Saxon, but the wolf wouldn't respond. He had never reacted like that during Marcus's troop's frequent visits.

Ian concentrated on summoning the elements while keeping his pace, counting on Saxon to be enough of a distraction that Falcon wouldn't notice. Clouds soon obliterated the sun overhead. A cool breeze swept up from the ocean and rustled the branches in the trees.

They reached the northern vortex structure in record time, and Ian held up near the door. Saxon snorted and paced, keeping himself between Ian and the guard. Falcon hadn't broken a sweat, and from what Ian could sense, his breathing wasn't labored.

At clap of thunder, Ian grabbed the door handle and bent over as if to catch his breath. His keen hearing caught the subtle click as the latch disengaged, further masked by the conjured thunder. Ian applied the merest pressure to ease the door open.

Falcon didn't break his attention on the wolf.

"Saxon doesn't seem to like you." Ian scratched the wolf behind the ears. Falcon didn't respond. "We better head back before this storm gets any worse."

"Or, you could vanquish it at will, Sire." The smug twitch at the corner of Falcon's mouth came and went. The guard walked over and tugged on the door handle. It latched with a click. He stepped back and stood at attention.

Ian's failed plan weighed heavily on his mind as they returned, and his thoughts raced faster than his legs. The Primary's elite guards were no fools.

"I'm tired of being a prisoner in my own home," Ian grumbled while he picked at Milo's dinner. Seated around the dining room table, no one had spoken for several minutes, and by the look of food remaining on their plates, everyone's appetites were depleted as much as their patience. A thick fog of tension had settled in the mansion.

Falcon must have reported Ian's ruse to Henrick, because everyone suddenly had a private escort wherever they went. With the grounds jam on the highest setting, the incessant scraping in Ian's core was as good as Chinese water torture; and, after nearly twenty-four hours, he'd had enough. He pushed his chair back and bolted to his feet. The guard across the room didn't flinch.

"Where's Henrick?" Ian commanded.

"Collecting the last of the test results," the guard said with unwavering calm.

Ian stormed into the kitchen. Dr. Mac was packing the unused blood samples. He then turned and tore off a printout from a nearby machine. "That's the last one," Dr. Mac said handing it to Henrick.

"Thank you for your cooperation, Doctor," Henrick said. He stuffed the printout into a satchel on the kitchen island counter, and then latched it.

"Are you finally done dissecting me?" Ian demanded.

"Sire, everyone is to remain under the Primary's guard until the results are reviewed. If your condition is found to be unchanged, as the good doctor claims, then you and the others will be released." Henrick whistled. A couple of the guards came in and grabbed some of the equipment. "They will be back for the rest. Do not leave the mansion until the remaining guards have been recalled." He followed the men out of the kitchen.

Dr. Mac collapsed into a nearby seat and rubbed his bald head, the tuffs of snowy hair over his ears appearing like ruffled feathers. Ian grabbed Dr. Mac's shoulder. "Did you find something?" he asked under his breath, unsure if there were any guards within earshot.

"Tell me, Ian, do you feel different?" Dr. Mac asked casually, but his rapid heartbeat gave his concern away.

Ian hesitated. "Yes," he whispered.

"Different how?" Mac indicated for him to take a seat next to him. Ian settled down but kept one ear to the hall beyond the kitchen. "I feel as if I'd walked around, all my life, with a half-full stomach. But for the first time, I now know what it feels like to be full."

Dr. Mac closed his eyes and gave into a tremendous sigh. "Good." He patted Ian's arm as if he'd gotten the answer right. "Don't tell another living soul what you just told me. Not Tara, not even Milo. This must stay between us."

"What's going on, Mac?" Ian said. "What did the rebels do to me?"

"There's no way to know until the jam is turned off." Dr. Mac stared out the archway. "The house arrest will be lifted soon. But we must hurry and find Patrick. I fear we don't have much time."

{38}

Patrick watched the crashing waves at the shoreline as the SUV sped down the winding dirt road. His hands were cuffed, but his thoughts ran wild, trying to find a way to escape again.

From what he could tell, they were on one of the smaller Greek islands with a much larger one looming in the far distance, across the ocean waters that reminded Patrick of the Caribbean. Wedged in the backseat between his body-building captors, he caught the best views whenever they rounded a corner, or took a sharp curve along the cliff. They soon left the ocean's edge and navigated inland. Enjoying an unobstructed view, with even clearer thoughts, Patrick saw one olive orchard after another. Bent-backed men led their donkey carts full of bushels of the hand-picked gems down the road. They made a sharp turn at the massive boulder where the wreck had been cleared. If it wasn't for the scrapes in the rock's surface, Patrick wouldn't have known it was the same location.

A large metal structure sat on the crest of a hill and the vehicle headed straight for it. A dust cloud billowed behind them, blocking any views from over Patrick's shoulder. The crazed driver skidded to a stop, apparently the only way he knew how to use the brakes. Everyone unbuckled their seat belts, and one of the men grabbed Patrick so tight that he winced. He was pulled out of the backseat, and it took some effort to remain on his feet as he touched ground. Dragged into the metal warehouse, Patrick collided with the man standing guard. Then he was brought to the middle of a wide open space where two chairs sat. A woman was tied to one of the chairs; her back was to them, and her hands were secured behind her. Patrick was thrown down into the chair beside her.

It was his mother!

Her soiled and damp gag looked as if she'd been there a while. Her typically coiffed hair was tangled and stuck out in all directions from under the knotted gag. One of the sleeves on her designer dress was ripped at the shoulder and the garment was rumpled and askew on her body. She opened her eyes and looked at him. They widened in terror.

"Wait!" Patrick yelled, but before he could set the men straight that he wasn't the Heir, they stuffed a rag into his mouth and tied a gag around his head so tight that both cheeks cut on his teeth. He tasted blood. Two men held his arms down, removed the handcuffs long enough to lace them between the rungs at the back of the old wooden chair, then secured them with a click. He tried to stand, but strong hands pushed him down from behind. "What do you want?" he tried to shout, but it came out muffled and incoherent.

What was his mother doing here? A vague memory rose to the surface of Patrick and his mother on her jet.

They called him Heir. They had to be Weir. Were they Aeros's men?

An invisible hand turned up the heat in the center of his chest as he took in his mother. He'd never seen her so haggard and depleted. He screamed, "I'm not the Heir!" at the top of his lungs, but the gag distorted his desperate plea.

A door opened at the opposite side of the warehouse and Patrick blinked at the blinding natural light. A thin older man, dressed in a white suit, sauntered in like he was in charge. The teenager brought up the rear. They approached with deliberate steps, and then paused a couple of feet in front of Patrick and his mother. What Patrick would have given to have a free hand, anything to punch the smirk off the kid's face.

The white-suited man tilted his face and stared at Patrick with nothing short of amusement. He was dressed in cream-colored suit pants and expensive shoes. His dark oxford shirt was opened at his throat and his silk tie hung loose. Long sleeves were rolled up to just below his bronze-skinned elbows.

"Welcome, Heir," he said in perfect English, tinged in a thick Italian accent. "I am Xercus." He paused when the teen brought over a stool. He sat down with the manners of royalty, smoothed out his pants, and further loosened his tie. Xercus leaned toward Patrick's mother and patted her knee, then waved a finger in Patrick's direction. "See, I told you he was unharmed." The man crossed one leg over the other and clasped his hands in front of him as if settling in to share pleasant conversation. He gave Patrick a wide smile. "We spent the better part of the night discussing you, your mother and I. Well, I have to confess, I monopolized our conversation given her gag and all." He rolled his eyes and chuckled. "That did put such a damper on our visit, didn't it?" He threw his arm over the back of the chair and gave her a wicked smile.

His relaxed demeanor clashed with the wild look in his eyes. It wouldn't be the first time Patrick had crossed paths with a crazed Duach. But insane or not, how could he have mistaken Patrick for the Heir? Patrick mumbled at the man.

Xercus clasped his hands. "Oh, you are fun." He jerked his chin and the man behind Patrick untied his gag. He slurped to catch his pooled saliva. "I'm not the Heir," Patrick blurted.

"Are you so sure?" The smile vanished, and Xercus gave Patrick a piercing stare. He got to his feet and stepped up, grabbing Patrick's shirt. His mother shrieked and struggled against her bindings. Xercus paused. "You mean he doesn't know?" A sheer look of glee brightened his face, and he unbuttoned Patrick's shirt. With a Cheshire cat of a grin, Xercus pulled back the edge of his shirt, exposing his upper left breast.

Patrick shivered when the man's finger brushed his skin, in spite of the sweltering heat. The teenager stepped next to Xercus and they stared at Patrick's exposed chest.

Baffled, he dropped his gaze. Through his chest hair, he saw a slightly raised image, like he'd been branded. A throb at his neck slipped into full throttle as he followed the outline and its three sharp points, but when he made out a sun trapped inside the triangle, his pulse slammed to a halt.

The strange heartburn he'd felt, ever since waking from the drugged sleep, reared its head like an awakened dragon. A rising plume of heat formed in the center of his chest and fought its way, ever upward, blistering his throat.

"A newborn core is the pits, is it not?" Xercus said with a sly smile.

{39}

Xercus sat down on his chair and waited until Patrick recovered. When he straightened up, Patrick looked at his mother. "Take her gag off."

"I prefer to talk to you," Xercus said. He pulled out a thin silver case from his pants pocket and removed a cigarette. When he placed it between his lips, the teen stepped up and flipped open a lighter. He lit Xercus's cigarette, flipped the lid back on with a flick of his wrist, then stepped back. Xercus took a long draw and released the carcinogenic cloud in a steady stream between his teeth, directed at Patrick's mother. "You did well, hiding him from everyone for what . . ." Xercus scrunched his face in contemplation, then regarded Patrick. "How old are you?"

"Twenty-five," Patrick said almost as an afterthought. His head wasn't in the moment, but scanning, reviewing, details of his life. He was the son of American billionaires. He'd grown up wanting for nothing; yet, he spent most of his life rejecting it, striving to forge his own way.

"This is a mistake. I'm not the Heir," Patrick said, fighting the urge to look at the Seal for fear that his eyes hadn't deceived him. The heat churned deep in the center of his chest. It was heartburn, the early warning signs of a heart attack, he reasoned. He looked at his mother, but she averted her eyes and hung her head. "Take her gag off," Patrick said. "I don't have your answers."

Xercus jerked his chin at Patrick's mother, and the guard untied her gag. She leaned forward and took deep breaths. "He might not have answers, but you do, don't you, Eve?"

Eve? The rising bile lodged in Patrick's throat. He stared at her.

"I find it hard to believe that she kept this, even from you. But then, she always was a wily one." Xercus's dapper poise morphed into uncertainty. "This turn of events is quite unexpected. It must be very troublesome for you." He pursed his lips and shook his head like someone surrounded by sorrow, yet immune to it. The man stood and looked between Patrick and his mother. "I'll give you two a few minutes to get . . ." he hesitated. "Reacquainted?" He gestured, and the guards filed out behind him. The warehouse door shut with an echoing clang.

It took several seconds for Patrick to gather his wits and look at his mother. She regarded him with sympathetic eyes that soon turned to steel. His mother had always been an enigma to him. Callous, yet gentle, self-serving, but generous when it suited her.

"We need to get out of here," she said.

"Stop!" Patrick shouted, but cringed at the pounding in his head. "I'm so messed up right now I'm going to puke!"

"That's your body adjusting to your awakened core. It's still forming, connecting to the earth. You're not fully developed and won't be for a while."

"You did this to me?" He shook his head. "Why?"

"It's a long story."

He settled back in his chair and focused on deep breaths, the only thing that eased the nausea. "Start at chapter one."

She scooted her chair around so they faced each other.

"Who are you?" he said.

"I'm your mother, Patrick. I always have been, always will be."

The maternal smile she gave him transported him back to childhood in an instant. It was JoAnna Langtree, not Eve, who sat across from him. It set his body at ease, but did little to stop his jockeying thoughts.

"You know about the Weir," he said. "If you're Weir, the rebel leader Eve, then you know Ian's the Heir."

"Earth has two. Ian is one. And now, its other has risen."

He closed his eyes and shook his head. "I'm normal . . . human . . . ordinary," he whispered.

"Your Weir birth name is Paerik. You come from a long line of the most powerful Weir. You were my greatest secret. No one on earth could know who you really were." She drew back and sat erect. "Not even your father knows."

"Is he Weir?" Patrick asked. His mother averted her eyes and didn't respond. His head wouldn't stop spinning. With every new revelation, a slew of questions rushed in. "Weir

Sars are born with a Seal," he said and gazed down at his chest. "Where the hell did this come from?"

"I suppressed your core. It lay dormant all these years." She peered at him closely. "You've had some memory loss. What is the last thing you remember before finding yourself here?"

"I was at the mansion." It took several seconds for reality to straighten Patrick's back. "You had Jaered shoot Ian." Anger shattered the disbelief, and the churning heat in Patrick's core returned with a vengeance. He fought his bindings and let loose a barrage of expletives. How long had it been? A day? Two? A week? It all rushed back in a crashing wave of memories. "Did Ian make it? Is he even alive?"

"Jaered revived him and kick-started your core at the same time."

The familiar steel returned to her eyes.

"Jaered brought you to me," she said without an ounce of remorse. "I raised your Seal and connected you to Earth."

"But Ian is okay?" Patrick said.

"He is well, but in grave danger." She looked around as if sizing up the room.

"What did you do to him?"

"There are some who would want control of Earth's Heirs, Patrick. Ian has served the Primary, but only remained safe as long as he was not a threat to him, or the Syndrion." Her shoulders wiggled, like her hands were doing something behind her. "If everything has gone according to plan, Jaered didn't just revive him; we've awakened the rest of Ian's powers."

Adrenaline swept in and energized every nerve. Patrick came alive. He needed a phone. He had to get word to Ian.

His mother stilled and stared past him. "Well, hello there."

Patrick glanced over his shoulder, but couldn't see. He felt a tiny hand tug at his handcuffs followed by slobbering licks. A second later, Epi's huge chocolate eyes appeared at his hip. "Epi. What the heck?"

"Find something to break these," his mother said, indicating behind her.

"I don't think he understands English, Mother." Patrick took advantage of the higher rungs on his chair and stood up as far as he could. When he tried to turn toward Epi, his chair came with him and scraped across the cement floor. It earned a glare from his mother. Patrick froze, listening, but only silence came from outside the walls.

The mutt trotted over to check out what everyone was looking at, sniffed at the base of the metal door, then clawed the cement as if wanting out. "Get back here," Patrick hissed at the mongrel. Epi strolled over, grabbed the dog by the scruff of its neck, and led him back to the group. The child tapped one of the wooden rungs behind Patrick's mother, and the dog bit down on it, planted its hind legs and, with a low growl, pulled.

Patrick rolled his eyes. "Oh for the love of —"

Splintering wood. The rung broke free. Epi grabbed it from the dog's mouth and tapped another one. The mongrel bit down and shook its head. Crack. Another rung appeared in the dog's mouth, but this time he wasn't ready to give up his prize and scooted away. Then he lay down, gnawing on it like a rawhide stick.

His mother stood and teetered for a second. She pushed her cuffs higher on her delicate forearms and rubbed her wrists, then took stock of Patrick's cuffs and the back of his chair. "Your rungs don't look as loose as mine." Footsteps faded. Scuffling came from behind Patrick. She returned and grabbed his cuffs. Metal scraping metal. "Oh, fuck."

Patrick suppressed a smile. He'd never heard his mother cuss before. A second later, his cuffs opened and he wiggled out of them. A bent nail landed on the warehouse floor next to his shoe.

"See if you can open mine," she said and turned her back to him. He grabbed the nail and studied the lock. "Come on, Patrick, we don't have all day," she hushed.

"Then you shouldn't have sent me to private schools," he snapped. He stuck the nail in the lock and wiggled it. When nothing happened, he looked over her shoulder. "What did you do to get it open?"

She gave him a sideways glance. "I just—"

A metal bang. Patrick turned. The teenager stood in the doorway. He shouted to someone behind him.

"Run!" Patrick pushed his mother toward the back door of the warehouse and scooped Epi up into his arms, taking off at a full run. A bullet struck the back wall, inches from where his mother held up at the closed door. Patrick came to a halt and raised one hand in surrender while clutching the child with the other. Barking. Growls. A yelp. When Patrick turned, the mutt lay motionless on the floor. Epi whimpered. Patrick cradled the boy with a heavy heart.

The teenager wiped the butt of his gun on his T-shirt and pointed the tip of the barrel at Patrick's mother.

"No!" Patrick shouted and stepped in front of her.

"Wait!" Xercus yelled from the open doorway. "She's mine."

One of the men grabbed for the boy, but Patrick resisted. Two more men stepped in and Epi was torn from Patrick's grasp. Epi screamed and thrashed about, but his frail attempts were no match for the muscled help.

"Take him out back. That one's mine." The teenager sneered. One of the men carried Epi out the back door. Xercus held up next to the teen at the center of the warehouse.

"You need me to cooperate, am I right?" Patrick said. "Don't hurt them and I'll do whatever you want."

Xercus grabbed the back of his chair and laughed. "You're quick to negotiate, especially when you have no idea what's at stake."

Patrick stilled. He looked at his mother.

"I've only kept her alive because my employer wanted information on the rebel forces," Xercus said.

"You're not after me, or my powers?"

"What powers? The ones that you used to escape last night and come here and free your mother? Oh, wait, you were using them, just now to get all of you out of here." He gave a

247

flourish wave of his hand and bowed. "By all means, Heir, demonstrate what you can do!" When Patrick didn't react, Xercus laughed. Even his men took heed with furtive glances. "It's obvious your powers are stifled, if you inherited any at all." Xercus reached behind him and removed a long barreled gun that reflected the bright sunlight streaming through the open door. "I was hired to get as much information as I could, and then kill the rebel leader." The tip of the gun turned on Patrick's mother. "I guess my employer will have to settle for half. I hope you enjoyed your final visit with Mommy." Xercus's finger tightened on the trigger.

Patrick's hand shot up. "No!" An explosion, deep in his chest sent a ball of energy erupting out of his raised hand. The scarlet shockwave burst outward, filling the warehouse, knocking everyone in its expanding path off their feet and onto their backs. The chair in front of Xercus flew up and crashed into him, knocking the gun out of his hand. He fell backward across the warehouse, then slammed into the far wall. The man collapsed in a heap on the cement floor. At the same time, his mother's chair collided with the teenager and together, they tumbled over and over until coming to a rest on top of Xercus.

Stunned surprise at his power and what it had done gave way to spikes of pain. "Owww!" Patrick pressed a fist to the center of his chest. The searing exhaust from his core burned his lungs and blistered his throat.

His mother put a gentle hand on his arm, and with tears in her eyes, slowly led him to the center of the warehouse. Her hands were free of the cuffs.

Both doors to the warehouse pushed open and people swarmed inside. The man who had taken Epi outside returned with the child clinging to his neck. A lollipop stick protruded from the boy's mouth. and he giggled when he saw Patrick. Someone whistled and the lifeless mutt sprang up onto its two back legs and barked in a spontaneous dance. A man tossed him a treat, and then patted him on the head.

The warehouse filled with bodies of all ages and races. Many were clothed as the field workers. Others in urban street clothes. A familiar flower pattern caught Patrick's attention. It was the woman from the balcony in town, minus her straw broom.

Xercus and the teenager were propped up against the back wall. A man pushed in and shone a penlight in their eyes, hovering like he was examining them. A moment later, he held up one thumb, and then another.

The last person to arrive was Jaered, but he lingered in the open door and didn't join the crowd. He gave Patrick a subtle nod, then left.

"For the greater good," Patrick's mother shouted.

"For the greater good," more than a hundred voices said in unison.

She raised Patrick's arm above their heads like he'd just won a boxing match. "I give you your Heir!" she announced in a voice that bounced off the steel walls.

"Long live the Heir," rang throughout the warehouse, and the crowd dropped to one knee. "Long live the Heir," they said and bowed their heads.

Patrick took in the bodies with their faces lowered in reverence. He'd only seen the Pur Weir treat Ian with such pomp and circumstance. "What is this?"

"You passed," his mother said.

"Passed what?"

"The Rising." She hugged him tight, her petite arms barely reaching around him. "The Primary had poor Ian whipped and tortured for his Rising." She looked up at him. "My version was much more humane, wouldn't you agree?" She pushed away from him before he could respond, and addressed the crowd. "Job well done, everyone!"

They stood and proceeded to slap each other on the back with smiles and laughter. Many of them worked around the crowd, shaking hands and exchanging stories.

Patrick stormed past them and headed outside with hurried steps, creating as much distance from the building, from his mother, as he could. He'd made it a few yards when he was stopped in his tracks by an elephant sitting on his chest. Denied air, he couldn't utter a sound and he bent over while a jackhammer pounded at the walls of his core. Then it stopped as quickly as it had appeared.

He fell to his knees, and he took deep breaths as the pressure in his chest corrected itself. Not more than thirty feet away, Jaered was holding Vael up against a parked car along the road. The Pur Sar dropped his head back and was sucking air. Jaered stole a glance in Patrick's direction, then said something to Vael. They took off down the road on foot toward a small, gathered crowd.

Pur and Duach cannot unite. They must stay apart. Patrick's spine sagged. The Curse had dropped him and Vael.

He wasn't sure how long he stared at the two men retreating down the road, their bodies growing smaller with every passing minute. A deep ache formed around his heart like a constricting fist.

The door to the warehouse opened, then closed behind Patrick and a moment later, his mother stepped next to him.

"You made me a Duach," he said. He could never go home.

{40}

Joule glanced at Ian from over her shoulder and, in spite of the concern in her eyes, gave a final cursory nod of good-bye. One of the elite guards helped her into the idling Jeep. It seemed as though a lifetime had passed since Ian and Tara visited the Congo to meet with the doctors Willoughsby. He had Joule to thank for being alive and had promised her he'd repay it by finding her father.

But first, he was determined to find Patrick.

Ian watched them drive off with unsettled thoughts. He'd tried to convince Joule to stay with them, but she insisted on going back to Africa. What awaited her at her research site? Her colleagues had to be scattered by now, if not killed. Why did her father desert her?

He slammed the mansion's front door on the Primary's retreating guards and turned the deadbolt for good measure. Given the mystery and secrecy around their skills, Ian doubted it would be a deterrent if they ever returned, but the act felt empowering.

It'd taken almost two days for the Primary to withdraw his small band of troops and give Ian and the others their lives back.

Saxon joined him at the front door. *Enemy gone?*

They weren't our enemy, Ian channeled. Saxon snorted.

"Tara, get the boys and set everything up in the great room again. I want to be ready to shyft when the jam is turned off," Ian said. She took off for the gym.

"What the hell was that all about?" Milo roared from the other room. The old caretaker had backed Dr. Mac up against the fireplace mantle and the lifelong friends were engaged in a stare down to rival any schoolyard brawl.

"You're just pissed off that I took over your kitchen." Dr. Mac slipped out from beneath Milo's arm and crossed the room, settling next to Marcus.

"I'm with Milo," Marcus growled. "My gut tells me you know more than we do."

Dr. Mac scoffed and relocated to the rolling arm of the living room chair. "I've already been interrogated by the Primary and that weasel Henrick. Don't start with me."

"Why were you interrogated?" Marcus said.

"Perhaps because it was my responsibility to inform them of Ian's illness." Dr. Mac reached for his mug, took a sip, and scrunched his face at the room-temperature beverage.

"The Syndrion had a right to know," Marcus said. "I had a right to be kept in the loop."

"Mac thought it could be contagious," Milo said. "That's why we didn't alert the Syndrion right away."

"But it wasn't a virus," Marcus said. "And you still kept the events quiet." Tara arrived with Xander and Pacman.

"You've been protecting Rayne, all this time," Marcus continued. "Hiding what she could do."

Who had confessed to Marcus? When Ian looked around the room, Milo was the only one who didn't make eye contact. What did it matter, now? Rayne was gone.

"I tried to buffer what happened, what we'd done, but from their questions, I suspect that my report didn't correspond with someone's." Dr. Mac tossed a disgruntled look around the room. "I thought we all agreed to report that Patrick and Rayne weren't even present."

"It wasn't me," Tara said.

"We came after the show was over," Pacman said.

Xander popped his gum. "We missed the fireworks."

"Had anyone thought to include Joule in that decision?" Ian asked.

Tara raised her hand. "I did."

"She might have slipped up, somewhere along the way." Marcus looked at the group expectantly. "And no one mentioned Vael as we agreed?"

Everyone nodded. Dr. Mac set down his mug and rubbed the back of his neck. "It's only a matter of time before you're in the Primary's sights. People have a way of disappearing. Am I right, Marcus?" But the Drion averted his eyes without comment.

"The Primary has always wanted an excuse to get rid of Patrick and Rayne," Ian said.

"It's worse than that," Dr. Mac said. "If the Primary learns that Patrick was involved—"

"—and survived the boost, and was taken by the rebels." Marcus shook his head. "The boy is in tremendous danger."

Ever since Vael had turned his back on the Pur, Marcus had been trying to protect his son from the same fate. If they found one, would they find the other? Could they save them both? Ian wondered if that wasn't the real reason Marcus was a willing participant in covering up the details.

"They had no right to put Ian through the meat grinder and treat us like traitors," Milo grumbled.

"Once the Primary had reason to be suspicious, he didn't trust anything we reported," Dr. Mac said. "Or anyone."

Xander didn't lift his face from his computer screen. "Or, the old geezer was just stalling while he tried to retrieve the data he stole."

"And walked away when he came up empty-handed." Pacman sucked on his licorice.

"He has a forty-eight-hour headstart," Ian said. "Whether he was able to recover anything or not."

"That's like, *forever.*" Pacman bit off a generous slice of his stick. "We've got some serious catching up to do." Clicking keys sliced into the tension that had settled on the room.

Ian grabbed Dr. Mac's arm. "Mac, a word, in private." Ian hurried him through the foyer and into the kitchen, then stood guard at the archway to make sure Milo's curiosity didn't bring him within earshot.

Dr. Mac grabbed a fresh mug from the cupboard and helped himself to the steeping pot of coffee on the counter.

Once convinced the others had given them some space, Ian leaned against the kitchen island. "We didn't know what we had, but the Primary took one look at it and knew it had to do with Eve." His voice drew a razor-sharp edge. "He wasn't the only one, was he, Doc?"

Dr. Mac returned the pot and stood, staring out the window. "When we arrived, I nearly died when I saw the information, floating in the middle of the room, for everyone to see." He looked down at the mug in his hand. "How did you know?"

"The look on your face," Ian said. "I caught the change in your heartbeat." He glanced over his shoulder and verified they were still alone. "Mac, how did you know it was about Eve?"

The old doctor looked down at his feet. "I'm not wearing my slippers. The Primary came unannounced. There was no time to change into my slippers."

Ian peered at him like he'd lost it. "What do your ragged bunny slippers have to do with anything?"

Dr. Mac faced Ian and in that instant, the man aged before Ian's eyes. "I always wear them when I come to see you. They were a gift, you see. A reminder of a promise I made someone a very long time ago." He walked outside and leaned against the patio railing. He stared down at his mug, but didn't bring it to his lips.

Ian stepped out and closed the door behind him. He sat on the railing next to Dr. Mac. "Who gave you the slippers?"

"Your mother," Dr. Mac said. "The night the Primary banned her to live on Thrae. You were only a few months old."

"My parents were killed in a car accident," Ian said gently, concerned that the pressure had finally taken its toll on the old doctor's mind.

"That's what the Primary wanted you to believe," Dr. Mac said. "But your mother is very much alive and living a world away, just beyond our reach."

The pulse at Ian's neck throbbed. "Why lie to me?"

"Because he didn't want you searching for her and learning the truth."

Ian clenched his jaw. "Marcus?"

"Other than the Primary, I'm the only one who knows. And if he finds out I've told you . . ."

Ian catapulted off the railing and reached the edge of the lake with pounding steps. Dark, billowing clouds blew in overhead. A thunderclap struck the surface. Sleet fell, stinging Ian's cheeks. Footsteps. "Why tell me this now?" Ian snarled.

"Because its time you learn the truth about who you are. What you are," Dr. Mac said. "Patrick isn't the only one in grave danger, Ian. If the Primary finds out that your powers are greater than presumed, he'll come after you."

A funnel formed over the lake and rose, spinning above the water, mimicking Ian's fury. The water at his feet receded, feeding the funnel.

A firm hand grasped Ian's shoulder. "My boy, you can't reveal to anyone what I've confessed."

Ian jerked his shoulder out of Dr. Mac's grasp. "Go," he said in a voice riddled with ice and stone. The sleet turned to hail and pummeled them both.

"I can help you find Patrick," Dr. Mac said with a raised arm to fend off the pea-sized ice. "Ian, you can trust me."

"I don't know who or what to trust anymore!"

A sizzling bolt of lightning struck behind the doctor, but he didn't flinch. "Then trust yourself," Dr. Mac urged. "But find Patrick before the Primary, or we're all doomed." He returned to the house with hurried steps.

Ian spread his arms and screamed. The funnel dropped on the lake in a massive splash that sent waves in all directions, crashing against the shore. Ian turned toward the battering hail and faced his pain.

{41}

Drained and numb, the storm receded and Ian turned to find Tara standing at the edge of the patio. When he approached, she didn't speak and together they returned to the mansion.

Milo tossed a towel at him as his soggy steps slapped across the kitchen floor. The others were gathered around the meal the old caretaker had fixed. Dr. Mac wasn't among them. The group remained mum as Ian passed by, headed for his room.

No one else knows the truth.

Rayne was gone, perhaps Patrick as well. If Ian's instincts were correct, Dr. Mac was one of the rebels and in league with Eve. The old doctor might have helped save Ian from the nanites, but did he have a role in infecting Ian in the first place? If the Primary lied to Ian about his parents, where did the lies start and end? Who could he trust?

Ian recalled the countless times the Primary had drilled Ian about what powers he'd discovered. He'd taken it to be frustration and the Primary's way of pushing him to try harder. If Dr. Mac was telling the truth, Ian had been under the Primary's microscope all these years. Was that why no one would tell him what powers to expect? What to develop?

He showered and changed into fresh clothes. When he walked back into his bedroom, a silver platter sat on his bed with Milo's culinary comfort. Ian walked by without as much as a glance.

Agitated by the constant pressure in his core, he snapped at Milo from the balcony. "Turn off the jam!" he shouted.

Milo appeared in the foyer and waved a wooden spoon at him. "I tried. They are overriding it at Syndrion headquarters."

Dr. Mac might have instilled doubt, but the Primary's actions were fueling it.

Ian hurried downstairs and into the great room to study the floating data. He focused on the columns and how Xander had arranged them.

Marcus joined him. A moment later, Tara arrived with a fresh plate of food. She set it on the coffee table. "For when you're ready."

Ian didn't respond, searching for what the Primary recognized earlier when he saw the data. He found the name of the car, Osera, and the company address in the third column. Ian looked at Marcus. "I can't ask you to cross this line."

"This isn't just about Patrick," the Drion said. "Eve has her claws in my son."

Ian's quest took them to Germany. The second they appeared, Saxon shook out his coat to stave off the frigid, long-distance shyft.

Lange Bäume's facility sat on a cliff overlooking the Rhine River. The location boasted deep waters for shipping their cars across the globe while supporting the quaint village beside the river. The manufacturing site was small, nothing like the larger automobile conglomerates in Cologne farther down the waterway. According to the boys' research, the privately owned company only produced custom-built luxury cars. The group arrived around three in the morning, and the sleepy town nestled next to the winding river had yet to stir.

Sparks flashed in the building's high windows, and the sounds of grinding metal coming from inside bespoke a lucrative business that never paused.

Saxon ran ahead and the trio followed. The wolf came to a halt at what appeared to be a back door with its overhead spotlight turned off. From a distance, Ian tapped into his keen eyesight to check for security cameras and spotted one above the door, but didn't see a light to indicate that it was on. If it was motion activated, it didn't move in response to Saxon. Nevertheless, they approached with caution. Ian conjured the lock away with a mere touch, and they slipped into the building without incident.

A small office sat at the top of a nearby metal staircase. The lights were off, and Ian held out his hand to stop Marcus from ascending the stairs.

Marcus threw him a baffled glance.

"If the plant is operational, why isn't there a supervisor on duty?" Ian said, just loud enough to be heard over the assembly line beyond the double-wide doors.

Tara shrugged. "Cutbacks?"

Marcus pulled out a handgun and led the way up the stairs, crouching low.

They paused before reaching the topmost step. The door to the office was ajar with splintered wood in the doorframe.

"Stay here," Marcus said, but the metal gears and conveyor-belt skids coming from the assembly room drowned his voice. The old general nudged the door wider. A dark, congealed pool just inside the office told Ian they were too late.

He stepped up to the railing across from the office and scanned the manufacturing arena. The glaring lights of the plant highlighted what he feared most. Bodies lay scattered next to the assembly line, while others slumped against walls or lay beneath the equipment as if a few tried to dive for cover. He stopped counting bodies at two dozen.

Ian shyfted beside a pillar, dropped to one knee, and pushed back a slumped man in overalls. A blackened patch in the center of the man's chest quickened Ian's pulse. Memories of murdered scholars rushed to the surface, and Ian took a whiff. He closed the dead man's lids and laid a gentle hand on his head.

The factory noise masked Tara's approach, and he wasn't aware that she stood over him until he looked up. Her expression gave him pause. "This is fresh blood."

"Who could have done this?" she said.

Ian stood and stepped around her to locate Marcus. The general was checking for a pulse at a victim's throat on the other side of the conveyor belt. "Someone with core blast powers," Ian said.

Marcus joined them. "This is what happened at the mansion a couple months ago, when the scholars were slaughtered. I didn't smell sulfur then, and I don't now. A Duach didn't do this."

Tara raised her gun and looked around. "Ning told me that it was the Primary's guard that night at the mansion."

Ian and Marcus exchanged stunned glances. "Why didn't you tell me?" Marcus said.

"Because he was a Duach psychopath, and I thought he was playing with my head." She lowered her gun. "But when they were guarding us, those guys gave me the creeps."

"We knew we'd be playing catch-up, but I wasn't expecting . . ." Marcus's gaze fell to the man at Ian's feet. "This."

"It could be Eve, covering her tracks," Ian said. Even now, it was so much easier to believe the faceless rebel leader capable of such atrocities, rather than the man who had watched over and protected him all his life.

"There'd be no reason for Eve to torture her own man," Marcus said and tilted his head in the direction of the upstairs office. "But the poor bastard didn't know anything."

"How could you tell?" Tara asked.

Marcus's jaw clenched. "There's not much left."

"So many people," Tara said.

"It's a message," Marcus growled. "One that even the most callous can't ignore."

Ian watched the grinding mechanical arms overhead, reaching for auto parts that weren't there. The whine of drills as they stretched into empty space along the ghostly conveyor belt sent a chill up his spine.

Smoke touched Ian's senses. He scanned their surroundings. "Marcus, we need to find the fire!"

The general took a whiff and his eyes widened. "Ian, we need to get out of here."

"Their families deserve more than ashes."

"Let the fire cover this up." Marcus grabbed his arm. "These are core blasts. It could expose the Weir."

Ian pulled his arm out of the general's grasp. "It's time the Weir stop thinking of ourselves and start putting others first." He ran upstairs and followed a row of rooms until he located the security office. The two murdered guards were slumped in front of still-active monitors.

Flames licked at the lower frame of what appeared to be a storage room. When Ian compared the monitor's number to a building schematic on the wall, he located the room at the back end of the facility. He stared at the screen, got a clear enough image through the rising smoke, and shyfted.

Ian appeared in front of the stacked boxes of supplies. He threw his arm up to shield his eyes and face while heat from the flames melted the plastic shrink wrap behind him. He found a fire extinguisher on the wall, pulled the pin, and pointed the nozzle at the fiery base. The flames closest to the ground extinguished, but what had caught on the column of wooden crates snaked its way higher. He fought the flames until the extinguisher sputtered with its last foamy breath and had nothing left to give.

The expansive room turned opaque as smoke obliterated everything beyond an arm's length. Ian choked and gasped, then dropped to the concrete floor, sucking in as much oxygen as he could before trying again.

Strong hands grabbed him and shyfted him beside the river. "We have to save them," Ian sputtered.

"Ian, you tried!" Marcus held on tight. "But I can't let you sacrifice yourself for a heap of corpses."

He stumbled to his feet and reached toward the river, conjuring a massive funnel cloud with raging, intense wind. He lifted his hands and the swirling mass carried up the bank. He tossed it at the facility and it sputtered against the outer walls, but only a fraction of it penetrated the few open windows.

Saxon ran up and knocked Ian to the ground, then licked the soot on his face as if thanking him for his failed heroics. Ian watched as the flames reached high above the building, and their wicked dance taunted him until the pounding in his head eased.

Tara reached out and helped Ian to his feet. Marcus made to gather them together for a shyft, but Ian broke away and pulled out his cell.

"What are you doing?" Marcus said.

Xander picked up before Ian could respond. "Xander, we were too late. I need you to tell me the rest of the companies and their locations."

"There's a lot, fearless leader. It'd be better if I text them to you."

Ian paused. "You and Pacman found a pattern to the rebels' thefts, am I right? That's how you traced the significance of their burglaries."

"Yeah, it was like getting an item that gained you access to the next level," Pacman shouted. Xander had put it on speaker.

A scuffle. Pacman's voice got louder. "We applied Xander's algorithm to figure it out."

"Do the same with this data," Ian said. "Then call me back ASAP."

"Will do!" The call cut off.

"What makes you think that this data is organized?" Marcus said.

"Rayne's research was all over the place," Tara added.

"Because Eve has proven that she's calculating and manipulative." Ian thought back to Dr. Mac. "Persuasive." Shouts came from the village. Lights popped on, one after another. "That makes her a woman with an agenda. And we need to figure it out and catch up fast, or the pile of bodies is going to get a lot higher."

{42}

Voices, loud and insistent, floated into the cabin. Patrick had no idea what Jaered and his mother were talking about, and he only half listened through the open door of the jet. If it were possible, he'd melt into the plush cushions and simply disappear. He'd have to see if that was one of his so-called powers. Still in denial about what had happened, he couldn't fathom having abilities that he'd spent the last four years envying of Ian. The thought of them terrified him.

He had the better part of the night to think about it and ended up convinced that Ian would reject him the second he learned of Patrick's fate. The pit deep in his gut festered. Tara, strong yet gentle, compassionate and kind, would kill for Ian. His mother had made him their sworn enemy. Every time Patrick's thoughts fell to Rayne, his heart sank. Gone were the hugs, the shoulder she leaned on, and the one she offered him in return. Their friendship could never be the same.

By midnight, Patrick abandoned the idea of stealing a cell phone or bribing someone to help him escape. He had nowhere to go.

Everyone on the island was devoted to his mother. To Eve. They bowed to her and gazed upon her with admiration. From his eavesdropping on conversations around him, her rebel force spanned the globe. If he did try and escape, how far could he get?

He still couldn't wrap his head around the fact that his mother was the rebel leader. He was Weir, always had been. Born a Duach Heir.

Patrick bolted from his seat, burst into the narrow bathroom at the back of the cabin, and puked into the toilet until there was nothing left to purge. He pulled the lever and blue chemical splattered about. A couple of drops struck his cheek. There wasn't enough pressure to rid the toilet bowl of the emotional upheaval. He closed the lid, sat down, and grabbed a towel from the dispenser to wipe his cheek.

A *knock* at the door. "Patrick, we're going to take off soon," his mother said, as if they were headed on vacation.

He stood and ran water into the sink, gargled with mouthwash, and rinsed his face. He opened the door and found her sitting in her favorite spot at the back of the cabin, sipping on what appeared to be an iced tea with a sprig of mint poking out the top of her glass.

"Did you get some rest?" she asked. "We have a long flight ahead of us."

Jaered stood next to the open door. "Are you sure you don't want me to shyft him there?"

"We have a lot to discuss," she said.

"Suit yourself." He threw Patrick a cautious look, then exited the plane. A moment later, the short stairs were raised, and the pilot swung the door closed and latched it from inside.

The engines revved to a deafening pitch, and the jet taxied. Patrick looked out the window. The runway was near the warehouse at the center of the small island. The jet rapidly picked up speed and lifted into the air. It circled around the island as dawn opened its eyes at the horizon. Colorful flashes below. Patrick pressed his face against the window. On one side of the small island, repetitive green flashes went off like sparkling fireworks. On the opposite side, red, and at the center of the island, pale, almost colorless bursts.

"We have several shyftors among the rebels," his mother said, gazing out her window.

"There's both Pur and Duach?" Patrick asked.

"We do our best to ignore the Weir's civil war. We choose . . . not to choose sides," she said. "Our battle is with Aeros. We are stronger when we don't battle ourselves." She ran her finger down the side of her glass. "A philosophy mankind has yet to adopt."

"What caused the pale lights?" Patrick asked.

"The rebel forces didn't originate here on Earth," she said. "They came from Thrae."

Ian hadn't told Patrick about Thrae. It had been Rayne, spilling what little she knew about its existence over margaritas one night. She said Jaered was from Thrae, and that's why he had no colored corona like the Pur and Duach Sars on Earth.

The rising sunlight spread across Earth's surface like a wakeup call. Patrick spotted several small surrounding islands. "Where were we?"

"An island near Malta. I own several, scattered here and there around the globe." She took a sip of her tea, then settled against her seat and released more than air in one long, continuous exhale.

"What do I call you?" He gave her a sideways glance and sat on the couch, facing her.

"You've always called me Mother, Patrick."

"Did JoAnna Langtree ever really exist?"

"I've been many people. Lived countless lives." Her fingertips played a nail-clicking tune across the side of her glass. "JoAnna Langtree was just one of hundreds."

He scoffed. "Drama queen doesn't suit you."

"I'm serious, Patrick. I'm more than two thousand years old." She stared as if daring him to look away first.

"Weir don't live that long," he said.

"Do you know about the Ancients?" she asked.

"Nemautis and the other scholars claimed that there were five. They'd found record of them in a book they were studying."

She got up from her seat and opened a nearby cabinet. Pressing her hand flat against the panel, it slid apart with a muted click. Patrick's breath caught in his throat when she removed the Book of the Weir and brought it over. She sat down on the couch next to him and lifted the cover. He'd forgotten how large it was. Opened, the book covered most of her lap and spilled onto Patrick's. Up close, the pages looked like they'd crumble if touched.

"You stole it," he said in disbelief, recalling her last visit and her desire to stay at the mansion with them, instead of a hotel.

"I merely verified it was there. A band of rebels infiltrated the estate while we were at the gala that night."

He clenched his fists. His chest heaved. "They murdered the scholars!"

"No," she shook her head vehemently. "By the time they arrived, the Primary's guards had already slaughtered the men. My team risked their lives to protect Milo and Marcus, and to secure the book."

"When Jaered kidnapped me a few months ago, he tried to tell me the Primary was responsible. I didn't believe him."

"The Primary's elite guards are ruthless and lethal. They keep his hands clean, and they obey only him." She turned a page in the book with delicate care. "I am one of the Ancients, Patrick, along with my two sisters, Gwynndol and Sophenna. Johann, the man you know as the Primary, is another."

It occurred to Patrick that he'd never heard his mother mention extended family. "That's four."

"Aeros," she said. She turned another page. "We originally came from Thrae, a sister planet of Earth's from another dimension. We believed ourselves to be ordinary. But then one day, during a particularly violent storm, something tragic happened." She turned to the next page.

There was a hand-drawn picture with a sun filling up much of the page, its rays striking people like arrows finding their mark.

"We were in an open field during harvest. There must have been a tear in the upper atmosphere because we were bombarded with solar energy. When we awoke, everyone else was burned beyond recognition. Our village destroyed, our crops, gone. The landscape, for as far as we could see, looked like it had been torched. But the five of us had survived without a mark on us." She pointed to an entry on the opposite page, as if reciting what was written in the strange language. "Aeros and his brother Johann discovered that they could do miraculous things. It began with growing plants at will, then manipulating animals to do their bidding."

Patrick's knee bobbed faster and faster. He pressed his hand down to make it stop. "I need a drink."

"We need breakfast." She closed the book and returned it to the safe in the cabinet. His mother pressed a button on the wall. The attendant exited the cockpit and stood in wait.

"Willow, we're ready," his mother announced.

The tall, thin woman disappeared behind the galley wall. Clinking glass and the subtle sounds of opening and closing cabinets and drawers could be heard over the engines.

Patrick stood and paced, alternating between rubbing his hands and rubbing his arms. "Why aren't you still on Thrae?"

"You have to understand, we were so much younger then." Eve grabbed her tea and slipped into her seat at the rear of the cabin. "Aeros adored Sophenna, always had. Johann eventually courted Gwynndol. Their offspring were the beginning of the Weir race. We must have survived because of a genetic mutation. It was passed on in their offspring. But the solar energy did something to us, the originals. We didn't grow old, while our children and their children did." She took a sip and grew pensive as if haunted by the past. "We couldn't remain in our village and were forced to scatter, reinventing ourselves every couple of decades somewhere. Everything changed when Aeros discovered a pocket of intensive energy, and he learned to manipulate it."

"He'd found a vortex," Patrick said. "And figured out how to shyft."

"Aeros and Johann mastered it over time, and then by accident, Aeros jumped dimensions. I eventually found the courage and asked Aeros to take me one day. He brought me to Earth. It was almost identical in every way to our Thrae, but the differences between plants and other creatures intrigued me."

"What kind of differences?" Patrick sat down and grabbed the edge of the couch when they hit some turbulence.

"Thrae had a species much like unicorns. Earth's version of course, were horses."

A nervous chuckle turned into giddiness. "And I suppose Thrae had dragons and trolls, Bigfoots and the Loch Ness Monster, too."

"All Earth names. On Thrae we called them by something different." She tossed him a knowing smile, but her tone held no amusement. "Understand that their sightings here on Earth were the folly of bored, self-proclaimed gods. The poor creatures were always returned to their natural habitats. I made sure of it."

"What'd they do, make you Thrae's warden?" Patrick smiled. The moniker seemed to fit his mother.

"I chose to stay on Earth. By then my sisters and their husbands had tired of each other. They found their amusements elsewhere. But I had a whole new world to discover."

Discover, or command? Patrick chewed on his lip and mulled it over.

Willow appeared carrying a small tray with the aroma of roasted coffee leading the way. She exchanged his mother's iced tea with a china cup of the steaming brew and handed one to Patrick, along with a bottle of aspirin, then disappeared into her galley.

He popped the painkillers, but could only take one sip at a time of the blistering liquid, and slowly worked the pills down his parched throat. His stomach gurgled for something more tangible.

It arrived a few minutes later. Willow set the table for them both and placed the western omelets, toasted sourdough bread, and fresh-fruit cups on the table, in front of his mother.

"Let's eat, Patrick. You need your strength." Eve leaned back when Willow opened the cloth napkin and draped it across his mother's lap. When he hesitated to get up from the couch, she cut into her omelet. "I don't bite, son."

"No, but you're capable of a whole lot worse." Patrick slowly got to his feet. Every movement taxed his exhausted muscles and the cabin swirled, taking his thoughts with it. He grabbed the seat backs and made his way to the rear of the cabin. He settled across from her, staring down at the meal, unable to draw upon the strength to cut into it. She spread jam on his toast and handed it to him. They ate in silence and for the first time in days, he had a glimpse of the familiar.

A jolt aroused Patrick. He opened his eyes to find that he'd dozed off on the couch. His mother was on her cell at the back of the cabin, and from the tone of her voice, it wasn't positive.

"Check on as many of the residents as you can. Arrange for food and whatever supplies are needed. Get them there stat!" She paused as if listening. "I agree. And Xercus, go through the normal channels and take precautions. For all we know, this is a trap and he's waiting to see who comes to their aid." She tossed the phone down on the table and pulled a shawl across her shoulders, then gazed out the window with an iron jaw.

"What's wrong?" Patrick swung his legs over and sat up, rubbing his face.

"Johann," she hesitated, "the Primary, has left me a message."

"What's with you and him, anyway?' Patrick stood and stretched.

"We have opposing views about Earth." She pursed her lips. "I believe that humankind needs the Weir's protection. He believes Earth's natural resources are more important."

"You can't exactly have one without the other."

"You'd be surprised to what lengths that man goes," she picked up her cell and ran her thumb across the screen, "to prove otherwise."

"You said the Ancients didn't age." Patrick yawned. "No offense, Mother, but you aren't a spring chicken anymore."

The corner of her mouth twitched, and she put her cell down. "We enjoyed youth for centuries, but were destined to watch loved ones come and go. After the first few generations, my sisters couldn't get pregnant any longer. I couldn't. The five grew restless over time. Sophenna was the only one who never left her beloved Thrae. Aeros spent much of his time between Thrae and Earth, but it was Johann who eventually followed me to Earth and settled here."

She pulled her shawl tighter around her shoulders. "Then, in the mid-twentieth century, just as we watched the Weir Sars decline on both planets and feared Thrae and Earth were at risk, a miracle happened." Her voice grew guarded. "Sophenna became pregnant. For the first time in centuries, we saw it as a sign that Thrae, and Earth, might survive, and that the Weir would flourish and nurture the planets once again. Jaered was the first to be born of an Ancient in almost two thousand years."

Patrick sat up with a start.

"A couple of years later, you." She gave Patrick the most glowing smile he'd ever received. "But it took some doing for Gwynndol," she paused. "For Ian."

Not only were Patrick and Jaered cousins, Ian, too? He slumped back and ran his fingers through his hair.

His mother rose from her seat and leaned against the table. "But the continuation of the Weir race came at a cost. We began to age, naturally, and not just us, but Aeros and Johann, too."

"Are you still immortal?" Patrick asked, shocked that it rolled off his tongue like discussing the weather.

"We haven't the courage to test it. You see, if bearing children affected us as one, what might happen to the whole, if one of us dies?

{43}

Ian shyfted Saxon to Wales. The boys' algorithm gave equal credence to two companies and had put them at the top of their newly revised list. Division of labor was prudent. Marcus and Tara had shyfted to Malta to investigate Sigrar Twal, the larger of the two companies; a shipping and export business that serviced Europe and the Baltic region. They had shipped half a dozen Oseras to retailers over the past year.

He hunched down in his jacket and lingered under the Dambrin Company's sign to get his bearings. They manufactured a whiskey called Coedhir. Coedhir had a reputation for being rare and quite expensive. Only a few cases were made available each year and, from what the boys discovered, they were purchased through private auction, never through retail. The company had been in business for more than a century, yet never expanded into other products or advertised in the world-wide market.

Ian pulled out his cell and texted Marcus as promised. *Arrived. Quiet. Will keep you posted.*

The hills curved along the horizon and encircled the wide valley with emerald-green pastures and wild flowers as far as he could see. Rock outcroppings jutted here and there, appearing as patches on a speckled canvas through the midday shower. Ian set off down the dirt, puddled path, following Saxon toward the small town that supported the facility. The smell of smoke quickened his pulse, but he relaxed when he realized it came from several chimneys in the village. The chill in the air tickled the back of Ian's neck, and he drew energy until the warmth in his core heated his limbs.

Saxon held up at the fringe of town and rested on the ground, licking his paw. Mud discolored the wolf's snowy coat, and when he stood at Ian's approach, Saxon's chest dripped with what looked like diluted chocolate paint.

"I can't take you anywhere," Ian said. He grabbed Saxon by the scruff of his neck and swiped his hands along the wolf's underbelly, conjuring the mud back to the puddle from whence it came. Saxon snorted and shook his coat, sharing the last of the muddy drops with Ian's jacket.

A rusty, weather-beaten truck pulled out from behind a cottage and turned in their direction. Ian stepped out of the way and gave a nod to the man, whose skin reminded him of a crinkled, brown paper sack. The man tipped his cap, then drove on with sputtering exhaust and squeaky shocks.

It struck Ian that in a town this size, everyone likely knew each other, yet the man didn't show surprise at Ian's presence. He took comfort in the calm, friendly atmosphere and counted on the Primary's guards not having gotten this far, at least not yet.

Saxon nudged him to keep moving. The gentle rain had everyone held up inside and they didn't pass a single soul until the third row of buildings where a middle aged-man leaned against a carved log post. He smoked a long curved pipe and released donut-shaped puffs that reminded Ian of Galen, and a nail pierced Ian's heart at losing his teacher, a father figure, to a Pur traitor. Galen had hailed from nearby Scotland, but that was a lifetime ago, and Ian wouldn't know where to begin, or how, to inquire about his mentor's childhood.

He strolled up to the man as Saxon leapt onto the deck where he stood and sniffed at the man's boots. "Hi," Ian said in English. It was futile to try and blend in since Ian was likely spotted as a foreigner the second they laid eyes on him. "Do you work at the company?" Ian pointed over his shoulder. "My father loves the stuff, and I hoped to get a tour and pictures while I was here."

The man's eyes scanned Ian like a Xerox machine. "The plant is closed. Weekday hours only." He shrugged and gave the guy the best disappointed expression he could conjure, then turned and headed back toward the facility.

Saxon caught up and together they battled the rain shower that had picked up a notch since he'd arrived. Gusts of wind swept his jacket around and he grabbed it, fumbling with the zipper. By the time they strolled back, the wind had become a full-blown storm. Ian drew energy into his core and tried to ease the worst of it, but he couldn't put a dent in the intensity. He ran the last few yards, then paused under a window. He made his way around the building, out of sight from villagers peeking through windows and possibly spotting his emerald corona.

A lower window, next to a door marked Deliveries gave Ian a chance to peek inside without climbing a trellis or standing on kegs. The overcast sky and absence of lights made it difficult to see, and Ian had to squint to make out the contents. He pinpointed a spot, and gave a short whistle. Saxon trotted up, and Ian grabbed his companion, then shyfted inside.

They appeared next to a large lidded vat with a shoot hovering above it. Fermented grains overpowered Ian's sense of smell, and he rubbed his nose on his sleeve. Saxon set out sniffing and exploring while Ian cocked his head and listened. Other than a low hum from another room and occasional drips from overhead pipes, the plant was on a hiatus. He located the main office, but paused at the old office fixtures and lack of modern technology. A single desk offered a stapler, a partially used pad for ordering supplies, and a ledger with handwritten numbers in columns with no headings. A couple of upright file cabinets looked promising, and he conjured away the locks, then flipped through tabs on folders. From what he could see, most of the information pertained to farms where they obtained the variety of grains used for their distillery. Nothing about the company itself. Not even letterhead.

A mom-and-pop operation with a handful of employees wasn't getting Ian any closer to finding Eve or her network.

He stepped out of the office and searched for his cohort. Saxon's snowy mound was plopped down on the balcony overhead with his snout stuck out between the railings. His eyes were closed. "So much for being my lookout," Ian mumbled. The wolf didn't acknowledge. Ian swore he heard snoring. Below the balcony were double-wide doors. Ian opened them and entered a large storage room.

Close to a hundred stacked kegs, at least two yards in diameter and four yards long, were piled on top of each other like a pyramid, filling the storage room from wall to wall. Ian gave up trying to calculate how much of the rare Scotch was being stored in this single space. He pulled out his cell and found the info that Pacman had texted him about the company. Why distribute so little each year when they obviously had made so much?

A change in the air. Ian twisted around. The Primary stood before him. Saxon came alive and growled. Stay, Ian channeled, but the wolf's agitation didn't settle. Saxon had never reacted that way to the Primary before. At movement toward the front of the facility, Ian understood. A few of the elite guard had come with the Primary.

"I won't insult your intelligence and ask why you're here," the Primary said.

"I'll extend the same respect," Ian countered.

The Primary took a couple of steps back and turned his face toward the balcony. "Saxon, join us."

Plodding paws faded overhead. They returned a moment later when the wolf made his way toward Ian, but remained tense and at the alert.

The Primary watched Saxon with interest. "Odd reaction," he said.

"He doesn't play well with your guards." Ian stroked Saxon, but it did little to calm the wolf.

The Primary walked up and ran his finger across the side of a keg. He rubbed his fingers together and took a whiff. "I don't partake." He took in the stored kegs with nothing short of disgust. "Such waste and depletion of Earth's resources. Let this be a lesson, Ian. How one chooses to live their life screams of what they hold dearest in their heart."

Standing this close, Ian stared at the leader of the Pur Weir and struggled to see him as the man responsible for so many deaths in Germany. His entire life, Ian had known him to be a man of peace and tremendous sacrifice for the good of the Earth. Not someone who would condone the slaughter of innocent people.

"I ordered you to stay away." The Primary's voice was eerily calm.

"She tortured me. I want to know why," he said.

"If I can trust the good doctor's report, it's obvious they tried something and failed."

"Why wouldn't you trust Dr. Mac?" Ian said.

"Why, indeed." The Primary faced Ian. "Tell me, how are you feeling since the attack?"

Ian kept his breathing steady, but caught the slight jump in his heartbeat. Was he the only one? "Tired, weak." He rotated his arm. "A little stiff."

"No change in your core?" he asked with a piercing stare.

Ian rubbed his chest. "No."

"Ironic, that the Duach and human were not present," the Primary said. "I'd gathered that you were all inseparable."

Ian's pulse quickened, in spite of his outward calm. "They have their own lives. I haven't been around much. Earth's needs have kept me busy."

"If they had." The Primary turned away. "I might have been forced to isolate them, check into their potential involvement."

"You've never trusted them," Ian said with blistering palms inside clenched fists.

"What concerns me is that you regard them as family." The Primary jerked his chin at someone behind Ian.

He half turned. Falcon stood stock-still and regarded Ian with indifference. "I always will," Ian said. "And if your allegiance is truly to Earth's Heir, you would protect them as you do me."

"The Pur's commitment is to Earth, Ian. Not man. Certainly not to the Duach. You would do well to remember that. It's imperative that we find Eve and put a stop to her rebel forces before they get any bolder." The Primary gestured toward the guard. "Falcon will accompany you home." The guard took a step closer. But Saxon growled and placed himself between Ian and Falcon.

Saxon, back down, Ian channeled, but the wolf ignored him and crouched as if ready to strike. *Saxon!* Ian channeled. *You'll get me in worse trouble than I already am.* A heartbeat later, the wolf compromised with inaudible snarls. "I know the way home," Ian said.

"I'd order you to stay there until we have a handle on the rebels." The Primary grabbed Ian's arm. "But you've repeatedly ignored my efforts to keep you safe. Perhaps it would be prudent to work together to locate her."

"You're the one with the boys' laptop and Rayne's research." At Ian's tone, the Primary's grip tightened around Ian's arm.

"You should have been forthcoming," Falcon said, but earned a disgruntled glance from the Primary. He returned to his stoic stance.

"I can't help you," Ian said. "This is as far as we got before you stole the information." Ian tuned into the Primary's heartbeat. "It was your men who murdered the factory workers, wasn't it?"

He released his hold on Ian's arm and looked Ian in the eye. "I had nothing to do with it." The man's heartbeat never faltered, yet Ian knew it was a lie. "You sound like it's a crime to protect the Earth," the Primary said.

"The end doesn't always justify the means," Ian said, unable to shake the image of the slain factory workers.

"I need to be able to trust you, Ian. Don't force my hand to take more extreme measures." The Primary signaled to another guard. "Komodo, I require your services." The guard approached. Ian recognized him from the estate. He had been assigned to shadow Marcus. Komodo followed the Primary into the storage room and closed the door behind them.

Falcon escorted them outside while Ian kept a firm hand on Saxon. "You have your orders," the guard said.

"I'm curious. What are yours?" Ian said, and looked beyond him into the distillery, but the elite guard shut the door on Ian without responding.

The Primary's message rang loud and clear. If he didn't cooperate, Ian would risk those closest to him. How could Ian not have known this side of the Primary? Had he selectively tuned it out? Would his eyes have been opened, if it hadn't been for Dr. Mac planting the seed?

Ian led Saxon around the corner of the factory and prepared to shyft home. Smoke filtered through a crack in the window at the rear of the building. The storage room had been set ablaze.

Flickers of crimson and amber light reflected in the windows. A second later, a couple of emerald flashes.

Ian called on his connection to the earth and the drizzle became a torrential rain. He held Earth's fire hose in place while he faced what he could no longer control or prevent. A clanking bell and shouts came from the village.

He texted Marcus for their coordinates. The second it appeared on his screen, he drew energy for the shyft and grabbed Saxon, pulling him close, sickened by the man he had respected and admired all his life. A man apparently capable of anything.

{44}

The Mediterranean sunshine blinded Ian the second he and Saxon appeared at the shipping dock. His soaked clothes clung to him. He stepped away from the wolf and ruffled his jacket, then thought better of it and took it off. Saxon shuddered, sending splatters of Welsh rain in all directions.

Ian found Marcus and Tara sitting on a park bench, overlooking the wharf. Massive cargo ships were docked in their berths. A couple of towering cranes swung toward their ships with rectangular crates being loaded. Others dwarfed their tugboat escorts as they made their way in or out of the harbor. Seagulls squawked nearby while the gentle lapping of the ocean licked the rocky pier behind them. The azure ocean waters reminded Ian of Rayne's eyes.

"What'd you find?" Tara asked when Ian took a seat next to her.

"No leads for Eve, but I ran into the Primary and his squad."

Marcus and Tara leaned toward him. "What happened?" Tara said.

"We exchanged words. He threatened me, and when I didn't back down, he tried to get me to help him find Eve." Ian looked at the ground. "I turned him down. He burned the place and left."

Tara grabbed his hand. "There weren't any—"

"No, it was the weekend. The place was deserted." Ian thought back to the amount of dust the Primary found on the kegs, but Ian had also noticed it on the equipment. Had it not been operational for a while?

"This is unbelievable. The Primary . . ." She settled back against the bench.

"Do you still have doubts he was behind it in Germany?" Marcus asked.

Ian shook his head. "Marcus, Dr. Mac said that people have a way of disappearing. What did he mean by that?" Marcus stood and took a few steps toward the water. Ian and Tara exchanged glances, then followed. "The raid on QualSton a few months ago. Other Duach sightings that you and the Drions respond to. What happens to them when you capture them?"

Marcus faced Ian. "I'm surprised it's taken you this long to ask."

"Marcus," Tara said tentatively.

The Drion's evasiveness sent chills up Ian's spine and he feared the truth. "You don't murder them. I can't believe you could be a part of something like that."

"We . . . relocate them," Marcus said. "To somewhere where they won't, and these are the Primary's words, not mine . . . contaminate Earth."

"You take them to Thrae," Ian said.

"That's a death sentence," Tara exclaimed.

"The Primary takes them." Marcus dropped his face. "He's a shyftor, but I've suspected for quite some time that he's capable of much more than that."

"He possesses powers, like Ian?" Tara said.

Ian stared at the gigantic, rusty cargo ships. Civilization populated the globe, in part through human trafficking, slavery, and relocating the persecuted. Had the Weir been incorporating the same brazen practices? "So Thrae is like his very own prison."

"Are they cared for?" Tara asked, her voice growing more shrill with each question. Ian wrapped his arm around her shoulder, but she pushed away.

"Tara, Ian didn't know," Marcus said. "Only the Syndrion are privy to this."

"But he does now." She turned on Ian. "You are the Heir, the leader of all Weir. It's up to you to protect everything that roams across the face of Earth. That includes man and Weir."

"The Duach are our enemies, Tara. They pollute and ignore Earth's needs, using its resources for their own gain." Marcus crossed his arms and jutted his chin at her. "Thrae is nothing more than a prison camp during our ongoing battle with them."

"You said yourself, only the Primary takes them. Who is policing their living conditions? Making sure their basic needs are met?"

"The Primary," Marcus responded.

"Yeah, well, Germany gave us a taste of how little he regards his enemies." She stormed off toward the water's edge.

Marcus's steeled resolve sagged at her parting words. He turned toward the ships. "The boys were mistaken; Sigrar Twal isn't the name of a company. It's a single ship. From what Tara and I could find, it had been in port for almost a week, but left for Spain yesterday."

"Making shyfting on board nearly impossible," Ian said.

"We'd have to know its exact location and its speed at the time of the shyft," Marcus said. "Otherwise we could end up appearing in a steel wall."

"Or in the middle of the Atlantic Ocean and miss the ship entirely." Ian headed for the shipyard. Marcus caught up to him. "Where are you going?"

"I can't return home empty-handed," Ian said. "I don't know how long the Primary stood in the foyer before he made his presence known. Even if he didn't retrieve anything from Pacman's laptop, he still had time to read the list. He may be old, but I'm betting his memory is still intact."

Marcus blocked his path. "Ian, this is turning into a waste of time. We're chasing our own tails. It's obvious Eve's connections are vast and her identity is well hidden. We need to approach this from a different angle."

Tara ran up, waving her cell phone. "The boys have something! I let them know about the glitch with the ship's name. They checked further and," she scrolled up on her screen, "they were able to tap into the ship's manifest and found that it didn't load cargo here in port. Only people. They sent me an attachment. Said that they got a picture off of a security camera." She tapped her screen. A second later, her eyes enlarged and she tilted her cell toward Marcus.

The black-and-white image was quite grainy but undeniably a screenshot of Vael standing between a man and a young woman as they boarded the ship. Marcus grabbed her cell and peered at the image. His knuckles turned as white as the surrounding seagulls. "We need to find that ship," he growled.

"Tara, get back in touch and see what the guys need to calculate a shyft onto a moving vessel, and then get them searching for it." Ian took off for the shipyard and this time, Marcus didn't try to stop him. Saxon sensed a change in mood and ran alongside. Ian's pulse picked up speed as he drew near with one single thought playing over and over. Was Patrick on that ship? But at Marcus's shout from behind, Ian's pace slowed and he stopped for the old general to catch up.

Marcus's expression screamed caution. They were about to infiltrate a ship filled with Eve's rebels.

{45}

The tingling eased, and they appeared on the aft deck of the Sigrar Twal. Ian and Marcus slammed into a cargo bin behind them, and it knocked the breath out of Ian. Tara missed the bin entirely and skidded down the deck on her back. Ian leapt after her and pinned her down until their bodies adjusted to the same speed as the ship.

"Whoa," Marcus shook his head and leaned against the railing.

Ian caught his breath while taking stock of where they had landed. The ship's railing was an arm's length away. If they had appeared three feet over, they would be swimming. "I can't believe that worked," he said, rubbing the back of his head where it had collided with the bin.

"At least the trip home won't be as hazardous." Tara sat up and swiped at the dirt on her jeans.

"Let's make sure we get home." Ian got to his feet, then gave Tara a helping hand.

"I don't see sentries," Marcus said. He and Tara drew their handguns. The trio made their way around the few cargo bins and found a staircase. They cautiously descended, and then paused at the bottom. Ian led them down a central passageway while reviewing the schematic of the ship that the boys had given him. There were crew quarters on the lower deck and then a few large, multi-bunk cabins toward the stern. Evening fast approached and he counted on most of the crew and passengers to be in the mess hall.

Aggravated that he couldn't make out sounds over the engines, Ian relied on shadows and changes in light before turning corners or stepping through open doorways. He hung back when they reached the hall leading to the cafeteria and crouched down under a stairwell.

Their intel indicated twenty-two passengers and twelve crew members. Ian was operating on the belief that they were all Eve's. He looked at Marcus and gave him three fingers to the brow, then pointed them down the hall and tilted them to the left, indicating where the mess hall door was located. Marcus nodded.

The cafeteria door opened and two men stepped out, laughing. One rubbed his stomach, and the other pried his teeth with a toothpick. They shut the door and headed in the opposite direction.

Ian waited until they disappeared around a far corner, then stood and headed for the mess hall door. He bent close, listening, but other than some laughter, he couldn't hear anything. Ian eased the handle and pushed with his hip, counting on the engine noise to drown the opening door.

A loud metallic scrape dashed their element of surprise. He bumped the door wide and walked in like he belonged there.

Three rows of rectangular tables sat end to end with attached benches like picnic tables. Ian counted nine people sitting on either side. No one looked up when he entered the room, otherwise engaged in their food or conversations next to each other.

A man wearing a long white apron with a tight-fitting knit cap walked in carrying a large pot and ladle. He headed for the nearest man, but came up short when he spied Ian. "Attention, Heir on deck!"

Everyone seated at the tables looked up or over their shoulders, rose, and stood at attention.

At the head of the tables, a middle-aged man in a navel uniform pushed his chair back and bowed with a fist to his chest. "Heir, we are honored by your presence." The others turned toward Ian and as one, lowered their gaze with fists to their chests.

Stunned, Ian didn't move. Marcus and Tara pushed in behind him. "At ease," the old general said from behind. The group sat back down and returned to their meal.

"He's not here," Marcus said under his breath. Ian scanned the faces for Vael. No one looked familiar.

The officer remained standing. "Would you like to join us? Tonight's meal is superb."

"Better hurry," the cook said. "This is the last sitting before I clean up the kitchen for the night."

"You know who we are?" Marcus asked.

"Yes, General. We are all Pur Weir," the officer said. "Although your presence is unexpected, you are welcome. I am Captain of the Sigrar Twal." He waved a finger and those closest to him grabbed their plates and relocated to the end of the table, making room for three guests. "Please join us. I imagine you are hungry."

A few stole glances in Ian's direction. He walked over and took a seat next to the captain. The cook left and returned with three fresh plates and silverware. Marcus and Tara sat down across from Ian.

"My son," Marcus said.

"He ate at the first sitting. He often plays billiards in the rec room after dinner," the captain said.

Ian stared at Marcus. "We're searching for a friend of mine. His name's Patrick," Ian said. At the mention of the name, the man next to Ian stiffened. He got up and grabbed his half-eaten plate of food, handed it to the cook, then left, closing the mess hall door behind him. A few others around the table exchanged uneasy glances. In spite of the casual welcome, Ian remained on the alert. Something wasn't right.

"He is not on board," the captain said. "I'm afraid you made the trip in vain."

"I don't suppose you could get me in touch with him," Ian said.

The man shook his head. "I'm afraid not."

"Then why don't you put us in touch with Eve," Marcus said. "We have a lot of questions."

Tara raised her fork and sniffed at the chunk of meat.

The captain gave her a casual smile. "Our chef has a reputation for using a wide variety of culinary spices, but I assure you, poison is not among them."

"Unless you're a rat!" the cook shouted while wiping down his kitchen.

"I need to talk to my son," Marcus said.

"Britta, please escort the general to the rec room," the captain said. A young woman no older than Tara rose and stepped away from the table. "Clear the room when you arrive and give them some privacy," the captain added.

Marcus and Tara stood. When Ian didn't, they paused.

"I'm going to stay," Ian said. "Go, talk to Vael." Marcus left, but Tara sat back down. Ian dug into his meal. "Will you answer my questions?" he asked.

"I doubt that I have the answers you've come for," the captain replied.

Tara stopped chewing. "Do you know who Eve is?"

"She guards her anonymity with an iron fist," the captain responded.

"That's not an answer," Tara said.

"It's the only one we're going to get." Ian took a swig from his water glass. "Where are you headed?"

"You obviously found us through our manifest. So you must know that we're traveling to Barcelona." The captain pushed his emptied plate away and settled back in his chair.

Ian stirred his food around with his fork while weighing their options. "This is delicious."

"I'm glad you dropped by," the captain said like they were long-lost friends.

Tara leaned her elbows on the table and stared at Ian with impatience. This wasn't getting them anywhere. If he could believe the captain, Patrick wasn't here. Neither was Eve. Ian tuned into the beat of the captain's heart. The man was as cool as an iceberg. If he knew anything that would get them one step closer to Patrick or Eve, they'd have to use force.

Ian set his fork down and pushed his plate to the side. "Can you at least tell me that Patrick's okay?"

"He's being treated well," the captain said with more sympathy than Ian had expected.

"Why was he taken?" Tara asked.

"I am not cleared to respond to that," the captain said. "But I can assure you that there's no reason to fear for him."

"The Primary is searching for Eve," Ian said.

"The Primary is often searching for her," he countered.

"This time it may be different. Last night, he slaughtered an entire factory of personnel to send her a message."

The captain's heartbeat picked up speed, but Ian had to give the man credit, his poker-plastered expression never changed. Ian needed him to be unnerved and to understand that following protocol was not in anyone's favor.

"If he catches up to Eve, my friend will be caught in the crossfire," Ian said. "I am desperate to find him before it's too late."

"Eve will already be taking precautions," the captain said as his heartbeat returned to normal. "You do not have anything to worry about." He got the cook's attention. "Pie anyone? You can have it warmed up, even a la mode if you prefer. It's made from cherries grown on Mount Rainier." He licked his lips. "Scrumptious!"

A crimson strobe lit up the room at the same time a screeching alarm sounded. An announcement for all hands on deck came from a loudspeaker.

"What's wrong?" Tara asked, bolting to her feet along with everyone else at the table. She withdrew her handgun from beneath her jacket. It occurred to Ian that the captain never had them frisked. A testament to his arrogance, or trust?

"To your stations," the captain ordered his crew. He stepped to a console on the wall and pressed a button. "Captain, here. What's the emergency?"

"Incoming," the woman stated in a clear and calm voice.

"Ship or aircraft?" he asked.

Static crackled. "Black Hawk helicopters, sir. Radar is picking up five."

Tara and Ian looked at each other. The Primary had found the Sigrar Twal.

{46}

Ian and Tara followed the captain down the hallway, stepping through one doorway after another, and then up two flights of stairs to the ship's bridge.

From the outside, the freighter appeared rusted and unkempt, yet the accommodations and instrumentation inside its walls were state of the art.

A man in greasy overalls and a scruffy beard stiffened at attention. "Captain on the bridge!" His shock when Ian followed stole the man's voice for a second. "And, Pur Heir."

"ETA?" the captain asked.

"Three minutes, sir." The woman never lifted her face from the radar screen.

"Are you equipped with weapons?" Ian asked.

The captain turned to Ian. "Sire, I recommend that you and your party shyft home immediately."

"I'm not deserting you," Ian said.

"Drion Marcus is still below with his son," Tara added.

"Permission to enter the bridge," Marcus said from the doorway.

"Permission granted," the captain said.

Marcus stepped in with Vael close behind.

"Please, this is our battle, not yours, General," the captain said. "As one commanding officer to another, I am ordering you off my ship."

"Not a chance in hell," Marcus said. "They wouldn't dare attack if it's made known that the Heir and a member of the Syndrion are on board."

Ian didn't share Marcus's optimism. "If there's trouble, you're coming with us," Ian said to Vael.

"Hell no!" he said. "I'm with them."

"Let me talk to them. This debate may be premature," Marcus shouted over the alarm.

A dark mass skirted across the row of windows, followed by two more helicopters. Their thumping blades rattled the windows with such tremendous force that Ian was shocked the glass didn't shatter.

"That's three," the captain yelled.

"Two are hovering at a distance, sir," the radar operator said.

"You can't afford to be found on board," the captain said. "Sire, I must insist that you and the others go."

Ian grabbed Marcus's arm and pulled him to the side. "Marcus, if you're not on the Primary's hit list, you will be if you're found on a rebel ship in the middle of the Atlantic."

"Rebels or not, these people are Pur Weir. I won't leave them to the same fate as the factory workers." Marcus regarded his son. "Vael told me things, Ian. The Primary has secrets. You and I need to talk."

"I'll confront them," Ian said. "You stay hidden. I'm not losing you, too. If things turn south, promise me you'll shyft Tara and Vael to the estate."

The old general nodded.

"Ian, you're not facing them alone," Tara said.

"You're at risk as much as Drion Marcus," Ian said. "They weren't surprised to see me in Wales. My presence isn't going to escalate things. Stay here, out of sight." Ian left the bridge and hurried downstairs. Once his feet touched the main deck, he took off, drawing them away from the bridge, while his thoughts searched frantically for the words to make this go away.

Storm clouds blew a gale over the deck. Waves struck the side of the Sigrar Twal. Sitting high in the water with her nearly empty hull, she rocked violently as Ian struggled to get his fears under control.

He reached the helicopter pad and waved his arms, shouting up at the circling force. One copter veered close and hovered about twenty feet off the deck. Ian planted his feet and stood facing it. The side door slid open and Falcon crouched low, looking at Ian. A moment later, the guard stood, signaled, and they lowered the helicopter onto the deck.

The blades revved down but did not shut off.

Falcon approached Ian with an automatic weapon slung over his shoulder. "You were ordered to remain at your estate, Sire."

"I rarely do what I'm told," Ian shouted over the helicopter's engine. "Eve is not here. They're a Pur Weir merchant ship and presently have no cargo of value. There's no reason for the Primary to take his frustrations out on innocent people."

"We were ordered to search the ship. That's what we intend to do." He lifted his gun like it was his calling card. "If they have nothing to hide, why interfere?"

"Because I don't approve of your methods." If the Primary was in one of the helicopters, he was staying out of it. They do his dirty work and he keeps his hands clean, Ian thought. "Where's the Primary? I demand to address this with him."

"He is meeting with the Syndrion."

Marcus hadn't been summoned. If Falcon was telling the truth, the old general was deliberately omitted from the meeting. Ian's chaotic thoughts crashed against a solid wall. They carried weapons. The general was a shyftor.

Ian turned and shyfted onto the bridge, but a wall of energy stopped him cold and he catapulted down the outside metal staircase. Ian landed hard on the upper deck.

Someone on the bridge had a jam.

Ian rushed up the stairs to the sound of gunfire and screams. He threw open the door and was met with a thick cloud of metallic air.

The elite guard's weapons were turned on the room, slaughtering the captain and his crew. Tara and Marcus were constrained to the side, struggling against their captors. Tara screamed at the carnage.

Ian burst into the room and tackled the closest guard. His bullets rose upward as the gun slipped from his grasp, and the guard fell into the gunman next to him.

Searing heat pierced Ian's side. His legs buckled beneath him and he slumped to the floor.

"You idiots! The Heir's been shot!" Falcon shouted from the open doorway.

"It must have been a ricochet," someone said.

They rolled Ian to his side. Tara fell to her knees and pressed her hand against the wound. "Stand back, you bastards!" She fought them off like a mother tiger. Her tears dripped on Ian's cheek and she sobbed while pressing down hard against his wound.

"Breathe!" Marcus cried while compressing Vael's bloody chest. He bent down and listened, and then continued his efforts to resuscitate his son.

Blood splattered the consoles and walls like a Pollock painting. Bodies with staring, lifeless eyes littered the floor. The captain's among them. "They were Pur. Our own people," Ian groaned.

"With allegiance to someone other than you," Falcon hissed.

The flyby wasn't a show of strength. It was to give their shyftors a visual location and a chance to match the speed of the ship, enabling them to appear on the bridge. While Ian was out on deck trying to ease the situation, they'd taken it from behind. He had cautioned the captain not to use force. He'd fed right into their hands.

Komodo grabbed Marcus's arm, but he pulled away and pressed down on Vael's chest wound. "Get a medic in here!" Marcus screamed.

"We're to take you to the Primary," Komodo said.

"No," Ian moaned and tried to get up, but blistering spikes shut his body down. "Drion Marcus was here to protect me," Ian said, but his plea came out in a whimper.

"We've been ordered to take him into custody," Falcon said from behind Ian.

Ian fought the looming darkness, but despair engulfed him and drew him into an abyss. This time, the rebel's blood was on his hands.

{47}

A finger against his forehead woke Ian from his dreamless sleep. Dr. Mac leaned over him with a core thermometer pressed to his chest.

"He's awake. Now give me some space and let me examine my patient!"

Falcon stepped back and took a stoic stance next to the bedroom wall.

"You're home," Dr. Mac said, shaking out his thermometer. "They brought me to the ship. I had to do surgery and remove the bullet before they could shyft you home and get you in your boost. The storm your condition elicited, made for a tricky surgery."

"You saw," Ian sputtered. It came out raspy, fretful.

Dr. Mac gave him a solemn nod.

"Vael?" Ian asked.

"He's not yet out of danger."

Ian closed his eyes. So much blood. "How long?"

"You've been in your boost two days. You're not completely healed, but close. I want you to take it easy and eat what Milo fixes you." Dr. Mac turned and glared at Falcon.

"Really, do you have to suffocate us both! Give the Heir some space. Does it look like he's going anywhere?"

Falcon stared at Dr. Mac with something short of contempt, then walked to the doorway and stood just outside the bedroom with the door wide open.

Dr. Mac laid a gentle hand on Ian's shoulder. "What were you thinking, my boy. Getting in the middle of this war?"

"It's like trying to put out a raging wildfire by myself." Ian kept an eye toward the hall. "But things came crashing down around me. People were slaughtered because of me."

"You must stop acting like you can take the world on by yourself. This is a hell of a lot bigger than you," Dr. Mac barked, but then paused and softened his voice. "You're not alone." Dr. Mac pulled back the covers and lifted the edge of the bandage. He pressed his fingertips next to the healing wound and ripped off the bandage. Ian winced at the momentary sting. Dr. Mac handed him his cell phone. "Get rid of this," the old doctor hissed under his breath.

Ian closed his eyes at his blunder. It was how the Primary knew where to send his guards. The tracking chip in his cell phone had led the way.

He grabbed Dr. Mac's arm and met his gaze, counting on the look in his eyes to convey how sorry he was that he had doubted him. He'd gotten Marcus arrested. Like hell he'd put Dr. Mac in more danger than he already was. "I give up. I won't get anyone else killed. The Primary and his hit squad can do their dirty work without me," Ian said loud enough to ensure that Falcon would relay Ian's message.

"I'm glad you've come to your senses." Dr. Mac cleared his throat and tilted his head toward the bathroom. "When you're strong enough, get cleaned up." He packed the last few instruments in his bag and latched it. "There's nothing else I can do. The rest is up to you." Dr. Mac's bent back straightened. "Now, your sorry bum has kept my other patients waiting long enough." He walked out of the room. "Next time, make an appointment before you step in front of a bullet!"

The Primary's guard fell in behind Dr. Mac and they disappeared down the hall.

Falcon escorted Dr. Mac home and never returned. The Primary didn't sequester Ian and Tara, probably in hopes that Ian would lead them to Eve.

Nothing eased Ian's guilt. Tara needed to release her own demons and chose to take what happened on the Sigrar Twal out on him in the gym. Ian welcomed the physical pain, unable to extinguish the emotional and mental anguish.

Ian had never seen her so full of unbridled rage. She came at him with a primal scream and kept swinging her sword, abandoning all protocol, like a wild, crazed animal.

Spent, Tara's sword clanged against the gym floor, and she fell to her knees. Ian gathered her up in his arms. "I'm sorry. I'm sorry," he moaned until he had no breath left and his voice silenced. She went limp beneath his embrace, unable or unwilling, to lift her arms in response.

Ian left her slumped in the middle of the gym and shyfted to his room. He showered amidst racing thoughts about how to connect with Dr. Mac in secret. One thing was for certain, the tracking chip would be left behind.

When Ian stepped out of the shower, he hesitated. The steam had revealed a hand-scrawled message on his mirror.

What's in a name?

He walked up and stared at it through his reflection. Had Dr. Mac left a clue?

The odor of baking bread filled Ian's bedroom, and a tray of warm rolls sat on his bed. He threw some clothes on and found Milo in the kitchen kneading a massive mound of dough, releasing his frustrations in a cloud of flour, creating rolls that no one would have the appetite to eat.

The caretaker slammed a fist into the dough and didn't remove it. "Don't take Tara," he said.

"What are talking about?" Ian settled on the stool across from him.

"I know Mac left you a message. I saw it when I went to check on you."

"Do you know what it means?" Ian said.

"Not a clue. The Primary's guard watched him like a hawk when he came to patch you up. Mac must have done it when he turned his back for a second."

"Why not tell me outright? Why make me guess at its meaning?"

"In case the bastard followed him into the bathroom when he took a piss! Hell I don't know how that old coot's brain works half the time." Milo stirred the contents of his boiling pot, but the spoon slipped, disappearing into the boiling liquid. He leaned against the counter. "Mac's in this up to his ass, isn't he?"

"He's never come out and admitted it, but I think he's—"

"Don't tell me," Milo snapped. A second later, the old caretaker fished his wooden spoon out of the pot. "Maybe you both still believe you can fix this, but there's been enough spilt blood to fill that lake out there. Tara's won't be added. You hear me?" Milo said.

"She won't forgive me." Ian looked at him. "She'll hate us both."

He grunted. "Better her wrath, than eternal silence."

"Take Saxon," Ian said. The wolf raised his head and whined. *I don't know where I'm going, or for how long,* Ian channeled. *I need you to protect them until I can return.* Ian slid off the stool. "It's not safe here, not anymore."

"I've got us some options that the Syndrion don't know about." Milo separated a glob of dough and rolled the sticky ball between his hands. "But we'll have to figure out a way to communicate that they can't track."

"Destroy Tara's cell phone. I think that's how they've been tracking us." Ian glanced toward the hallway. "Do the boys know about Marcus?" Ian said.

"Tara told them."

"I need them to help me figure out the clue," Ian said.

"They're asleep in the great room. Why those two prefer couches and chairs over the beds upstairs is beyond me. Get them up. It's past five in the afternoon." Milo pulled a tray of golden-crusted rolls from the oven and took a whiff. "They can't go home," he said. "Without Marcus's protection, the Syndrion will torture them to find out where you've gone."

"I know." Ian followed the amber glow of a virtual screen into the great room.

What's in a name? Ian stood, staring at the floating data while trying to decipher Dr. Mac's cryptic clue. He walked around the columns, as if looking at it backward, then forward again would somehow bring it into perspective.

Ian scratched along his jaw. Something about the names. "Xander!"

A snort came from the couch behind him. Pacman had curled up in the chair.

"What?" Xander said and rubbed his eyes. He sat up and gave into a silent, wide yawn that wiggled one ear.

"How do I rearrange the data?" Ian asked. He poked at one of the words and its pixels dispersed, then corrected themselves.

"Here." Xander hunted and pecked something out on his laptop with one hand while ruffling his hair with the other. Several key strikes later, he leaned back. "Have at it."

"Did you save what was up here?"

"Does a sunbathing chimp use banana oil?"

Ian hesitated, unsure how to respond, but Xander indicated to go ahead with a backhanded wave. Ian pinched the floating pixels, but they dispersed between his fingers.

"It's not grab and squeeze," Xander said on the heels of a shrill yawn. "Think of a touch screen on a tablet. Just use the tip of your finger and drag it to where you want."

It took a bit of practice, but Ian soon got the hang of it. He separated all of the proper nouns into two columns, one for the company names, and the other with the product names. Then created a column for the women's first names, and another for last names. He stood back and studied the four columns.

What's in a name? He mulled over the clue, but the longer he stared, the warmer his core grew, and gusts of wind rattled the windows. He walked away and paced behind the couch. What's in a name?

"Hell, those two are gobblygoop to me," Xander said, wiggling fingers at the foreign companies and international product columns. His mumbled attempt at pronouncing the Maltese shipping company name ended in garbled sounds. Ian lobbed the correct pronunciation at him from over his shoulder. Xander then tried the name of the whiskey, but Pacman spoke up from under a curtain of sleepy eyelids and pronounced it correctly. "I looked that one up," he added.

"What does it mean?" Xander said lying down on the couch. He threw his arm over his eyes.

"Long trees," Pacman said, stretching out in all directions over the rolling arms of the chair. A second later, he went limp like a rag doll. "Why would anyone name a gut-burning drink after trees?"

"Whiskey is made from trees?" Xander asked from under his arm. "I'm sticking with beer."

Pacman shushed his underage drinking confession.

"It's made from a variety of grains," Ian said. Pacman opened one eye and turned it toward Ian. "That's what I found when I got there," Ian said without breaking a step.

"Seems stupid calling it *long* trees." Xander rolled over, pressing his face into the couch cushion. "Wouldn't it be tall trees," he mumbled.

Ian's steps came to an abrupt halt. He stared at the list while his thoughts scrambled to open and dust off drawers of old lessons, rapidly applying the multiple languages he'd learned from his years growing up in Europe.

A pattern emerged at the same time a chill coursed through his limbs. The truth stared him in the face. It was here all along. There had been no need to track the rebel leader across the globe. Ian sank to the arm of the couch. He'd wasted so much time on a goose chase of his own making.

He knew where to look for Patrick, but even more disturbing—he knew who Eve was.

{48}

Ian grabbed a picture of Patrick and his mother, taken at their estate in the Hamptons. The Langtrees had residences all over the world, but Ian had never visited any of them. Patrick never cared to. The photo was all that Ian had as a starting point until the boys could get him addresses if the Hampton residence came up empty.

He set the photo on the foyer table, focused on a location, and shyfted to the spot depicted in the image. Ian appeared on the back patio where its concrete railing attached to the back of the house.

It was after 10:00 p.m. on the east coast, and the chatter of katydids greeted him. At the hoot of an owl, Ian looked up and counted five smokestacks along the expansive roof. His heart sank when he peered through the window and didn't find lights on; only ghostly sheets covering the furniture. It struck him as odd there were no security lights outside or, from what he could tell, inside. Were there motion detectors?

Ian took the chance and shyfted inside the great room, but stood still, listening and searching for security cameras. Other than the rhythmic ticktock coming from a grandfather clock at the front of the house, the mansion slept.

The boys were the only ones to know where Ian had gone. They were hiding out in Rayne's neighborhood at a small rental bungalow with enough supplies, including licorice, gum, and gift cards for pizza delivery, to last a month or more. Ian was counting on them playing video games and to not sticking their heads out the door for weeks.

He had wanted to spare Tara and Milo the truth. That JoAnna Langtree had duped them all. But if he were honest, it was pure selfishness, wanting the confrontation to be his alone. His head swam, unable to fathom that her answers could make sense of it. The woman he'd thought of as a surrogate mother had Ian tortured, burned alive from the inside out. How could she do that and still look him in the eye? At that instant a revelation hit him: she had been at the mansion when the Book of the Weir was stolen.

Ian set out combing the downstairs. In almost every room, pieces of JoAnna's past came to light. He discovered framed awards, letters of congratulations, and more than one diploma in the study. He was shocked to find that she graduated from Yale with an archeology degree. Patrick had never shared any of his parents' lives with Ian. It struck him that there was nothing about his father on display anywhere. His parents had lived separate lives for decades.

In the center of the study, a lanyard hung from an intricately carved sculpture depicting a mother wolf fending off a looming bear. The chiseled date on the side indicated it was from the fifteenth century. The statue was displayed prominently on a podium. He fingered the pass, out of place in an otherwise meticulous room. It felt like an invitation.

He grabbed the lanyard and stuffed it into his pocket, then made his way up the winding staircase to check the bedrooms. When he stepped into the last one at the far end of the east wing, he paused and sniffed. Cleanser and furniture wax had permeated the house, but this odor was isolated to one bedroom.

The scent led Ian to a bathroom where it was at its strongest inside the tub. He ran his finger along the inside and a purple crust came off on his finger. When he opened the medicine cabinet to check inside, a hand-scribbled message appeared on the opposite mirror. Ian closed the cabinet, and the message disappeared. He opened it again and realized that the moonlight's reflection was what made it visible.

Ian left the cabinet open and peered at the scrawled lines. The top word was smeared. He took the first letter to be a capital *K* and made out what he could only guess was the word, *Kyre*. The word below it was nearly intact and much clearer than the one above. *Alive.*

He resumed his search, while mulling it over. It wasn't a name from Rayne's research. Was Dr. Mac here earlier? Was this another clue? Ian stopped in his tracks. Was the K really an R? His pulse quickened as he examined the word in his head. The r between the y and e could have been the letter n. Was the top word Rayne?

Adrenaline fueled his legs. He searched the mansion more thoroughly, and chose to retrace some of his steps with renewed eyes. But his elation had fizzled by the time he reached the lowest level and discovered nothing that would get him one step closer to finding Eve. Ian didn't get a signal in the cement basement, so he returned to the back patio and called the boys using the burner phone. Pacman picked up.

"Whoa, Tara's turned psycho," Pacman said. "It's kinda sexy."

"She isn't e-mailing you to get a date," Xander shouted from nearby. "She's figured out that we helped the Heir." Scuffling. Xander's voice grew louder. "But you're our bro and our lips are sealed."

"Promise me you'll get me a date with her," Pacman yelled. "Once you save the world and all!"

"Where am I going next?" Ian said over an explosion in the background. He hoped it was coming from a video game.

"You would think that billionaires would have a slew of palaces, but if they do, they're not in their names," he said. Xander popped his bubble gum close by. Squealing tires, muted shouts.

He fingered the pass in his pocket. "Try cross-referencing the women's names with residences. And add Kyre to the list."

"Already on it," Pacman said. "We'll keep you posted."

"We've got your back, fearless leader—" the call ended, cutting off Xander's parting words.

Ian pulled the pass from his pocket and looked the museum up on his cell, found the address and business hours, then shyfted to Denver, Colorado. The mountain time zone was a couple of hours earlier than New York and the hustle and bustle of late-evening downtown traffic filled the air. Ian stepped out from behind the sign at the entrance and peered through the glass front doors. Security lights lit up hallways beyond the lobby where a towering T-rex skeleton stood to greet patrons with a toothy snarl. The museum had been closed for more than an hour, but security might be doing a sweep.

He shyfted behind a tall sign in the lobby and increased the electromagnetic energy in his core to wreak havoc with security cameras. He grabbed a map at the information counter, then hurried deeper into the museum, impressed by the displays and featured exhibits.

Voices and the sound of a motor moving along the floor came from the second story. He pulled the pass from his pocket and studied it further. It struck Ian that JoAnna was significantly younger in the picture of her at the museum. Egyptian Studies was listed underneath her photo, and he wondered if an internship had brought her here decades earlier. Ian referred to his map and found the indicated hall. It took him by the minerals exhibit where dim lights glinted off of milky quartz the size of a knight's shield and an amethyst bigger than his fist.

Ian stepped into the Egyptian exhibit at the end of the hall and came to a halt. JoAnna stood in the middle of the room, looking down at a mummy lying in a glass case.

Patrick's mother didn't look up. "She had the most contagious laugh. I made sure she found a good home." She planted a two-finger kiss on the glass case, just over the mummy's face. "Hello, Ian."

"JoAnna," Ian said. He glanced around and listened to the room. There were only two heartbeats, the racing one was his. He approached with caution. "Or would you rather I call you Eve?"

"Eve, please." A relaxed smile defined her lips and she rested her arms on the mummy case. "Did you enjoy learning about me? Patrick didn't know I had a career as an archeologist before devoting myself to my new role as JoAnna Langtree. He had no idea that his socialite mother used to dig in the dirt, uncovering artifacts." She looked at the mummy. "Friends, across the globe." She rubbed the palm of one hand. "The calluses took their sweet time to fade."

"Where is he?" Ian demanded.

"You'll see him soon. I wanted a chat first." She sat on a bench and patted the seat beside her. "Like old times."

Was she remembering their first encounter? Ian on a park bench beside a proud mother bragging about her son. She crouching down to smell the yellow roses before leaving the park.

"We didn't meet by chance, did we?"

"I leave very little to chance," Eve said.

"You introduced Patrick into my life. Nurtured our relationship. Why?"

"To keep friends close, and potential enemies, even closer." She pursed her lips. "You and Patrick had to learn to work together, but more importantly, to trust one another.

Given who you are and who he was to become, it was critical that you not be enemies."

"Why kidnap your own son?"

"He needed to discover his path for himself. You couldn't be a part of that." She stood and approached. "But your destinies have always been entwined." She locked her fingers together and pressed them into a fist. "Now, you must learn to work together as a team."

"We've always been a team, JoAnna." Ian caught himself. "Eve. You never had faith in him, not like I did."

"You're wrong, Ian. I've always known what Patrick was capable of." A bright flash reflected in her pupils. Strong arms locked around him from behind and lifted him off his feet.

"Play nice, boys," Eve said.

A frigid blast of magnetic energy engulfed him. The shyft robbed Ian's gasp as the air sucked from his body. The second they appeared, an arctic shudder rippled through Ian and he was shoved onto a hardwood floor. He rolled onto his back and faced Jaered. "You bastard!"

"Really, that's the best you've got?" Jaered gave him a smirk. "I expected a lot worse."

Ian got to his feet. "You burned me up from the inside out!"

"You got your payback, and then some!"

It took a second for Ian's thoughts to catch up to his rage. "Rayne. Is she all right?"

"No, thanks to you." Jaered flexed his shoulder. "After nearly killing her, I'd kiss that relationship good-bye."

Ian dropped his head and rammed it into Jaered's abdomen, lifting him off his feet. He then fell on top of him, pummeling him with his fists.

Jaered threw his arms up, blocking the worst of the blows, but suffering others. Blood splattered across the polished floorboards. He managed to wrap his legs around Ian. With a twist of his hips, he flipped Ian onto his back, then pinned his arms down. "You fight with your emotions. I've got my work cut out for me."

Ian fought the constraint, but Jaered was incredibly strong. He soon relented. Ian went to draw power, but his core sputtered. He growled.

"Super jam. You aren't going anywhere." Jaered got off of him and licked a drizzle of blood at the corner of his mouth. He pressed a palm to his jaw and winced. "Eve figured we'd kill each other if we had our powers."

Ian got to his knees and coughed. The pressure didn't ease and made it impossible to draw a deep breath. It was the high-powered jam, not Jaered, that crushed his core. "Turn it off!" he barked.

Jaered chuckled and walked away.

The rebel had shyfted them to a small indoor basketball arena. There were several rows of seats flanking both sides, rising from the hardwood floor at the center. A narrow platform, midway up gave way to an upper level of rows. Arched windows highlighted the curved ceiling and topped off the impressive building. Basketball hoops faced each other from opposite ends.

Movement in the topmost row. Patrick sat, staring at Ian. His friend's hands were free from restraint, and he kept rubbing his palms across his legs. The distance couldn't mask Patrick's terror.

Ian scrambled to his feet.

Jaered chose a seat in the first row, center court. He plopped down and stuck his legs out in front of him, then reclined back like settling in for a show.

Ian took off, rushing up the stairs.

Patrick waved his hands, "Ian, stop! Don't!"

"I wouldn't do that if I were you," Jaered called out.

"Fuck you!" Ian shouted from over his shoulder.

"Then have at it." Jaered raised a thumb into the air.

Ian cleared the lower level, crossed the platform, and kept climbing.

Patrick got out of his seat and backed up. He pressed his fist to his chest. "Ian, please," he moaned.

The heat in Ian's core intensified. It took a second to realize, it wasn't from exertion. His steps slowed. When he turned into Patrick's row, the walls of his core shuddered and constricted. He stopped and leaned against the back of the seat—stunned.

Patrick grimaced and met Ian's gaze.

The unspoken truth passed between them as Ian stared at his friend, measuring the distance that would forever define their relationship. A bridge that neither could cross.

Ian backed down the steps until his core returned to normal. Patrick sank into a nearby seat and buried his face in his hands. Ian glared at Jaered across the way. The rebel's smug attitude was gone.

"You made him a Duach," Ian snarled.

"He always was." Jaered got to his feet and wandered out to center court. "We need to talk."

"Ian, listen to what we have to say." Patrick descended the stairs at the far end of the arena. "This isn't about the Pur and the Duach. This is so much greater than that."

It was the same thing Jaered told Ian weeks earlier. He closed his eyes. The rebels had gotten to Patrick. His mother had made him Ian's natural enemy. Keep your friend close, but your enemy closer. He didn't know who to trust anymore.

Ian descended the steps, retreating from Patrick, searching for an exit. When he reached the platform he paused. "Where's Rayne?"

"On Thrae," Jaered said. "The fire forced me to parashyft. It was either that, or die."

Ian's legs threatened to buckle. She was in the one place he couldn't go. He'd lost the two people closest to him. He stumbled down the stairs, picking up speed as rage flushed his despair.

"Ian!" Patrick shouted and hurried after him, but Jaered waved at Patrick to stay back.

Ian reached the bottom step and took off for the closest doorway. He ended up in a hall and followed the exit signs until he came to double-wide metal doors. He shoved them open, but threw his hand up, blinded by brilliant, natural light. He didn't get but a few yards before coming to a halt. Shock cemented his feet to the ground. The super jam extended beyond the arena. Unable to draw energy to shyft, Ian found he couldn't pull enough heat into his core to warm himself. He shivered and rubbed his arms.

A wall of ice stood not fifty yards away, spilling over an ocean cliff. Frigid blasts of wind rocked him on his feet. The back of the iridescent-blue glacier swept up toward jagged mountain peaks zigzagging across the horizon. They framed the valley where the arena stood, the only building in sight.

Footsteps from behind. Ian didn't turn around. "Where am I?"

"Greenland," Jaered said. "Listen, I know you don't trust me."

"Trust?" Ian scoffed. "Even hate doesn't come close." He shuddered and his teeth chattered when a strong gust swept over him.

"I've given you reason, I admit that," Jaered said. "But Rayne is stranded on Thrae. We need to get her back to Earth before Aeros hunts her down and kills her."

"You're the rebel. You do it." At a sideways glance, Ian caught something in Jaered's hand. A remote. "Turn off the jam. You don't need me. You've got your new Sar."

A fury rose in Jaered's eyes and Ian swore his iris's turned to flames. "You don't get it," he snarled. "I can't go back, and he's not strong enough, not yet." Jaered pointed toward the door. "You're the only one who can save her."

"I nearly killed her," Ian said. His voice drained with the last of his warmth. "I thought I had."

"If you leave, she is as good as dead. But not until Aeros has his fun. He's *our* enemy, yours *and* mine." Jaered pointed the remote at Ian like an accusing finger. "Either work with us to save her and defeat him, or go back to the Weir's senseless civil war, fueled by the shortsighted and closed-minded." He tossed the remote at Ian's feet. "Your choice." He let himself inside without looking back, and the metal door shut with a ferocious clang.

Ian wasn't sure how long he stood, staring at the remote.

If he didn't return, what would Milo and Tara's fate be? Would the Primary hunt them down, imprison them, like he had Marcus. Or worse?

He didn't trust Jaered, but Patrick changed everything. Shyft home, screamed in his head, before it's too late, but the home he knew didn't exist any longer and the image of Rayne in the fiery vortex was too vivid to ignore. If he was responsible for her being trapped on Thrae, how could he walk away?

He returned with uncertain steps, shutting the door behind him. Patrick and Jaered sat in the stands at opposite sides of the arena, hunched over with their heads hung low, like opposing counsel awaiting a verdict.

Ian came to a stop under the basketball hoop and swallowed hard. "How much time does she have?"

"I don't know." Jaered came alive and got to his feet. "Not long."

Ian pressed the button on the remote. The god-awful pressure lifted, and he took a deep breath while drawing energy into his core. "I can't leave Earth—it'll self-destruct."

"That's just the tip of an iceberg of lies," Jaered said. He descended the stairs, but held back from the bottom step.

Patrick started down. "There's so much you don't know. Rayne isn't the only one on Thrae. Your mother is there, too."

Ian's nostrils flared. "I need the truth. No more lies."

"Show him," Jaered said.

Patrick hesitated, then slowly unbuttoned his shirt, pulling it back and exposing his left breast.

When Ian found his voice, it came out barely above a whisper. "I suspected there might be two." He looked at Patrick. "But you . . ."

"There's more to this than rescuing Rayne," Patrick said. "It's about saving Earth."

"It goes way beyond that." Jaered pulled his T-shirt off. "This is about saving the universe."

The Heir's Seal on the Thraen's chest turned Ian's thawed pulse to ice. He pressed a fist to his left breast. With three Heirs standing on the floor of the arena, in the formation of a triangle, he finally grasped what Dr. Mac tried to tell him. The world, hell, the universe was vast, but for the first time in his life, Ian wasn't alone.

***

Glossary

Book of the Weir: A volume of letters and notes kept by the Ancient Weir Counsel. It is rumored to include secrets to the Sars powers and predicts the coming of the Heir.

boost: A device that draws elements from the planet, such as calcium or proteins, to aid in healing. The boost is fueled by the energy stored in a Sar's core.

Channels: A set of identical Weir twins who share a genetic marker with a Sar. The three are able to communicate telepathically or, when standing close enough together, the Sar may receive visions or eavesdrop on the thoughts of others.

core: Sars are born with a core, deep in the center of their chest. It allows them to control, and contain, energy drawn from the planet. Not all cores are alike, and therefore, it dictates what power they yield. If a core extinguishes, the Sar dies.

core blast: Known as the Dragon's Breath during the Dark Ages. A core power that enables a Sar to draw and manipulate energy from below the surface of the planet. Scholars believe, from the center of the Earth.

corona: A colorful gas that's created when a Sar uses a vortex. If a Pur steps into a vortex field and draws energy into their core, the gases turn green. When a Duach uses the field, the gases turn red.

Curse: An unpleasant, often excruciating reaction when a Pur Sar and a Duach Sar come in close proximity to each other. Developed by the Ancients, it prevents the Duach and the Pur from stealing each other's powers, a barbaric practice which often results in death.

Duach: \dū-ôk\ A rebellious group of Weir who use their powers for self-gain. They are considered the black sheep of the Weir and are despised by the Pur for their narcissistic ways.

Heir: The Ancients predicted the eventual decline of the Weir race and predicted the coming of the Heir, the last Sar born to the Weir. Prophesy stated that he would be born with the most powerful of cores, and thus, inherit all of the combined powers of the Weir Sars that came before him. Since the Weir keep the energies of Earth in harmony, the planet would continue to survive.

mark: In ancient times, known as a Seal. A triangular image of raised skin found on the left breast of Sars. Only the Heir's mark is a triangle that houses a sun. Weir males born without a mark are powerless.

paral: Someone from Earth and someone from Thrae who are the mirror image of each other.

parashyfting: Crossing into an alternate dimension during a shyft. A powerful vortex stream or field is required. Only Sars born with the shyfting power can parashyft.

Primary: The head of the Syndrion.

Pur: \pūr\ Thought of as the original and longest practicing of the Weir. They continue to work tirelessly for the good of the planet and to lessen man's impact on the world and other living creatures.

The Rising: A Weir practice, designed to draw a Sar's powers to the surface. Only held in the event of a Sar not discovering their powers naturally.

Sar: A firstborn Weir male who's inherited a core, granting them control over a single Earthly power. Most Sars control plants or animals. Sars born with rare powers, such as shyfting or core blast powers, are the most revered and sought after.

shyft/shyfting: \shift\ The ability to teleport. The Sar's core allows him to use one of thousands of vortex energy fields or streams found across Earth in order to move around the surface of the planet.

shyftor: \shif-tor\ A Sar born with the shyfting power doesn't need a vortex to shyft over short distances.

Somex: \sôm-ex\ A Sar born with the somex power can control neurotransmitters in the brain that affect consciousness.

Syndrion: \sin-drī-un\ The Weir counsel. Ever since the Duach broke away from traditional practices centuries earlier, the current Syndrion is made up of only Pur Sars. Representatives from each continent serve on the counsel.

Thrae: \thrā\ Earth's twin planet in an alternate dimension.

vortex: A specific location where energy fields emanate from the planet surface and circulate on invisible gases.

Weir: \wē-er\ Magical stewards of the Earth who have lived quietly among humans for more than two thousand years. Their purpose is to ensure harmony between Earth's various energies and all living creatures. With each generation, there are fewer Weir Sars born with a connection to the Earth. The Weirs' power is dwindling, and along with it, their control of Earth's combined energy. As a result, natural disasters are on the rise in frequency and intensity.

A Message from the Author and a Sneak Peek Ahead

I hope you enjoyed reading Sleight of Hand, Book Three: The Weir Chronicles. To get caught up on the series, don't miss Fade to Black, Book One or Masks and Mirrors, Book Two of The Weir Chronicles available wherever books are sold.

To receive the latest news about the series, visit my website at www.sueduff.com. Add your name to the fan email list to receive notices about book events, the latest information on upcoming novels in the series, and more.

Here's a peek at the next exciting adventure in the series, *Stack A Deck, Book Four: The Weir Chronicles* appearing winter, 2017.

Rayne stumbled, but the tight pull on the tether in either direction helped to keep her on her feet. The dust clouds swallowed up Liem and Gwynn. The pressure of the cord around her waist was a miniscule beacon of comfort and safety.

They made their way along the protective side of the dome. The meteors, that weren't dissolved by the field, bounced over them as they came sliding off the sloped dome. Rayne took shuffling steps, but Liem's constant tug on the rope forced her feet to keep moving. The pull of gravity taxed her muscles, but she barely noticed. Her attention remained on controlling her pulse. She needed to conserve her oxygen.

"How are you doing?" Gwynn's voice sounded in Rayne's ear.

"I'm okay," she said, but it came out raspy.

Gwynn had warned Rayne not to touch the dome for fear she'd corrupt the only thing keeping the Thraens alive. The shower of meteors made that a challenge. Many were the size of microwaves. Rayne couldn't help but stoop whenever they came crashing toward her. Miraculously, they bounced over their heads and landed a few feet away, kicking up clouds of dust. Gwynn had promised they would, thanks to the curvature and power emitted from the dome.

"I'm getting more activity ahead." The edge in Liem's voice put Rayne on the alert.

"Retrace your steps to find Rayne, then we'll turn around," Gwynn said. "There's no need to take chances. The power grid is holding up on this side."

The ground shook with a tremendous shudder underfoot. It stopped Rayne in her tracks. She peered up, through the dust cloud. A boulder, the size of a small car, slid down the slope with sizzling scrapes. They were directly in its path.

"Run!" Gwynn shrieked.

Acknowledgements

I am so lucky to have a marvelous support team who help me pull pages off my computer, then mold them into books and digital pages for the fans to enjoy. Special recognition goes to Karri Klawiter for her mind-blowing covers, Steve Parolini, editor extraordinaire, Stephanie Viola, who patiently cleans up my grammatical messes, Matthew Woolums for his detailed Beta reads and valued insight, and Sami Jo Lien of Roger Charlie for her tireless efforts to keep this series in the public's eye. Thank you, the Tattered Cover Writer's Group in Littleton, Colorado, for your never-ending support of my work and this series. I'm blessed to call you friends, as well as colleagues.

To my awesome family, countless friends and fans, your enthusiasm makes everything about writing worthwhile.

ABOUT THE AUTHOR

Sue Duff dreamed of dragons and spaceships before she could read, and it's only natural that she combines both fantasy and science fiction as her favorite writing genre. She is the author of The Weir Chronicle series with the first three books, FADE TO BLACK, MASKS AND MIRRORS and SLEIGHT OF HAND available wherever books are sold. Check out her anthology short story in TICKTOCK, Seven Tales of Time, coming March, 2016. When she's not writing, she can be found walking her Great Dane, getting her hands dirty in her garden, or creating something delicious in her kitchen. She calls Colorado home. Check out her blog, A Cook's Guide to Writing, and her other musings at www.sueduff.com. Follow her on Facebook at Sue Duff-Writer, Tweet along at https://twitter.com/sueduff55, view her Instagram pics and emoji strips at sueduffauthor, or connect with her at sueduffauthor@gmail.com.

Book cover by Karri Klawiter.

CPSIA information can be obtained
at www.ICGtesting.com
Printed in the USA
FSOW01n1055080716
22522FS